BLACKSTONE AND THE FIREBUG

Recent Titles by Sally Spencer from Severn House

THE BUTCHER BEYOND

THE DARK LADY

DEAD ON CUE

DEATH OF A CAVE DWELLER

DEATH OF AN INNOCENT

A DEATH LEFT HANGING

DYING IN THE DARK

THE ENEMY WITHIN

GOLDEN MILE TO MURDER

MURDER AT SWANN'S LAKE

THE PARADISE JOB

THE RED HERRING

THE SALTON KILLINGS

THE WITCH MAKER

Writing as Alan Rustage

RENDEZVOUS WITH DEATH

BLACKSTONE AND THE TIGER

BLACKSTONE AND THE GOLDEN EGG

BLACKSTONE AND THE FIREBUG

Sally Spencer

writing as

Alan Rustage

severn House

This first world edition published in Great Britain 2005 by
SEVERN HOUSE PUBLISHERS LTD of
9–15 High Street, Sutton, Surrey SM1 1DF.
This first world edition published in the USA 2005 by
SEVERN HOUSE PUBLISHERS INC of
595 Madison Avenue, New York, N.Y. 10022.

British Library Cataloguing in Publication Data

Rustage, Alan, 1949-
    Blackstone and the fire bug
    1.   Blackstone, Sam (Fictitious character) - Fiction
    2.   Police - England - London - Fiction
    3.   Extortion --England - London - Fiction
    4.   London (England) - Social life and customs - 19th century - Fiction
    5.   Detective and mystery stories
    I.   Title II. Spencer, Sally, 1949-
    823.9'14 [F]

    ISBN 0-7278-6245-6

Typeset by Palimpsest Book Production Ltd.,
Polmont, Stirlingshire, Scotland.
Printed and bound in Great Britain by
MPG Books Ltd., Bodmin, Cornwall.

Prologue

It was a warm spring day. Outside the Palace of Westminster, the general populace strolled by, enjoying the mildness of the air. Inside the Palace – and more specifically, inside the House of Lords – it was an entirely different matter. Here, the air was thick with an oppressive heat which had been generated more by anger and indignation than by the weather.

From his place on the Government benches, Lord Salisbury, the Prime Minister, watched as Lord Clitheroe, one of the rising stars of the Liberal Party, climbed confidently to his feet from the benches opposite.

'My Lords, I must once again address the issue of the war in Southern Africa,' Clitheroe said.

There were cheers from the Liberal benches and theatrical groans from the Conservative seats. Both sides were making a loud enough noise, the Prime Minister thought, but there was no doubt which of the two sounded the more spirited – and it was not his own party.

'I have said from the very beginning of this conflict that the war against the Boers of Southern Africa is an immoral war,' Lord Clitheroe continued.

The Boers! Lord Salisbury repeated silently – and with some disgust. Who would ever have thought that a bunch of farmers of Dutch descent could ever have been moulded into such an effective military force?

'I make no apology for my choice of words,' Clitheroe thundered. '*Immoral* was what I called it, and *immoral* is what it is.'

There were roars of agreement from those peers sitting on

the red benches behind him, but scarcely a murmur of dissent from the Government benches which he faced.

'Why are we fighting it? Because the Boers are evil?'

'No!' the Liberals cried.

'No,' Clitheroe repeated. 'A thousand times no. They are an honest God-fearing folk, living in states they themselves created – states which only exist because of their efforts. Shall I tell you how this came about?'

'Yes,' called the Liberals obediently, though they knew the story as well as Clitheroe did himself.

'When the Boers decided that they no longer wished to live under British rule, what did they do? Did they attack us, as we are now attacking them? No! Instead – because they are a peaceful people – they withdrew. They trekked into the interior of Africa, where out of virgin territory they single-handedly established the Transvaal and the Orange Free State. And why did they do this? Because they are simple farming folk who wish for no more than to be left alone to grow their crops.'

The Noble Lord had been speaking for nearly two minutes, and had still not mentioned the gold, the Prime Minister noted. He wondered if this were some kind of record.

'I will tell you why we are fighting – why we are sacrificing British lives and Boer lives,' Clitheroe continued. 'It is because gold has been discovered in those peaceful, ordered Boer states. *Gold*, My Lords. And this Government – this wicked, unprincipled Government – will go to any lengths, and commit any injustice, to get its hands on that precious commodity. But this government's plan simply hasn't worked, has it?'

There were more cries of 'No!' from the Liberal peers behind him. The Government supporters continued to be mute.

'It hasn't worked,' Clitheroe said passionately, 'because the Boers are fighting for a just cause, and because they *know* their cause is just. This small, gallant army of farmers has the mighty British Empire *on the run*. Mafeking, Ladysmith and Kimberley are all under siege. Under siege!'

'Shameful!' cried the men behind him.

'As early as last December – when the full extent of the

2

disaster began to reveal itself – I called for the Secretary of War to be impeached,' Clitheroe continued. 'Yet there he sits even now – cloaked in his mistakes, cloaked in his failures! I call on him, yet again, to resign – to make way for a man who will sue for peace! I call for him to go – and for his rotten Government to go with him.'

The Prime Minister risked a sideways glance at his Secretary of War. Yes, he was indeed still sitting there, though only a few months earlier even Salisbury himself would have put the man's chances of political survival at virtually zero.

Amid loud cheers from his own side, Clitheroe sat down. The Lord Chancellor, who, from his Woolsack, had a view of both sides of the House, scratched his nose, then said, 'Lord Lansdowne?'

From the Government benches, Henry Charles Keith Petty-Fitzmaurice, 5th Marquess of Lansdowne, 6th Earl of Kerry, Viscount Clanmaurice and – for the moment at least – Secretary of War, rose to his feet.

'The noble Lord would *give away* Southern Africa if he could,' he said contemptuously. 'And what else would he be prepared to cede? India? Canada? I believe that if his party took power, Her Majesty the Queen would have so little to rule over she could *walk* round her entire empire in a day!'

There was some laughter from the Government benches, but it seemed merely childish and defiant when compared to the roar of anger which rose from the benches opposite.

'Would the noble Lord complain so bitterly if we were *winning* the war?' Lansdowne asked scathingly. 'I think not. While having no wish at all to compare him to a rodent, I cannot help but note that it is always the rats which leave the sinking ship first.'

There were cries of 'Shame!' and 'Withdraw!' from the other side of the House.

'But, in fact, the ship is far from sinking,' Lansdowne continued. 'As the House is well aware, we have already captured Bloemfontein, the capital of the Orange Free State.'

'And what about Mafeking?' the Opposition jeered. 'What about Ladysmith and Kimberley?'

3

The Secretary of War smiled. 'It is interesting that you should raise that question,' he said, 'because I was just about to announce to the House that General Roberts's forces have relieved Mafeking this very day – and that the relief of Ladysmith and Kimberley are expected to follow very shortly.'

It was as if a huge bucket of cold water had suddenly been thrown over the Opposition, the Prime Minister thought. Now the roars came from the Government side of the House, and it was the Liberals who had fallen unnaturally silent.

'There will be dancing in the streets when the news is announced,' Lansdowne said. 'Dancing in the streets! And what will My Lord Clitheroe do? Will he join in with the celebration, and show himself to be a hypocrite? Or will he instead choose to mourn the triumph of Her Majesty's brave soldiers over our enemies?'

Nicely done, the Prime Minister thought. He had been right to keep Lansdowne on, despite all the calls for him to go. True, he had done it partly for selfish reasons – if Lansdowne had fallen, it was likely that the Government would have fallen, too – but it was gratifying to think that in saving his own administration, he had also saved the hitherto distinguished career of Henry Petty-Fitzmaurice.

One

The police constable whose nightly beat took him along Tooley Street – and down the lanes which ran off it – was called Dobson, but was known to all his colleagues as Dobbin. This nickname was arrived at not so much because it was a variation on his true name – 'Dobbo' would have been the obvious choice if that had been the case. Rather, it was in recognition of the fact that he was not exactly the brightest button on the tunic – that, like a stolid carthorse, he was reliable but uninspired.

Yet however slow-thinking he was – and even though many other men would undoubtedly have assessed what was going on more rapidly – it was Dobbin Dobson who first came across the fire in the Imperial Tea Company's warehouse at the far end of Battle Bridge Lane.

It was the flickering glow in the warehouse office that first caught his attention, if not his interest.

He walked on. Some careless clerk had obviously left the gaslight burning when he went home, he thought, and the clerk in question would doubtless be in trouble for it come the morning.

Yet did gaslights burn as brightly – or as irregularly – as the light he'd just observed? he asked himself when he'd taken a few more steps.

He spun round smartly on his heel – as they'd taught him to during his training – walked back to the window, and peered through it.

A large table dominated the centre of the office, and in the middle of that table a small fire was merrily eating its way through a small mountain of stacked documents.

The constable instinctively grabbed the bars on the window

and gave them a good hard tug. He was wasting his time. The bars were made of solid steel and were embedded in thick concrete.

'The door,' his slow brain told him. 'Try the bloody door!'

The door was iron, rather than steel, but was just as solid as the window-bars, and was very definitely locked.

Dobson returned to the window. The fire had gained a stronger hold even in the short time he had been away, and at the very moment that this thought crossed his dull mind, the big table collapsed with a crash which rattled the windows.

The constable fumbled in his pocket for his whistle. But what good would that do? His nearest colleague would be streets away, and the Night Patrol Sergeant could be anywhere on the patch. And this wasn't even a job for the police. What was wanted was the Fire Brigade – and damn quickly!

There was a public phone box on the corner of Tooley Street, Dobson recalled – and though he was even less famed for his athletic ability than he was for his intellect, he reached the box in record time.

He was sure there were worse places than Tooley Street that a fire could choose to break out, Leading Fireman Harris thought as he put down the phone and hit the alarm button.

There *had* to be worse places, he assured himself, as the bell shrieked on every floor – and in every room – of the fire station.

But he couldn't help wishing that – just at that moment – he could think of even one of them!

Within a second of the alarm going off, every man in the fire station was on the move. In the recreation room, a chess game was abandoned, and billiard cues – already lined up for a shot – clattered on to the table. In the gymnasium, barbells were carefully – but swiftly – placed back on their stands, and a fireman about to leap the vaulting horse pulled himself back at the very last moment.

Down in the stables, a groom touched the spring which released the horses from the cords securing them to their stalls, dropped collars over their heads, and pulled the blankets off their backs.

6

'Calm, my beauties,' he cooed softly. 'Keep calm.'

Firemen converged on the tackle room, reaching for their helmets, pulling on their boots and tucking their short axes into their belts.

The engineer was already at work in the garage, checking that the fire engine's boiler was burning strongly enough to generate the pressure necessary to pump water. When the groom arrived with the horses, he stepped aside to allow the other man space to strap the animals between the shafts. By the time the crew arrived, the horses were in place and eager to be going.

The whole operation had been, as it always was, frantic but efficient – pandemonium, certainly, but *organized* pandemonium.

The garage doors swung open, and the horses pulled the tender out on to the street.

It was a little under three minutes since he'd sounded the alarm, Leading Fireman Harris thought, as he braced himself against the rocking of the tender. That was good by anybody's standards – but was it good *enough*?

He was too young – as were the rest of his watch – to remember the Great Tooley Street Fire of 1861 personally, but the details of it were burned into his brain, as they were burned into the brains of all his comrades.

The fire of 1861 had started in Cotton's Wharf, but within minutes had spread to Hay's Wharf – a full two hundred yards downstream. The problem, as the fire-fighters had appreciated from the start, was that the warehouses were packed with all kinds of highly flammable material – cotton, sugar, tallow, rice, spices, jute, hemp, and even saltpetre!

The fire engine in the present crisis dashed up Southwark Bridge Road, and turned on to Union Street, while Harris relived the disaster of the past – a disaster which had occurred before he'd even been born.

They were all old men now – those whom he'd spoken to about it – some of them so old they were hardly able to remember their own names. But when they talked about the blaze, it was as if they'd just come away from it.

The tallow had been the worst, they'd said. It had liquefied

7

with the heat, and then flowed into the river. There'd been so much of it that it had actually set the Thames on fire!

Imagine that – Old Father Thames on fire!

And Harris, whose business it was – and who had seen more fires than he could count – found it almost impossible to conjure anything quite so horrific.

And what about Tooley Street itself? he'd asked these old men.

Strike them dead if they were lying, they'd replied, but Tooley Street had been ankle deep in molten grease and tallow!

The engine turned on to Borough High Street, and now Harris could see the red glow in the night sky over Battle Bridge Lane.

'Leading Fireman Harris was the man in charge at the big Tooley Street fire of 1900,' he heard a voice from the future say in his head. 'And what a right bloody mess he made of it, as well!'

It had taken two whole weeks for the Brigade back in 1861 to completely extinguish the fire, he remembered, and the damage it had wrought had been terrifyingly immense.

Eighteen thousand bales of cotton had been destroyed, five thousand tons of rice had been reduced to ashes. Nobody had blamed the Fire Brigade for that, of course – at least, not openly.

The engine had reached Tooley Street, and the driver's mate was ringing his bell furiously to alert the crowds of people who had already started to appear on the street.

In 1861, people had hired boats to go out and see the burning river from closer to, Harris thought grimly. They'd taken risks even a fireman wouldn't have taken, and a fair number of them had lost their lives because of it – more, in fact, than had lost their lives in the Great Fire of London.

Well, that wasn't going to happen this time – not on *his* watch.

The tender turned on to Battle Bridge Lane, and the full extent of the task ahead of him was now visible to Harris for the first time.

The fire had completely engulfed the ground floor of the

tea warehouse, and had spread to the first floor. Thick smoke billowed from the windows, carrying with it the acrid smell of burning tea.

If it had been the other way round, Harris thought – if the fire had started at the top and then worked its way down – he might have been able to save something. As it was, the best he could hope for was to stop the fire from spreading.

The driver reined in the horses a dozen yards from the building; his mate stopped ringing the bell. It was time, Harris thought, to find out just how good a *leading* fireman he really was.

'Masterton! Higgins! Get the hose down to the river!' he bawled at the top of his voice.

The two firemen obeyed instantly.

'Woddle! Smith!' he shouted at two other members of the crew. 'Do whatever needs to be done to keep the crowd out of the way!'

The fire had almost reached the second floor. It was going to be a real proper bugger to put out.

At the end of an hour's hectic, dangerous work, the fire was under control, and Leading Fireman Harris could relax a little, confident that his name would not, in fact, live on in infamy, but might even merit being mentioned – approvingly, and in passing – to future generations of young, eager, trainee firemen.

He had already decided that the blaze had probably been started deliberately, and shuddered at the thought that – if it was not, in fact, an insurance fiddle – a firebug was perhaps on the loose in London.

What he did not know – *could* not know – was that the fire formed only a small part of a much more elaborate and carefully formulated plan; that it was the opening shot in – or perhaps an early warning beacon of – a campaign aimed at bringing London, the mightiest city in the modern world, the hub of the greatest empire ever created, to its knees.

Two

Leading Fireman Harris stood looking up at the blackened shell of what, until a couple of hours earlier, had been a thriving tea warehouse. The owners wouldn't be pleased, he thought. Like most people who knew nothing about fire fighting, they'd probably complain that the firemen should have got there sooner – that since the blaze had gutted the building, they'd failed to do their job. But how little they knew! The true measure of his team's success on the job, Harris told himself, was that the fire had not been allowed to spread beyond the warehouse – that there hadn't been another disaster like the one in 1861.

Part of that success had been due to the dedication, courage and skill that he and his colleagues had demonstrated, Harris thought, but part of it – and there was no point in pretending otherwise – was down to pure luck.

He looked at the crowd which had gathered to watch the fire, and was being held back by a number of uniformed constables.

They were the usual bunch he would have expected to appear at that time of night. There were common prostitutes, hoping for one last customer before they returned – half-drunk – to their tuppenny boarding houses. Standing shoulder-to-shoulder with them were some of those potential clients – men who didn't care how rough – or how hurried – the sex was, as long as it was cheap. There were working men who were planning to appear at the docks before dawn, in the hope that this would be their lucky day – that the foreman would select them to unload the ships, to grunt and strain for twelve long, hard hours, in return for a few coppers. And there were the dock workers who had secured work the *previous* day, stayed in the pubs until closing time, and then – unable or unwilling to go home – had bedded down on the street.

Tramps and vagabonds, waifs and strays. They had all been drawn to the fire as a moth is to the candle flame, and though there was no longer a blaze to watch, they seemed reluctant to leave the scene of all the excitement and return to their own drab lives.

The crowd parted slightly, to allow a man to pass through it. He was a tall bloke, Leading Fireman Harris thought, watching his progress. Very tall – maybe as much as six feet or six feet one. He was thin, but not skinny – muscle and bone, and scarcely an inch of fat – and had a large nose and a square chin. Harris put him in his early thirties, but decided he could be wrong by at least five years either way. What was certain – from both his purposeful stride and the way that his deep eyes missed nothing – was that he was a copper.

The tall thin man came to a halt a couple of feet from the stocky firefighter. 'I'm Inspector Sam Blackstone,' he said. 'Who are you, and are you the one in charge?'

'Leading Fireman Harris,' the fireman replied. 'And yes, I am the one in charge.'

Blackstone looked up at the building, and Harris waited for the inevitable comment about the Fire Brigade getting there a little too late.

'Could have been much worse,' the Inspector said. 'You've done a good job, Mr Harris.'

'That's not what the owners will be saying in the morning,' Harris said fatalistically.

'People like that are never happy,' Blackstone assured him. The Inspector took a packet of cigarettes out of his jacket and offered it to the fireman. 'What I don't understand,' he continued, when they'd lit up and inhaled the smoke deep into their lungs, 'is what *I'm* doing here.'

'You mean they haven't told you?' Harris asked, surprised.

Blackstone shook his head. 'No, they haven't. I'm like you – part of the poor bloody infantry. The brass never tell us more than they need to – and sometimes, not even that. So all I *do* know is that a constable knocked me up at my lodgings, and said my boss wanted me down here as quickly

11

as possible – if not sooner. So what's it all about?'

The fireman reached into his jacket and pulled out a buff envelope. 'We found this on the tender,' he said simply.

Blackstone took the envelope from Harris, crossed the road and positioned himself under the nearest gaslight.

There was an address of sorts on the envelope, written in irregular block capitals. 'INSPEKTOR BLACKSTONE, SCOTLAND YARD,' it read, and underneath, the writer had added 'URGENT' and underlined it three times.

Blackstone slit the envelope open with his thumbnail. There was a single sheet of paper inside, and as he read it, a deep frown came to his face.

The Inspector folded the note carefully, slipped it back into the envelope, and then returned to the spot where Leading Fireman Harris was still standing.

'You said this note was found on your engine?' he asked.

'That's right,' Harris agreed.

'When, exactly?'

'Must have been about an hour or so ago,' the fireman guessed.

'And how long *could* it have been there before you noticed it?'

'That's a bit difficult to say. We were all very busy fighting the bloody fire, you see.'

Blackstone sighed. 'How many people were already here when you arrived on the scene?'

'There was quite a crowd. There always is at fires. It's better than the music hall for some people.'

'So how did you stop them from getting in your way?'

The fireman laughed. 'They cleared out of the way quick enough when they saw our horses coming,' he said. 'Nobody wants to be trampled by a big shire horse, then run over by the wheels of the fire tender as an encore.'

'But they came back, presumably,' Blackstone said.

It was Harris's turn to sigh. 'They *always* come back,' he admitted.

'So how do you control them?'

'I put a couple of my lads on the job. I can usually ill afford to spare them, but there's very little choice in the matter.'

'And that works, does it? The crowd obey them?'

12

Harris looked down at the ground. 'Well, you know,' he said, almost in a mutter.

Blackstone nodded. 'I think I do,' he agreed. 'What you're actually saying is that you give the job to the toughest-looking lads you have, and if the crowd doesn't do what they want it to, they get a bit menacing.'

'Something like that,' Harris admitted reluctantly.

'And quite right, too,' Blackstone said. 'You can't have civilians getting in the way of professionals, when they're trying to do their job. So that's what happened tonight, is it? You put a couple of your lads on intimidation duty, and the rest of you tackled the fire?'

'That's about it,' Harris agreed. 'Mind you, they didn't have to do it for long, because your blokes got here very quickly, considering they were on foot.'

Blackstone looked at the crowd of onlookers, which was now starting to thin out a little. 'Your lads will have kept them as far away from the engines as my lads are doing now, will they?' he asked.

'At least as far,' Harris agreed.

Which meant that none of the gawpers were within twelve feet of the engine, Blackstone thought.

'Where *exactly* was this note?' he asked.

'Wedged between the driver's seat and the side lamp.'

'So it was *placed* there, rather than *thrown* there?'

'It must have been.'

'I'd better go and have a word with a few of our concerned citizens,' Blackstone said.

But, as if they could read his mind, the remaining spectators were already starting to make themselves scarce.

Three

Dawn was just rising over the river, and the two men – the tall thin one, and the shorter, nearly stout one – stood at a coffee stall on the Thames Embankment, half a mile up-river from New Scotland Yard.

This particular stall was one of hundreds of such establishments, all of which were only open in the hours between the pubs closing their doors at midnight and opening them again at five o'clock the next morning.

And there was very good reason for the stalls' limited business hours, Blackstone thought, grimacing at the taste of the grey-brown brew which was swilling around in his cup.

It was widely rumoured that the coffee was actually made from ground-up acorns – though he himself doubted it came from anything as wholesome as that – and no one in his right mind would have patronized the stall at all, if there'd been any other alternative.

'What's this so-called "coffee" we're drinking taste like to you?' he asked Patterson.

The chubby Detective Sergeant sniffed at the surface of the liquid in his cup. 'I've had worse,' he pronounced.

'I'd like to know where,' Blackstone said. He took the letter Leading Fireman Harris had given him out of its envelope, and handed it over to his Sergeant. 'Well, since you've already proved that you're an expert on coffee, I'd like to know what you make of this.'

Patterson held the letter a fair distance away from his face. He was a man who loved anything which smacked of modernity – from telephones to horseless carriages – but even his passion for technology was not strong enough to make him admit openly that he needed reading glasses.

'NICE FIRE, AIN'T IT, INSPEKTOR BLACKSTONE?' he read. 'I'M REAL PROUD OF THE JOB I DONE.'

'Well?' Blackstone asked.

'Give me a chance, sir,' Patterson said. 'I've only read the first two lines so far.'

'You'd have finished the whole thing by now, if you didn't have to squint so much,' Blackstone said. 'But even from the first couple of lines, you must have formed an opinion. How do they strike you?'

'I'm not sure,' Patterson admitted. 'It could be no more than a practical joke.'

'So the bloke who wrote the letter just happened to be walking along Tooley Street, saw the fire, and came up with the idea of playing a joke on us, did he?' Blackstone asked.

'It's possible.'

'And he also happened to have on his person an envelope, a piece of paper and a pen? Not only that, but he also found a desk or table, with sufficient illumination, to sit down and write what is – in many ways – a carefully constructed letter?'

'When you put it like that, sir, it doesn't seem entirely likely,' Patterson admitted.

'So what's altogether more probable, Sergeant, is that he did actually start the fire as he claims?'

'Yes, I suppose so.'

'Which makes him?'

'A firebug. A . . . what's the proper term for it . . . a *pyro-maniac*.'

'And a very good one,' Blackstone said.

'Oh, I'm not so sure about that,' Patterson said airily. 'If he'd been *that* good, he'd have burnt the whole street down.'

'He was good enough to get into a heavily barred warehouse, and to secure it again when he'd finished his work,' Blackstone pointed out mildly.

'Pardon, sir?'

'The constable who spotted the fire tried to get into the warehouse himself, and couldn't. Which means that our man picked the lock, went inside, and locked up again when he'd finished. That suggests more the very careful mind than the wandering nutter.'

'But you can't dispute the fact that he really failed in what he was attempting,' Patterson protested.

'That's where we differ,' Blackstone countered. 'I don't think he did at all. I think he achieved exactly what he wanted to achieve.'

'And what makes you think that?'

'Well, for a start, there's the place he chose to start the fire,' Blackstone said. 'Of all the lanes that run off Tooley Street, there's only one – Battle Bridge Lane – which you can reach the river from. All the others have buildings standing between them and the Thames.'

'So what?'

'So if the fire had been on any lane *but* Battle Bridge Lane, the firemen would have had considerably more difficulty drawing water from the river. And it's not only the building he chose that's got me worried – it's the point in the building at which he decided to start the fire.'

'Come again?'

'Once he was inside, why didn't he go up a floor, to where the tea chests are stored? Tea's very dry stuff. It burns absolutely beautifully. So why start the fire in the office?'

'Maybe he didn't think. Or didn't know . . .'

'He'd done *a lot* of thinking. In fact, I'd go so far as to say he considered every angle, even down to the timing of the fire.'

'Sorry, sir?'

'The warehouse is on the constable's regular beat. He goes past it at pretty much the same time every night.'

'And what does that prove?'

' I believe it proves that our firebug wanted him to discover the fire.'

'Maybe he didn't know about the constable's beat?'

'He knew about *me,* well enough to address me by name.'

'True.'

'And there's another thing about the timing. It was high tide when the fire was started.'

'Is that significant?'

'Yes, I think it is. There was nothing random about it. It was a deliberate choice.'

'I can't see that,' Patterson admitted.

'Can't you?' Blackstone replied. 'Then let me ask you this – what's the difference in water height between high and low tide?'

'I've never really thought about it. Around five feet? Or is it closer to ten?'

'It's *twenty feet, nine inches*,' Blackstone said. 'At low tide, it would have taken the fire crews longer to pump water up from the river. But I don't think he *wanted* it to take them longer. I think he wanted to make it as easy for them as possible.'

'But why would he want to do that?'

'He didn't want to make us angry, because there's no telling what angry men will do.'

'Then what *did* he want to do?'

'To *worry* us.'

'You've lost me again,' Patterson confessed.

'Read the rest of the letter, then maybe you won't be,' Blackstone suggested.

'THIS IS ONLY THE START,' Patterson read. 'JUST TO SHOW YOU WHAT I CAN DO WHEN I CHOOSE TO. IF YOU WANT TO SLEEP PEACEFULLY IN YOUR BED AT NIGHT, YOU'D BETTER TELL THEM RICH BASTARDS IN THE GOVERNMENT THAT I SHALL WANT PAYING TO DESIST. AND HOW MUCH IS IT GOING TO COST? ONE HUNDRED THOUSAND POUNDS!'

Patterson whistled through the slight gap in his front teeth. 'One hundred thousand pounds!' he repeated. 'That's a lot of money!'

'More than you and I will ever see if we work for a thousand years,' Blackstone agreed.

'WHAT YOU'VE GOT TO DO WHEN YOU DECIDE TO PAY UP IS TO PUT AN ADVERT IN THE CLASSIFIED SECTION OF THE TIMES,' the letter continued. 'ALL IT HAS TO SAY IS THAT SAM HAS SOME SHEEP TO SELL. AS SOON AS IT APPEARS, I'LL CONTACT YOU.'

'What do you make of the style of the letter?' Blackstone asked.

'He's trying to sound less educated than he actually is,'

17

Patterson said. 'He spells "Inspector" incorrectly, but he seems to have no difficulty with "peacefully". And though he uses "them" when he should have used "those", he has no problems putting his apostrophes in the right place.'

'So he's educated and he's skilful,' Blackstone said. 'And we know that he's serious, because of what's happened tonight. All of which seems to suggest that if "them rich bastards" don't cough up the money, as he's demanded, there are going to be more fires. And do you think they will cough up the money, Patterson?'

'Not a chance,' the plump Sergeant said.

'Not a chance,' Blackstone agreed. 'Which means we've got to catch the clever little bleeder as soon as possible.'

'If we're put in charge of the case,' Patterson pointed out.

'We will be.'

'You sound very sure of yourself.'

'I am. First of all, our firebug has singled me out himself, which makes it almost certain we'll be given the case. And even if he hadn't done that, it would most likely have been assigned to us, because it's a bastard. And why are we given the bastard cases?'

'Because we're the best there is?' Patterson asked unconvincingly.

'Try again,' Blackstone said.

'Because you've got up so many important people's noses that we're *always* going to be given the bastard cases,' Patterson said, almost stoically.

'Correct,' Blackstone said. 'So since this is going to be our investigation whether we like it or not, where do you propose we start?'

Patterson's brow furrowed. 'Difficult,' he said. 'We *should* start by talking to the witnesses, but according to you, they've all done a runner.'

'Correct again,' Blackstone confirmed.

'So we'll just have to wait until he *does* strike again, and hope he leaves a clue next time,' Patterson said gloomily.

'Wrong!' Blackstone told him. 'The first thing we do is get a description of our firebug.'

'And where do we get that description from?'

'Either from one of the firemen who held the crowd back at first, or from one of constables who took over from them.'

'But how will any of them know what the firebug looks like? You can't expect them to remember everyone who was there.'

'I don't,' Blackstone agreed. 'But the firebug will have done something to make himself stand out from the rest, won't he?'

'Will he?' Patterson asked, sounding puzzled.

'Pigs might fly on occasion, but generally most other things don't,' Blackstone said enigmatically.

A smile of comprehension slowly appeared on Patterson's face. 'Of course he'll have done something to get himself noticed,' the Sergeant said. 'We wouldn't be standing here now if he hadn't.'

Four

Sir Roderick Todd, the Assistant Commissioner of Police, gazed across his desk through eyes which – amazingly – managed to seem simultaneously bleary and aggressive.

That'll be the opium, Blackstone thought, hands clasped behind his back, shifting his weight from one foot to the other.

If a constable – or even an inspector – had a serious drink problem, he reflected, it wouldn't be long before the man was brought up on charges and then ignominiously kicked off the Force. But when it was an assistant commissioner who was addicted to drugs rather than alcohol – when it was a man from the right background who belonged to all the right clubs – those in charge chose to look the other way. It wasn't right – it wasn't *fair* – but it *was* the way of the world, and there was absolutely no point in fretting about it.

Sir Roderick blinked three times, as if he hoped that might clear his head, then said, 'You and I have not met since our little adventure in Russia, when we were investigating the case of the missing golden egg.'

Or to be more accurate, when *I* was investigating the case of the golden egg, and *you* were getting in the way, Blackstone thought. But aloud, he said no more than, 'That's right, sir.'

'Of course, I wasn't there for the conclusion of the investigation – in for the kill, as you might say – because I'd been called back to St Petersburg for consultations.'

'Fortunately, I managed to struggle on without your help,' Blackstone answered, only *just* preventing a small smile from coming to his lips.

'Not that you can be said to have actually *solved* the case on your own,' Sir Roderick said harshly. 'The simple truth is that the solution fell into your lap. Isn't that true?'

'Quite true,' Blackstone agreed. 'Circumstances contrived to make it so simple that even a child of five could have solved it.'

Sir Roderick studied the Inspector's face for any signs of sarcasm and, failing to find them, sighed and said, 'It's a wise man who knows his own limitations. And you are very limited indeed, Blackstone.'

'Still, I do my humble best,' the Inspector told him.

'What puzzles me is why this arsonist should address his letter to you,' Sir Roderick said.

'I can't understand it, either,' Blackstone replied.

'Unless, of course, he wanted you to be assigned to the case, because he knew that you would have less chance of catching him than most of the officers under my command.'

'Best not to fall for his tricks, then,' Blackstone suggested.

'I beg your pardon?'

'Don't assign me to the case. Give it to someone who's much better at detecting.'

Sir Roderick looked momentarily uncomfortable. 'That *was* my first thought,' he admitted, 'but the Commissioner disagreed. He seems to feel you should be given a chance to prove yourself.'

'That's very generous of him,' Blackstone said.

'I think so too,' Sir Roderick agreed. 'More than generous. So, given that I'm stuck with you, might I ask how you propose to conduct your investigation?'

'It's early days yet, sir,' Blackstone said cautiously.

'I should tell you that the Government is highly unlikely to give in to the arsonist's demands.'

'I rather thought it wouldn't.'

'But at the same time, it is anxious that there should be no more unfortunate incidents.'

'I'll do my best to see that there aren't,' Blackstone promised.

'Yes, but will your best be anything like good enough?' Sir Roderick wondered.

Of course it wouldn't! Blackstone thought. The firebug was both intelligent and professional. He would torch at least one more building before they caught him, and probably more. It was even possible that they would *never* catch him.

'You have had a certain amount of success in the past,' Sir Roderick continued grudgingly, 'though I have to say that I believe those successes came more through luck than judgement. But whatever their cause, you cannot afford to rest on your laurels, Inspector. Failure will not be tolerated. It would be no exaggeration to say that your head is on the block with this one.'

It would be no exaggeration to say that, with idiots like you in charge, my head is on the block with every case I investigate, Blackstone thought. But he wisely kept his opinions to himself.

It was generally considered that Man was essentially a conservative creature by nature, and the four constables who worked the night-shift patrol out of the Lant Street stationhouse certainly seemed to subscribe – if only by example – to this view. As much as any reindeer or summering bird, they were locked into a migratory pattern which never varied. The police canteen expected them when they came off their shift at six o'clock, and was already preparing their heavily subsidized – and heavily larded – breakfast when they walked through the door. Their wives expected to hear their clumping footfalls outside their back doors at just after eight. And between-times, when the food was settling, and bed was but a future promise, the officers would pay an early morning visit to the Goldsmith's Arms.

The pub was usually very quiet at that time of day. The casual labourers, having supped a sustaining pint, would be queuing up outside the docks, ready – if not willing – to work. The costermongers, on the other hand, would not yet have sold enough off their barrows to be able to convince themselves they had earned a drink. Thus, it was not uncommon for the officers to have the place completely to themselves.

On that particular morning, however, they were not as alone as they might have thought. Had they glanced in the large mirror at the back of the bar, they would have spotted in it the reflection of the plump young man who was sitting quietly – beyond the partition wall – in the saloon bar.

The moment the public bar door swung open, the barmaid

– who knew her regulars and knew what they liked – reached for the beer pump and began to pull the first of four pints.

'We don't want that rubbish today, Doris, darlin',' called one of the constables from the doorway.

'What rubbish?' the barmaid asked, mystified.

'The *ordinary* bitter,' the constable replied. 'Today, it's *best* bitter or nuffink.'

Best bitter cost a ha'penny more a pint than the ordinary – and they all knew it.

'Are you sure about that?' the barmaid asked sceptically. '*Best* bitter, you want?'

'Never been more sure of anyfink in me life,' the constable replied confidently. 'And while you're at it, you might as well set up four whisky chasers as well.'

The other constables looked at him dubiously. 'What's got into you, Jethro?' one of them asked as they approached the bar. 'Best bitter?'

'Men like us – men who do a *real* man's job – deserve the best,' Jethro Quail said.

'That's as maybe,' his companion responded. 'But we're all on a constable's pay, an' if drinkin' best bitter today means there's no money for ordinary bitter tomorrer, then I'd prefer to drink *ordinary* bitter on both days.'

'So it's the money what's botherin' you, is it?' Quail asked, slightly contemptuously.

'You're damn right that it's the money what's botherin' me,' the other constable said.

'Then worry no more.' They had arrived at the bar, and Quail reached into his pocket. 'Have you got change for a gold guinea, Doris, my love?' he asked, holding the coin out for the barmaid to see.

Doris shook her head. 'I'd be lucky to have change for one of them at the *end* of the day,' she said. 'At this time of the mornin', there won't be more than a couple of bob in the till.'

'Well, that *is* a problem,' Quail said, his voice indicating that he didn't really consider it a problem at all. 'Don't suppose there's any chance of you givin' me credit, is there?'

'I'm sure the landlord won't mind if I put a few drinks on the slate,' the barmaid said.

Quail grinned at his companions. 'Ain't that just the way fings are in this life?' he asked. 'If you've got tuppence in your pocket, you're nobody. But if you've got a *gold guinea*, the world's your oyster.'

It was the four constables' practice to have two swift pints of bitter and then leave for home, but since Jethro Quail was footing the bill, they were in no hurry to depart that day, and it was not until half-past nine that they rose, fairly shakily, to their feet and headed for the door.

The slightly plump man, having already emerged from the door of the saloon bar, was waiting for them outside.

'If being mean was a hanging offence, you'd die innocent,' Patterson said genially to Constable Quail.

'What's that supposed to mean?' Quail demanded, with the aggression which comes to some men through drink.

'Merely that you seem to have treated your comrades almost royally this morning,' Patterson said.

'An' what if I 'ave?'

'I was just wondering how you possibly managed it on a police constable's wage.'

Quail staggered slightly, then raised his arm and poked Patterson in the chest.

'Listen to me, Fatso,' he slurred, 'It's none of your business how I choose to spend my money. Do you even know how much a police officer earns?'

'As a matter of fact, I do,' Patterson said.

'Well, ain't you a clever boy!' Quail sneered.

'There's nothing clever about it,' Patterson replied, reaching into his pocket and pulling out his warrant card. 'I know because I was a constable myself, once. Now, of course, I'm a sergeant – which means that I outrank you.'

The temperature on the street suddenly dropped by several degrees. Quail screwed up his eyes and attempted to focus them on the warrant card which was being held out for his inspection.

'Detective Sergeant . . . Detective Sergeant Patterson,' he said, after some effort.

'That's right,' Patterson agreed.

The flushed look had drained from Quail's face, and he was beginning to grow quite pale. 'Look, Sarge, I don't want no trouble,' he said.

'I think it's a little late for that,' Patterson told him. 'I'm on my way to Scotland Yard, and it would probably be best if you came with me.'

Five

Blackstone looked up at the man standing in front of his desk. Constable Quail had narrow, cunning eyes, the Inspector thought. Cunning – but not necessarily very intelligent. They were the kind of eyes which could spot an opportunity when they saw it, but yet were unable to communicate back to the brain the dangers which might be involved in taking such an opportunity.

'There's been a mistake, sir,' the constable said, unconvincingly.

'Has there?' Blackstone asked.

'Yes, sir, there has.'

'And what, if I may be so bold as to enquire, is the nature of this mistake?'

'Sergeant Patterson seems to fink I stole the money. But I didn't. It was mine, to do with as I wished.'

'Quite so – even if what you wished to do was squander it on getting your comrades drunk,' Blackstone said dryly. 'But what I still don't understand is where the money came from.'

'I saved it up, sir.'

'You must be very thrifty indeed to have saved so much on a constable's salary.'

'I am, sir. "Make do and mend", that's my motto.'

'And when you'd saved up enough, you took it to the bank, and exchanged it for a gold guinea.'

Quail, who clearly thought he was going to get away with it after all, could not resist a slight smile. 'That's right, sir.'

'And when exactly did you change all these copper coins that you'd been saving up for gold?'

'Yesterday.'

Blackstone leant back in his chair. 'Why?' he asked.

'Why what, sir?'

'Why change it *at all*? I could understand you going to such trouble and inconvenience if you were going to save the money, but that wasn't your plan at all, now was it?'

'I . . .'

'Yesterday, you changed copper for gold, and this morning, in the pub, you tried to break up gold for copper. Wouldn't it have been easier simply to keep the copper in the first place?'

'I suppose so,' Quail said sullenly.

'Unless, of course, you'd never made any such exchange,' Blackstone said. 'Unless what really happened was that someone handed you the guinea sometime last night. Isn't that what really occurred?'

'No, sir.'

'What did he look like?' Blackstone wondered.

'What did *who* look like?' Quail countered.

'The man who handed you the letter, of course,' Blackstone said, as if it should have been obvious to anyone.

Quail's jaw dropped. 'How . . . how did you know?' he asked.

'I feel almost shy pointing this out to you, but I *am* a detective,' Blackstone said diffidently. 'A very good detective, as a matter of fact. But even if I'd been the most bumbling investigator ever born,' he continued, his voice suddenly as hard as flint, 'even then, I'd still have been able to work it out. You know what I'm talking about, don't you?'

'No, sir,' Quail said, but now he was looking down at the ground, as if he wished it would swallow him up.

'One of the first things the leading fireman did when the engines arrived on the scene was to instruct two of his men to see to it that the spectators were kept well back from the fire,' Blackstone said. 'Then, when you and your comrades appeared, you took the firemen's place. There was no way that any of the crowd could have got within more than five yards of the engines, was there?'

'I suppose not.'

'Yet someone *did* get close enough to the tender to be able to carefully place a letter between the driver's seat and the near-side light. Now who do you think that might have been?'

'Could have been one of the firemen,' Quail mumbled.

'It could indeed,' Blackstone admitted. 'But, as far as I'm aware, none of the firemen who were there last night had a shiny new guinea in his pocket just a few hours later.'

Quail shuddered. 'But I didn't know that I was doin' anyfink wrong, sir,' he said.

'Just because you're a bloody idiot yourself, don't think to tar me with the same brush!' Blackstone said sharply. 'Of course you knew you were doing wrong! Nobody would give you a guinea for simply doing what was *right*! But what I am prepared to believe – if you decide to co-operate with me – is that you didn't know just *how* wrong it was.'

Quail's jaw was beginning to tremble uncontrollably. 'Am I in trouble?' he asked.

'That's not really the question any more,' Blackstone told him unrelentingly. 'What we're really here to decide, Constable Quail, is whether you just get kicked off the Force . . .'

'*Just* get kicked off?'

' . . . or whether you go to prison as well.'

'He said it was a joke he was playin' on one of the firemen,' Quail said, almost blubbering now. 'Nuffink more than a joke.'

'A joke he was prepared to pay a guinea to see carried out,' Blackstone said. He slammed his hand down hard on his desk. 'Tell me what the man looked like, you miserable creature!'

'He . . . I'd say that he was about my height, sir.'

'Age?'

'Probably in his early thirties.'

'Well, that certainly narrows it down a lot, doesn't it, Sergeant?' Blackstone said to Patterson.

'It certainly does,' Patterson agreed. 'There can't be more than a few hundred thousand men in London who match that description.'

'You'll have to say a lot more than that if you're to escape the ball and chain,' Blackstone told Quail.

'He . . . he had short brown hair, sir.'

'More!'

Quail hesitated.

'In some prisons, they don't even have an exercise yard, you know,' Blackstone growled.

28

'Sir . . .' Quail pleaded.

'You could be incarcerated for ten or fifteen years and never get to smell fresh air,' Blackstone told him. 'But you won't want for exercise, because where there's no yard they use the treadmill instead.'

'He . . . he wasn't dressed very well, sir,' Quail said reluctantly.

'*I'm* not very well dressed,' Blackstone countered. '*Sergeant Patterson* isn't very well dressed. There's nobody below the rank of Superintendent who can *afford* to be well dressed.'

'He . . . he was dressed a lot worse than you an' the Sergeant, sir. His clothes was almost rags.'

'So he looked like a tramp?'

'Yes, sir.'

'But you knew he couldn't *be* a tramp, didn't you?'

'Well, I . . .'

'Because tramps don't usually have gold guineas on them to hand out to bent constables.'

'I . . . I really think he *was* a tramp, sir.'

'Pull the other leg, Constable, it's got bells on,' Blackstone said contemptuously.

'It was his *smell* that made me think he must be the real thing, sir,' Quail insisted.

'It's the easiest thing in the world to make yourself stink,' Blackstone said impatiently. 'It's hotting up in London now, and anybody who doesn't wash for a couple of days is almost *bound* to stink.'

'But he *didn't*, sir. That's the whole point,' Quail whined.

'Didn't what?'

'Didn't stink.'

'You're wasting my time,' Blackstone told him.

'No, sir, he smelled clean – but it was a very special kind of clean.'

'And what's that supposed to mean?'

'I thought he was a real tramp because he had the smell about him of the kind of soap they always use at the workhouse.'

Six

The grim, imposing walls which surrounded St Saviour's Workhouse sent a chill running down Blackstone's spine every time circumstances caused him to walk past the place.

And why wouldn't they? he asked himself, looking up at those walls once more. What else did he expect, for God's sake?

He had been brought up in Dr Barnardo's orphanage. How could he – or any of Barnardo's children – ever forget that? Was it any wonder that thoughts of the workhouse – *another* institution in which he might *end* his life – were his constant, dark, companions?

Of course, it was by no means inevitable that he would finish his days in the workhouse. If he managed to hold on to his job long enough to collect a pension, he could look forward to spending his last few years in only *relative* poverty.

But that was unlikely to happen – because he'd had too many brushes with his superiors to believe that his luck would last for ever. There'd come a point, he was sure, when even his reputation as a thief-catcher wouldn't protect him any longer, and he'd be unceremoniously shown the door.

He supposed he should save up for that eventuality, but his salary was not large, and much of what little he received was immediately passed on to help support the work of Dr Barnardo's.

He supposed, too, that he could have accepted a few of the numerous bribes he'd been offered over the years, but he knew that if he'd succumbed he would have found it impossible to hold his head up high ever again. He hadn't even been able to force himself to take the money that the Russian agent, Vladimir, had offered him – ten thousand pounds, with no strings attached – because even though it would merely be a reward for having done the *right* thing – the honourable thing – he'd sensed that in accepting it he would cease to be his own man.

So, looking into the far-from-distant future, there were only two alternatives beckoning – death or the workhouse. And he had already decided that, of the two, he would much prefer death.

But he was neither dead nor infirm yet, he reminded himself, as he strode purposefully up to the workhouse gate. He was still employed, and still vigorous – and he had a job to do.

The man who opened the door was stocky, and in his late forties. He had hard, shrewd eyes, and an unyielding stance. He was, in other words, the kind of man who'd been employed as gatekeeper since the beginnings of history, and would continue to fulfil that role until the world came to an end.

Blackstone showed the porter his warrant card, and then produced a pencil sketch which the police artist had drawn from Constable Quail's description of the man who'd bribed him.

'Yes, I've seen the bloke,' the porter said, after studying the picture for a few seconds. 'He's been here as a "casual".'

'When?'

'Must have been three nights ago, which means he will have been put back out on the street again yesterday morning.'

'How can you be so sure of that?' Blackstone wondered.

The porter shrugged. 'Because that's the way the system works,' he said, as if it were the most obvious thing in the world.

'Explain the system to me,' Blackstone said.

'We let them in here at six o'clock at night, though they'll have been queuin' up for long before that.'

'Why?'

'There's only so many places to be had, and on a busy night – especially when it's cold or wet – we have to turn dozens away.'

'I see.'

'Anyway, once they've been admitted through this door, they're taken straight to have a bath – an' believe me, some of them really need one. Then they have their supper, an' are sent to bed. They're got up early the next morning, given their breakfast, then they're set to work.'

31

'What kind of work?' Blackstone asked, knowing it was probably irrelevant to the case, but feeling a kind of morbid fascination anyway. 'Cleaning? Kitchen work? Things like that?'

The porter chuckled. 'They should be so lucky,' he said. 'Cleanin'? Kitchen work? Them's the plum jobs that are reserved for the regular inmates. The casuals are usually set to pickin' oakum.'

Picking oakum! Blackstone repeated silently – and with a small sense of horror.

Unravelling rope, so that the separated strands could be used as part of the waterproof lining for boats.

What a truly soul-destroying job!

'They have their dinner, then it's more work, then supper an' then bed. On the *third* day, we give them their breakfast, an' they have to leave.'

'Why?'

'Because that's the policy. An' they're not allowed re-admission for another two clear days after that. That's policy again.'

'Where would any of us be without *policy*?' Blackstone pondered. 'How could any of us live our lives without the arbitrary rules which are imposed on us by people who never have to feel the effect themselves?'

'Exactly!' the porter agreed, missing the point.

'You're sure that the man in the sketch *was* actually one of your casuals?' Blackstone asked.

'Positive.'

'How can you be *so* certain?'

'Because some of the paupers draw attention to themselves, whether they mean to or not.'

'And he did?'

'Yes. That's what I'm sayin'.'

'*How* did he draw attention to himself?'

'It was durin' the search—' the porter began.

'What search?' Blackstone interrupted.

'Before they're admitted to the workhouse, they have to be searched,' the porter explained.

'Why?'

The porter shook his head at Blackstone's amazing ignorance. 'We're lookin' for two things when we search. The first is money – because if they got more than four pence on them, they can afford to pay for lodgin's somewhere else, so they're not allowed in.'

'And the second thing?'

'Cigarettes, tobacco and pipes.'

'Why should you be looking for anything like that?'

'Because if they've got some, we take it off them.'

'Fire regulations?'

The porter shook his head. 'No.'

'Then what's the reason?'

'Because most of them enjoy a good smoke.'

'I'm not following you,' Blackstone admitted.

'You're not meant to *enjoy* yourself in the workhouse,' the porter said. 'That's the whole point of it. The Guardians don't want anybody treatin' it as a soft option, so they make it so unpleasant that only them as is really desperate will ever think of tryin' to get in.'

Maybe, just before I'm due to hand my pistol over to the police armoury for the last time, I'll use it on myself, Blackstone thought.

'I was tellin' you about searchin' this bloke in the picture,' the porter reminded him, seeing he was lost in some kind of reverie of his own.

'Of course you were,' Blackstone agreed, as his brain shifted from thoughts of a grim future to thoughts of the grim present reality.

'The first thing I do, before I get down to searchin' them, is ask them where they slept the night before,' the porter said. 'They all say "nowhere", because they're afraid that if they say anyfink else, it'll jeopardize their chances of gettin' in. An' that's just what this bloke said – "Nowhere, sir." That's when I started to pay him particular attention.'

'Why?'

'Well, for a start, it really seemed to stick in his craw to call me "sir". An' then there was the fact that he didn't look tired.'

'Why should he have looked tired? It was only six o'clock in the evening, wasn't it?'

'Them as has been sleepin' rough always look tired,' the porter said. 'They never get a good night's rest on the street, because the police is always movin' them on. An' even if there's no coppers around, they're frightened to fall into a deep sleep, because if they do, they'll more than likely wake up in the mornin' – if they wake up at all – without their boots.' The porter paused. 'But I'd probably have forgotten him, even with them two things, if it hadn't been for the search.'

'What did you find when you searched him?'

'Nuffink. He had threepence ha'penny in his pocket, an' not a trace of smokin' equipment.'

'Well, then?'

'But it was more how he *reacted* to the search than the search itself. The regular casuals are well used to it. They don't particularly like it – who would? – but, on the other hand, they don't actually mind it too much, neither, if you see what I mean.'

'Yes, I think I'm getting the picture,' Blackstone said.

'They try to hide their tobacco from me, an' I try to find it,' the porter continued. 'If I *don't* find it, then they consider that they've got one over on me this time. An' if I *do* find it, they fink that's fair enough. It's what you might call a game we play.'

'And this one didn't like the search?'

'He pretended it didn't bother him, but you could see that it did. At one point, he almost pulled away, then he bit his lip an' let me finish. Shall I tell you somefink else?'

'Please do,' Blackstone said patiently.

'His clothes were old an' tattered enough – even some of our paupers would have turned up their noses at wearin' them – but they were very *clean*. An' that's not usual. Most folk who live on the streets find it almost impossible to keep clean, even if they want to.'

'He could just have been to the public bathhouse, couldn't he?' Blackstone asked.

The porter shook his head, almost pityingly, as the full extent of Blackstone's ignorance continued to reveal itself.

'Why would he spend some of what little money he had at

the public bathhouse, when he knew he'd be gettin' a bath here for free?' he asked.

'So he wasn't what he seemed.'

'That's what I've been tryin' to tell you.'

'And what did you do about it?'

'Do about it?' the porter asked.

Blackstone sighed. 'You knew for certain that he wasn't your typical pauper, didn't you?'

'Yes?'

'That, in all probability, he wasn't even a pauper at all?'

'Yes?'

'So what did you do about it?'

'Nuffink. This place runs smoother than any factory I've ever heard of – paupers in, paupers bathed, paupers fed, paupers bedded. There's no time for what you might call "investigation". If he's got less than fourpence in his pocket an' he hasn't been to St Saviour's for the last two days, then any man what wants to come in can come in.'

'If he'd had a gold guinea on his person, would you have found it when you searched him?' Blackstone asked.

The porter laughed. 'If he'd had a gold guinea to his name, he'd probably have booked in at the Ritz instead of here.'

'That's a very interesting observation, but could you just please answer the question?' Blackstone said firmly.

'You'd be surprised where these paupers hide their stuff,' the porter said. 'Some of them have hidden pockets, but I'm on to that trick. Then again, there's some who stick their pipes an' tobacco up their backsides.'

'And you find that, too?'

The porter laughed. 'The workhouse don't pay me anyfink like enough to go searchin' up there,' he said.

'So you didn't give him an anal examination?'

'I most certainly did not. An' I didn't go lookin' up his bum, neither. But even if I had, it's unlikely I'd have found a gold guinea, now isn't it?'

The porter was probably right, Blackstone thought. But if the man hadn't had the money when he entered the work-house, he'd certainly acquired it three days later, by the time he appeared at the scene of the fire.

Seven

The tall Inspector and his slightly dumpy Sergeant were walking down the Embankment towards their office in Scotland Yard. Blackstone had no idea what was on Patterson's mind, but his own was starting to fill up with memories of his days soldiering in India.

All that the old India hands had talked about on the long, gut-churning journey across the two choppy oceans which divided Southampton from Calcutta had been their destination.

'It's a land of contrasts,' they'd repeated endlessly. 'A real land of contrasts.'

And young Sam Blackstone, who – with the arrogance of youth – thought he knew the answer to nearly everything, had replied, 'But isn't every land a land of contrasts?'

The old sweats hadn't bothered to argue the toss. They'd simply laughed at him and said, 'Just wait till you get there, young feller-me-lad. Just wait till you see it all for yourself. It's not like anywhere else in the world, and nowhere else in the world is anything like *it*.'

He hadn't been in India long before he knew *exactly* what the men on the ship had been talking about. There were displays of wealth which would have made the London rich go green with envy, but at the same time there was poverty which was beyond the imaginings of even the most oppressed British pauper. Temples of incredible beauty existed in a sea of squalid slums which made the slums of the East End seem like palaces.

Ah, India! India! The days had been pure hell. But the nights – the nights – had come close to being paradise.

The nights hid the ugly side of the country. They were cool, so that – for a few hours at least – a man could live in peace

36

with his own skin. The night air had been filled with smells – exotic spices, wood smoke, jasmine – all melding together into a richness which intoxicated.

London, at night, was an entirely different creature. It was during the hours of darkness that the vicious side of the capital emerged – that the great beast of criminality, having rested for most of the day, crawled out of its den and claimed the city as its own.

Most of the murders in London were committed at night. And not only the murders. Most rapes and burglaries were night-time affairs – as were virtually all arson attacks!

The Inspector looked up at the sky. If the firebug did intend to strike again soon, he had only a few more hours to wait.

The room had no windows, and his captors had not considered it necessary to leave him with any kind of artificial lighting. Thus, for hours on end, the prisoner existed in almost complete darkness.

They fed him three times a day, and while he ate, his jailer stood in the doorway, the illumination from his oil lamp giving the prisoner just enough light to see his plate.

Perhaps he wasn't given food three times a day at all, he thought. It was impossible to gauge time in this dark universe which had become his home. So possibly the meals came only a couple of hours apart. Or possibly a couple of days. Perhaps, even, two were brought close together, and then there was a considerable gap before the next one was delivered.

He did not feel particularly hungry whenever they brought him his food, but then that was no guide at all to the time between meals. He had done nothing – *could* do nothing – to work up an appetite, and when he *did* eat, it was only in order to keep up his strength – in case the chance of escape should present itself.

But escape *wasn't* possible. He knew that deep in his heart. They were too careful – too rigid in their routine.

If only he knew *why* he was being kept there, he agonized.

If only he knew what he had done wrong – or what they planned to be his ultimate fate.

He had never been a particularly good man, he reminded

37

himself. In truth, he had done many things of which he was ashamed. Worse than that, he accepted that if he were eventually released from his captivity, he would probably do those things all over again.

But surely, whatever he had done or not done, he had done *nothing* to justify this!

He was constantly replaying the last few precious hours of his freedom in his mind.

Had there been any indication then that this was about to happen?

He did not think so. He did not think that even his *captors* had envisaged this fate for him at the time.

So what had happened to suddenly change everything – to turn his world upside down?

Was it something he had said?

Something he had done?

It had to be – though he could not imagine what that *something* was.

He heard the heavy steps of his jailer in the corridor outside his cell. It was time to eat again.

He suspected that they were drugging his food, but he ate it anyway. Because if life was such hell with drugs, he could not even begin to imagine what it would be like without them.

They were almost at the gates of Scotland Yard when Blackstone turned to his assistant and said, 'I'd like your opinion about what I discovered at St Saviour's Workhouse.'

'I think it's odd,' the Sergeant replied.

'Odd?' Blackstone repeated, almost incredulously. 'It's *odd* when Sir Roderick Todd smiles at us. It's *odd* when it doesn't rain on public holidays. I think all this goes a little beyond *odd.*'

'Then it's *very* odd,' Patterson conceded. '*Most* odd. *Extremely* odd. Odder than a gorilla in a convent.'

Blackstone grinned. 'I think that's taking things a little too far,' he said. 'But it's certainly a puzzle. If the porter is right, and the man he admitted to the workhouse is the same one who gave Quail the guinea – and I'm almost sure he *is* right – then we have to ask ourselves who the bloody hell that man was. And why the bloody hell he chose to stay at St Saviour's at all.'

'Clean clothes, wasn't over-keen on being respectful to a mere porter, not used to being searched – the bloke was obviously not what he was claiming to be,' Patterson said.

'Brilliant!' Blackstone said dryly. 'And do you think you could be just as helpful on my second question?'

'You mean, what drove him to seeking admission in the workhouse?'

'Exactly.'

'He was in hiding.'

'From whom?'

'From us, I should think. That's who most people who go into hiding are actually hiding *from*.'

'That would make some kind of sense if he went into the workhouse *after* the fire,' Blackstone mused. 'Then he might have had a *reason* to hide. But *before* the fire we weren't looking for him. Why should we have been, when we didn't even know that he existed?'

'It's a mystery, all right,' Patterson said. 'But then, if it wasn't for mysteries, we'd both be out of a job.'

'Very philosophical,' Blackstone said. 'I appreciate a bit of philosophy now and again.'

'Yes, I think it's always a good thing to take a slightly wider—' Patterson began.

'Especially when I'm trying to solve one of the most difficult cases it's even been my misfortune to have to deal with,' Blackstone interrupted. 'Philosophy can be very useful in situations like that.' He paused to light a cigarette. 'I can't help thinking I missed something vital at the workhouse.'

'Like what?'

'To tell you the truth, I've absolutely no bloody idea.'

'Then maybe you didn't actually—'

'But I've got this nagging feeling that there's something I should have said – or something I should have done.' Blackstone took a drag of his cigarette. 'It'll come to me,' he said, without a great deal of conviction. 'How are your own inquiries going, Sergeant?'

'Not particularly well,' Patterson admitted. 'I haven't been able to talk to any witnesses to the fire, because – as you saw for yourself – they all melted away before we had time to take their names and addresses.'

'Has the Fire Service been of any use?'

'I can't say they have. Don't get me wrong,' Patterson said hastily, as if he feared he might be misunderstood, 'they're willing enough to help. But, quite honestly, they're as stumped by the whole thing as we are.'

'Oh?'

'It's the *nature* of the fire that's flummoxing them, you see. According to Leading Fireman Harris, every professional arsonist has his own particular way of going about the job – his own *methodology*, if you like.'

'Methodology,' Blackstone repeated. 'That's one of those big words – like marmalade.'

Patterson grinned. 'Would you prefer it if I called it leaving his own "mark"?' he asked.

'Definitely,' Blackstone said.

'All right. Each arsonist leaves his own mark. He stamps his name on his crime as clearly as if he'd actually signed it. So Mr Harris can look at a fire scene and say, "That's the work of Joe Bloggs." And even if he *can't* do that – even if it's the work of a man who's never been arrested before – he can still say, "The person who set this fire in Pentonville was the same one who set a fire in Notting Hill five weeks ago." '

'But he can't do that in this particular case?'

'No. Because the arsonist didn't leave any distinctive mark. Mr Harris thinks that what was used to start the fire in the tea warehouse was nothing more than a bunch of rags soaked in paraffin. He says that's a bit like trying to do fine engraving with a stone chisel. From his viewpoint, it all seems very crude and very sloppy. Mr Harris says that any professional firebug worth his salt would be ashamed to admit that the warehouse fire was his own work.'

'Hmm,' Blackstone said thoughtfully. 'What's the word from our friends in the criminal fraternity?'

'I talked to a couple of our best informers, and they're as much in the dark about it as the Fire Brigade is.'

'So they can't tell us anything?'

'They did say *one* useful thing.'

'And what was that?'

'Like the Fire Brigade, they've no idea who started the fire – but they're pretty sure it wasn't one of the normal jobbing arsonists.'

Ominous, Blackstone thought. Very ominous.

He'd been wondering why memories of India had chosen to visit him on that particular day, but now he thought he knew.

It was because some part of his mind had started making connections that the rest of it hadn't even begun to consider.

Yes, that was it! This case reminded him of the kidnapping of the Indian prince, right off the streets of London, two years earlier.

Blackstone tried to pin down exactly why his brain should want to tie together a kidnapping and an arson attack.

The first connection was obvious, he told himself. Then, as now, he had come up against a blank wall when searching for leads – had been assured by his most reliable underworld contacts that whatever else the criminals were, they weren't Londoners.

But there was something else, too. The kidnappers of two years earlier hadn't snatched the Prince immediately. They'd pulled off two other jobs – one relatively simple and the other only slightly complicated – before attempting the big one. And this new case had the same sort of feel about it.

The warehouse fire was no more than a *trial run*. The arsonist not only intended to carry out his threat to set more blazes, but he was planning to make each fire more spectacular than the one which had preceded it!

'You've gone very quiet, sir,' Patterson said. 'What's on your mind, if I might ask?'

'I was thinking how vulnerable this city of ours is,' Blackstone replied.

'Vulnerable?'

'How exposed it is, if you'd prefer that. London's simply not set up to handle a war on its own doorstep.'

'A war?' Patterson repeated. 'Have I missed something in the newspapers? Who's about to invade us?'

'The firebug,' Blackstone said grimly. 'And he's not *about* to do anything – he's already started.'

41

Eight

The Prime Minister looked down the long mahogany table, around which were gathered the members of his cabinet.

These were men who wielded immense power, he reminded himself. They could send hundreds of thousands of men to war – and had very recently done just that. The fate of the millions of subjects who made up Her Majesty's empire rested in their hands. The future prosperity and strength of Great Britain would be determined by the decisions they made.

Was it not, therefore, reasonable to expect that they should exude the air of being exceptional – that there would be something about them which would make them stand out from the crowd?

Of course it was reasonable!

And was that expectation fulfilled?

Not at all!

The longer the Prime Minister was in politics, the more he was learning to despise most politicians. And though a prime minister selected his ministers personally, it was not much of a choice when the pool contained more minnows and sticklebacks than it did pike and salmon.

He let his eyes wander further, resting for a moment on each member of his team. The President of the Board of Trade – a stickleback, if ever there was one. The Home Secretary – a minnow. The Chancellor of the Exchequer – a tadpole, and a worried one, at that.

Oh, where were the giants of yesteryear, he asked himself – the men who had served under Palmerston and Disraeli?

Dead, most of them!

And all he was left with was a Cabinet made up of milk-sops and time-servers.

There were notable exceptions, of course. Austen Chamberlain, the Colonial Secretary, was *almost* a big fish. And then there was Lord Lansdowne, the Minister of War.

Lansdowne, who had the floor at that moment, was a pike. There was no question about that. He spoke well, and had a good mind. He *looked* like a true statesman – and when the time came for the Prime Minister himself to step down, Lansdowne would be a very strong candidate to replace him.

'In his most recent communication, General Roberts has informed me that everything is going exactly to plan,' the Minister of War was saying. 'He has assured me that, barring any unforeseen circumstances, the war should be over by the end of the year at the latest.'

The Prime Minister reached into his pocket, took out a silk handkerchief, and mopped his brow.

What was it the Duke of Wellington had said about the Battle of Waterloo? he wondered. Something to the effect that it had been 'a damn close-run thing'.

Well, that was what this war had been, too. If it were lost, the Liberals would be proved right, and the Conservatives wouldn't see government again for another thirty years. But it wasn't *going* to be lost. Lansdowne had promised victory by Christmas, and the electorate would show its gratitude by keeping in office the government which had fought it.

'The annexation of the Transvaal and the Orange Free State will not only considerably enhance the Empire territorially, but will also keep German expansionism at bay,' Lansdowne continued. 'Then, of course, there is the gold. We will gain control of the mines already in existence, and establish our claim to any new ones which may be discovered. And gold, I need hardly remind you, gentlemen, is one of the products which truly lubricate the world.'

Other ministers – overly fond of hearing their own voices – might have said much more, the Prime Minister thought. *This* minister, choosing to end on a high note, shuffled his papers into a precise pile, then fell silent.

There was one other matter still to be dealt with.

The Prime Minister cleared his throat. 'We appear to be facing a new – and totally unexpected – problem on our own

43

shores,' he said. 'You have all, I take it, seen the reproduction of the note which was handed in to Scotland Yard?'

The men around the table nodded their heads.

'And what should be our response?' the Prime Minister asked.

'The police should lock the blighter up,' the President of the Board of Trade said, looking reproachfully at the Home Secretary, who was – ultimately – in charge of such matters.

The Home Secretary looked uncomfortable. 'Scotland Yard is doing all it can,' he said awkwardly, 'but investigations of this nature take time to come to fruition.'

'And in the meantime, we must simply endure these attacks – assuming there *are* more?' the President of the Board of Trade asked.

'Regrettably, yes,' the Home Secretary agreed.

'I take it that none of you would consider, even for a moment, giving in to the arsonist's demands?' the Prime Minister said.

More head-nodding, and several cries of 'Certainly not,' and 'I'd rather burn in hell.'

'I think we should pay the ransom,' the Minister of War said.

He couldn't have created a greater sensation, the Prime Minister thought, if he had stood on the table and shown his bare backside to all his colleagues.

'Pay it!' the President of the Board of Trade demanded. 'Pay one hundred thousand pounds!'

'Just so,' the Minister of War agreed calmly.

'But . . . but that's outrageous,' the Chancellor of the Exchequer spluttered. 'Just think of what it would do to my budget.'

'Besides, if there is one thing I have learned during my time in office, it is that we can never give in to criminals,' the Home Secretary said. 'If we paid this scoundrel what he is asking for, what is to stop him demanding more?'

'Why should he, if we *do* give him all he asks for?' the Secretary of War asked reasonably.

'Because that is the way the criminal mind works,' the Home Secretary said. 'The criminal is motivated by unlimited greed. Give him a hundred thousand pounds and he will want a million. Give him a million, and he'll be asking for the crown jewels next. I am surprised a man of your calibre – a man who has been Governor-General of Canada, and Viceroy of India – should have failed to grasp that simple fact.'

'Why *do* you think we should pay the ransom, Lansdowne?' the Prime Minister asked.

'Because it will buy us time,' the Minister of War replied.

'Time? Time for what?'

'Time to cement our victory in Southern Africa.'

'Don't see what one thing's got to do with the other,' the Chancellor said. 'Or am I just being stupid?'

Yes, you *are* being stupid, the expression on the Minister of War's face said – but the look was only there for a split second, and then was gone.

'The two matters – the war and the arson attacks – are very closely related, my dear chap,' he said, 'as I'm sure you will appreciate yourself – if you take a second to think about it.'

'Will I?' the Chancellor asked, mystified.

'There is no doubt about it,' Lansdowne assured him. 'But perhaps to save time, I should spell it out a little more clearly.'

The other members of the Cabinet nodded, some trying to indicate by their expressions that while *they* understood, it might be wise to make it clearer for the benefit of their dimmer colleagues.

'There are two key elements to winning any war,' Lansdowne said. 'The first is to have a large, well-trained army—'

'We already have that,' the Chancellor interrupted. 'And it's costing the Exchequer a fortune.'

'. . . and the second element is to ensure that the army is adequately *supplied*,' Lansdowne continued, as if the other man had never spoken. 'We are still in the process of shipping out men and materiel to Southern Africa, and I would not like to see that supply route disrupted in any way.'

'And how do you think it might be?' the Chancellor asked.

'In any number of ways,' Lansdowne said.

'For example?'

'For example, the arsonist may choose to attack the docks next. Or the arsenal.'

'Is that likely, do you think?' the President of the Board of Trade wondered, sceptically.

'I don't know,' the Minister of War confessed.

'Well, then?'

'But I simply do not wish to run the risk that it might happen.' The Minister of War turned his head slightly, so that his next remark was made directly to the Prime Minister. 'Pay the blackmailer. A hundred thousand pounds is a great deal of money, as has already been pointed out, but once we have our hands on the Southern African mines, we should be able to extract gold worth that much in a year – two years at the very most.'

'Can you guarantee that?' asked the Chancellor of the Exchequer, who was still doing the figures in his head.

The Minister of War shrugged. 'In mining, as in politics, there is never a guarantee.'

'As far as politics is concerned, that is not strictly true,' the Chancellor countered. 'If I need to raise taxes to cover a hundred-thousand-pound hole in my budget, I *guarantee* that we will lose the next election.'

'As we would certainly lose it if the war started going badly,' the Minister of War responded.

Tempers were becoming strained, and it was time to step into the breach, the Prime Minister thought.

'Does anyone else have an opinion on the matter?' he asked.

'Who is in charge of the investigation to hunt down the arsonist?' the President of the Board of Trade asked.

The Prime Minister looked quizzically at the Home Secretary.

'The case is being conducted by an Inspector Blackstone,' the Home Secretary said.

'And is that the same Inspector Blackstone who saved the Queen's life a year or two ago?' the President of the Board of Trade asked.

'He was certainly *instrumental* in saving her life,' the Home Secretary answered cautiously.

'Well, then, I think we can leave the whole matter in the

46

hands of this estimable policeman,' the President of the Board of Trade said.

The Minister of War snorted in disgust. 'You cannot put the fate of our foreign policy in the hands of one man,' he said.

'Why not?' the President of the Board of Trade asked. 'If one man can disrupt it, then surely one man can *prevent* it being disrupted.'

'I think it might be best to put the matter to the vote,' the Prime Minister said. 'All those in favour of paying the blackmailer, please raise one hand.'

The Minister of War raised his hand as instructed, and saw that it was the only one which had been lifted from the table.

'All those against,' the Prime Minister said.

A positive forest of hands were lifted.

'The mood of the meeting seems to be very clear,' the Prime Minister said. 'The Cabinet has decided, almost unanimously, to put its faith in Inspector Blackstone.'

The Chancellor of the Exchequer – regarding a day on which he had saved money to be just as valid as a day on which he had raised some – smirked.

The Home Secretary, on the other hand, looked distinctly worried, despite having helped to vote the motion down.

And the Minister of War's face had turned almost black with rage.

'You should learn to take your reversals in better part, Lansdowne, old chap,' the President of the Board of Trade said.

'Oh, should I?' the Minister of War replied tartly. 'Well, we'll see whether or not you can all be quite as sanguine about the situation the next time the arsonist chooses to strike.'

Nine

Good Queen Bess had been on the throne of England when the Dutch sloops had first begun to supply London with that most popular of Cockney delicacies, the eel. And – save for the occasional interruption to the trade brought about by periods of war between the two countries – the Dutch had continued to provide eels ever since. Thus, the small ships now anchored in the Thames off the Billingsgate Fish Market differed only slightly from the ones that William Shakespeare himself might have observed from the doorstep of his theatre, three hundred years earlier.

The sloop anchored nearest to the fish market that night – a favoured position, since it would be the first to be unloaded in the morning – was named the *Golden Tulip*. It was captained by a big-bellied Dutchman who went by the name of Hans van Diemen, and who – as Big Ben chimed two o'clock, a little further down the river – was standing on the deck of his craft, smoking his pipe and gazing across the dark water.

His gaze was not a merely idle one. It was, in fact, very intent, and the object of that gaze was two bobbing lights, which his eyes had been following ever since they left the shore.

He knew what the lights signified. They were warning lights on the bows of two small skiffs, and the watermen in charge of those skiffs were slowly making their way towards the *Golden Tulip*.

Watermen, as far as the captain understood it, were licensed only to carry passengers whose business was on the river, but these two had a very different – and even more slippery – cargo in mind for that night.

The racket they were involved in was both good for them

48

and good for the people who dealt with them, Captain van Diemen reflected, as he took another pull on his pipe.

In less than thirty minutes, the watermen would be returning to the shore with their boats loaded down with eels. In another couple of hours, their illicit cargo would have already been divided up amongst a dozen or more costermongers, who would be calling out to passers-by that they had on their barrows the freshest eels anyone could ever hope for. And an hour or so after that, all evidence of any wrongdoing would have been eaten.

As a result of this simple process, he himself would make a little money, the watermen and costermongers would make a little money, and the costermongers' customers would get their eels at a more-than-usually-reasonable price. No one suffered, save for the owners of the cargo and the management of Billingsgate Market – and they could easily afford to stand the loss.

The two skiffs had now drawn level with the sloop. Looking down, the captain could see that each boat contained only one man – which meant harder work rowing, but a bigger space for cargo.

Both the rowers were dressed entirely in black – a wise precaution. And though they were close enough to hail him, neither of the men had yet said a word, which was also wise for men who were not entirely sure of the situation they were going into.

The captain began to lick his lips at the thought of the extra cash which would come to him as the reward for his willingness to grab an opportunity when it was offered to him.

'Have you brought the money?' he called down.

The skiffs bumped against the side of the sloop, but still the watermen maintained their silence.

'My crew will not hear you, however loudly you speak,' the captain said heartily. 'I got them all good and drunk last night. They'll be out cold until the morning.'

The watermen made no response, but now there was a banging noise – which only they could have produced.

What, in God's name, was their bloody game? Captain van Diemen asked himself.

It *sounded* as if the men were hammering something straight into the side of the sloop.

But why would they do that? Didn't they realize that even men as drunk as his crew undoubtedly were would be bound to wake up if this thundering noise continued? Didn't they understand that if his men *did* wake up, they would soon grasp what was going on, and demand a share of the profits for themselves? Had they any idea of how much it would disappoint him to split this unexpected windfall, rather than keeping it all for himself?

'You need do nothing to the ship,' the captain shouted down to the watermen below. 'I will throw you a rope with which you may moor your boats.'

The banging continued.

'I have hung a rope ladder over the side of the ship,' the captain said, now sounding slightly desperate. 'If you wish to come aboard, you have only to use that.'

One of the men below climbed – rather awkwardly – into his companion's craft. The original occupant of the lighter used his oar to push the boat away from the *Golden Tulip* – and the two men began to row towards the shore.

'What are you doing? Where are you going?' the captain called after them. 'We had a deal.'

But what kind of deal could it be, if they left not only the eels but also one of their boats?

The men were rowing rapidly – almost *desperately* rapidly, it seemed to van Diemen – towards the shore. And though there was no real reason to worry – yet – the captain felt a drop of moisture fall on to his hand, and realized that he had begun to sweat.

The explosion – when it came – was not excessively loud, but echoing across the silent river it seemed enormous. The *Golden Tulip* rocked slightly, and then the captain, looking over the side, saw that flames had begun to lick at the sides of his ship.

Blackstone stood on a landing jetty a short distance from Billingsgate Fish Market, studying the blackened and semi-submerged wreck of what had once been a Dutch sloop called the *Golden Tulip*.

'She's playing havoc with the river traffic,' said Leading Fireman Harris, who was standing next to him.

That was true enough, Blackstone thought. The other Dutch sloops were having to execute complex and ungainly manoeuvres in order to get around the wreck and reach the jetty where the porters were waiting impatiently to unload their cargoes.

And other craft on the river were suffering, too. Barges, instead of simply going with the current, were forced to veer away and fight against it. Steamers, rather than ploughing proudly on, were compelled to halt their engines until more sluggish boats had negotiated the hazards.

The sinking of the *Golden Tulip* had, in effect, created a traffic jam as dense as any that might be found on any other busy London thoroughfare.

'The river authorities say they're sending a tug to deal with the problem,' Harris continued, 'but even if they succeed, it'll be hours before things get back to normal.'

Which was just what the arsonist – if indeed it *was* the same arsonist – would have wanted, Blackstone thought.

'What exactly happened?' he asked.

'As far as I can piece it together, two blokes moored a skiff to the sloop in the middle of the night. There was some sort of explosion, then the sloop caught fire,' Harris said. 'It could have been worse, I suppose.'

'Hard to see how it could have been *much* worse for the *Golden Tulip*,' Blackstone commented.

Harris grinned. 'True,' he agreed. 'But the fire could so easily have spread to the other sloops, as well.'

'And why didn't it?'

'There's two reasons. The first was the alarm was raised quickly, because the captain of the *Golden Tulip* was, as it happened, up on deck when the fire actually started.'

'Up on deck?' Blackstone repeated. 'At two o'clock in the morning?'

'Apparently so.'

'Did he give you any explanation for it?'

'He said he was having one last smoke before he finally turned in for the night.'

'And what time would he have begun to supervise the unloading of his cargo in the morning?'

'I've never been a fish porter myself, but I'd guess it would be some time between five and six o'clock.'

'Five or six o'clock,' Blackstone said reflectively. 'Hmm, this captain certainly doesn't seem to need much sleep. What was the other reason the conflagration wasn't any worse?'

'The floating fire station.'

'What about it?'

'It just happened to be moored nearby. If it had been further up river – as it often is – we'd have been in a real mess.'

'Is there any connection between this fire and the one in the tea warehouse?' Blackstone asked.

Harris looked dubious. 'On the face of it, I'd have to say that no, there wasn't,' he said. 'The fire in the warehouse, as you know yourself, was a bit of a botched job.'

'Or *appeared* to be a bit of a botched job,' Blackstone mused.

'Appeared to be?' Harris echoed. 'What do you mean?'

'What about this one?' Blackstone asked, ignoring the leading fireman's question.

'This one is much more sophisticated,' Harris told him. 'As I said, the captain reported hearing an explosion.'

'So there was a bomb on the skiff?'

'Yes, but probably not what you immediately think of when you hear the word. I'd guess it was an *incendiary* bomb. In other words, it was a bomb intended to spread a fire rather than blow the ship up.'

'Would it be difficult to make a bomb like that?' Blackstone wondered aloud.

'Any bomb's difficult to make if you don't know what you're doing,' Harris said, 'but for someone with a little experience of working with explosives, it shouldn't have presented too much of a problem. The trickiest part would have been the timer, and I do think our blokes slipped up a bit there.'

'Do you? Why?'

'It went off before they reached the shore again. If I'd been setting a bomb like that, I'd have made sure I was on dry land before it ignited.'

'Still, they got away with it,' Blackstone said.

'Seem to,' Harris agreed, 'but the fact remains that they so easily might not have done.'

Sergeant Patterson appeared at the end of the jetty. He was red-faced, as if he'd been running. 'We've found a body in the river, sir,' he told Blackstone.

'What kind of body?' Blackstone asked.

The question seemed to throw Patterson a little off balance. 'A *dead* one,' he said.

Blackstone sighed. 'They're always fishing bodies out of the Thames,' he said. 'Sometimes there seem to be more of them in the river than there are in the morgue. But does this particular stiff have anything to do with our investigation?'

'Yes, sir, I think it very well might,' the Sergeant replied.

'Then we'd better go and have a look at it, hadn't we, Sergeant?' Blackstone said.

Ten

The corpse had been placed on a long stone slab which was normally used to display skate and haddock. He was lying on his back, his lifeless eyes fixed on the ceiling of the fish hall. Porters rushed past, being careful not to bark their knees against the slab, but otherwise paying the dead man no attention at all. The constable posted to stand guard over the body wrinkled his nose almost continually – as if to say that if he never smelled fish again, it would still be too soon.

Blackstone looked down at the slab. The dead man was wearing a dark loose jacket, a dark pullover, and dark trousers. His face and hands were covered with some kind of black grease, but even with his camouflage, it was obvious that he was not – as the Inspector had hoped he might be – the man who had spent two nights in St Saviour's.

Blackstone paced from one end of the slab to the other. The dead man was around five feet nine inches tall, he estimated, and though the grease on his face covered up many tell-tale signs, the Inspector would still have guessed that he had been about thirty-five.

'He got himself entangled with the supports under the pier,' Patterson said. 'If he hadn't, the tide might have carried him several miles down river by now.'

'Cause of death?' Blackstone asked crisply.

'It's always possible he drowned,' Patterson replied, 'but if I had to place a bet, I'd put my money on *that*.'

'That' was a large piece of metal which was firmly embedded in the corpse's chest.

Blackstone crouched down to get a closer look at it. The end which had pierced the body was slightly tapered, almost like a knife blade. The other end was much chunkier. Strands of a lighter-coloured, less substantial material were clinging to the chunkier end, and when Blackstone prised one of them free, he found that it was a sliver of wood.

'So what do you think it is?' he asked his assistant.

'Looks to me like part of the whatchamacallit that the oar of a skiff rests in,' Patterson said.

'Rowlocks,' Blackstone said.

'I beg your pardon, sir, but I don't think you can dismiss my suggestion as easily as that,' Patterson protested.

'I said "rowlocks", not "bollocks",' Blackstone told his Sergeant. 'The whatchamacallit that the oar of a skiff rests in is called a *rowlock*. And I think you're right – that's exactly what it is.'

I'd have made sure I was on dry land before the bomb ignited, Leading Fireman Harris had said.

But either by design – or by accident – the two arsonists hadn't done that. And one of them had paid the ultimate price for it, because it was more than possible that this rowlock had come from the skiff which had blown up.

'Of course, we still don't know whether or not this particular attack has anything at all to do with the Tooley Street fire,' the Inspector pointed out to his assistant.

'Maybe if you looked in his pockets, you might find something to tie him in with our investigation,' Patterson said, with the verbal flourish of a magician producing a rabbit from his top hat.

'Brilliant!' Blackstone said dourly. 'And to think that you're still only a detective *sergeant*.'

He reached into the dead man's pocket. The cloth was good quality, but was also soaked through, and felt unpleasant against his skin. Nor did he particularly relish the fact that the further his hand entered the pocket, the more his knuckles were pressed against the stiff, dead meat which was all that was left of the living, breathing man of a few hours earlier.

His fingers brushed against something slimy.

A fish? No, it was the wrong shape for a fish.

Blackstone grasped the object by its corner, and extracted it carefully from the pocket.

What he had in his hand was a thin, rectangular package,

wrapped in oilskin. The Inspector stripped away the oilskin, and found an envelope – addressed to himself – inside it.

'Well, that clears up any questions about whether or not the two incidents are related,' he told Patterson, showing him the envelope.

The letter itself presented no major surprises.

'HOW MUCH DAMAGE DO YOU THINK I'VE DONE WITH THIS NIGHT'S WORK, MR BLACKSTONE?' the note read. 'AND HOW MUCH MORE DAMAGE DO YOU THINK I'LL DO THE NEXT TIME? IF I WAS YOU, I'D TALK TO MY BOSSES ABOUT PUTTING THAT ADVERTISEMENT IN THE PAPER.'

'He was obviously planning to leave this note somewhere we'd be bound to find it,' Blackstone said. 'Then he got a little distracted, due to being unexpectedly killed.'

'Anything else on him?' Patterson asked.

'I won't know till I've looked, will I?'

Blackstone searched the dead man's other pockets, and came up with a modest haul. There was a packet of cigarettes – so thoroughly drenched with Thames water that even the most desperate of smokers would think twice before trying to dry them out – and a sodden box of safety matches. There was an iron nail, approximately six inches long. And there was an expensive embossed card, with raised printing on its face.

Blackstone examined the cigarettes first.

'Woodbines!' he said in disgust. 'Just about the most popular fags around! If this had all happened in one of those detective novels that everybody seems to be reading these days, it wouldn't have been bloody *Woodbines* he had in his pocket at all.'

'Then what would it have been?'

'It would have been an exclusive brand which could only be obtained from one tobacconist in the whole of London. And this tobacconist would not only have had perfect recall, but would have been able to tell us the name and address of the person who bought the cigarettes.'

'But it wouldn't have been the dead man who bought them,' Patterson said, falling in with the game. 'It would have been the dead man's *boss*, and through him we'd have been able to crack the whole case wide open.'

'Exactly,' Blackstone agreed. He turned his attention to the iron nail. 'They probably used a nail just like this to fix the skiff to the *Golden Tulip*,' he said. 'This one would have been the spare, in case they got clumsy and dropped the first one into the water.'

'And this kind of nail is only sold in one ironmonger's shop in the whole of London,' Patterson said.

Blackstone laughed. 'Regrettably not. But maybe the card will tell us something we don't already know. "The Austro-Hungary Club, Soho," ' he read. 'What's that? Some kind of club for foreigners? A home-from-home for Central Europeans?'

Patterson shook his head. 'It's got nothing to do with Austria-Hungary at all,' he said.

'Then what exactly *is* it?'

'It's a gambling club – a very *expensive* gambling club.'

'How do you know so much about it?' Blackstone wondered. 'Had the odd flutter there yourself?'

'On my pay?' Patterson scoffed. 'I've never even walked through the door. But I know a bloke who has.'

Of course he did, Blackstone thought. Whatever the topic under discussion, Patterson always knew 'a bloke' who'd done it, whether the 'it' in question was riding a horse in the Grand National or walking barefoot half-way to the South Pole. It was Patterson's contacts which made him invaluable to his boss – that and his unquestionable loyalty.

'So what more can you tell me about this club, other than the fact that it's expensive?' he asked.

'What more *is* there to say?' Patterson asked. 'It's where the rich go to lose their fortunes – and the chancers go to try and win one.'

'Who runs it?'

'Now that I *don't* know,' Patterson admitted.

'You disappoint me,' Blackstone said.

'But I have met the man who fronts for the owners,' Patterson said quickly, in an attempt to salvage his reputation. 'His name's Maurice Dunn. He's a minor aristocrat with friends in high places.'

'And you're certain he isn't the owner?'

'Positive. He's the one who signs the bills, but I doubt he's got the brains to run a coffee stall, let alone a gambling club.'

'And what about our friend here?' Blackstone asked, looking down at the corpse on the slab again. 'Is he the sort who might be welcomed at the Austro-Hungary Club?'

'Hard to say,' Patterson pronounced cautiously. 'He's not badly dressed, but not exactly well dressed, either. Still, if I was planning to set fire to a Dutch sloop in the middle of the Thames, I don't suppose I'd go about it dressed in my best bib and tucker.'

'If you had one,' Blackstone said.

'If I had one,' Patterson agreed.

He reached out and picked up one of the dead man's hands. He ran the index finger of his own free hand over the man's palm, then bent closer in order to examine the fingers.

'No calluses,' the Sergeant said when he'd finished his inspection. 'His fingernails aren't broken, either. So I think we can say for certain that whatever he did for a living, it had nothing to do with manual labour. But that's not the same as saying he was well-heeled enough to have been welcomed with open arms at the Austro-Hungary Club. He might be no more than a clerk – and a clerk's weekly wage wouldn't even cover a single minimum bet at the baccarat table.'

'Maybe we'd better pay a visit to this club ourselves,' Blackstone suggested. 'When does it open for business?'

'I shouldn't think you'd find much activity before ten o'clock tonight,' Patterson said. 'And that's at the earliest.'

'Then that's when we'll have to drop in on it,' Blackstone said.

He turned round to face the uniformed constable, who was still sniffing loudly as a way of displaying his dislike of fresh fish.

'Have the people at the morgue been informed that they need to pick this bloke up?' he asked.

The constable took one more sniff, in case his superior had missed the point. 'Yes, sir, they have,' he said.

'Then there's not much more that we can do here,' Blackstone told Patterson. 'We might as well go outside and get a breath of fresh air.'

The constable watched the two detectives walk to the door and out into the bright autumn sunlight.

'It's all right for some,' he said, under his breath.

Eleven

The morgue's resemblance to the fish market that he had so recently left was just a little too close for comfort, Blackstone told himself, as he lit up a cigarette in what he already knew would be a futile attempt to keep the stink of formaldehyde at bay. Here, too, there were cold stone slabs – and men whose job it was to gut whatever lay on them.

The chief 'gutter' in this particular establishment was Dr Donaldson, and he was already bending over the corpse which had been fished out of the river. He was a huge man, in his early thirties. He had a sandy complexion, and red hairs sprouted in profusion on the backs of his extremely large hands. It was difficult to picture him ever carrying out a delicate operation, Blackstone thought, but since most of his work involved sawing through hard bone and slicing thick cartilage, he was probably ideally built for the job he now had.

The doctor looked up, and grinned at Blackstone. 'Another day, another cadaver,' he said cheerily. 'Why do you always have to bring me such gruesome cases, Sam? Is it too much to ask that, just in a while, you could give me a nice clean poisoning?'

'You'd still have to cut him up, however he'd been killed,' Blackstone pointed out.

'True,' Donaldson agreed. He looked down at the body again. 'Nasty. Very nasty. But at least it will have been quick.'

'So it was definitely the piece of metal which killed him, was it?' Blackstone asked.

'No doubt about it,' the surgeon confirmed. 'Even without cutting him open, I'm sure that the bloody thing has pierced his heart. Like I said, it will all have been over in a moment – a bolt from the blue, in a manner of speaking.' The doctor chuckled at his own humour, then fell silent for a second. When he spoke again, it was to say, 'We've been working together for quite some time now, and you've always found me very co-operative, haven't you, Sam?'

'Very co-operative,' Blackstone agreed, but with a hint of caution in his voice. 'Is there a reason you asked that?'

'They've got a very good morgue over at University College Hospital, you know,' the doctor said.

'I'm sure they have,' Blackstone said, mystified.

'You haven't seen it yourself?'

'No.'

'You should. It's an education.'

'There are some parts of my education I'd be quite happy to neglect,' Blackstone told him.

'Well, it takes all sorts to make a world,' Donaldson said, with a shrug. 'Suppose I were to suggest to you that the autopsy be carried out at UCH, rather than here. Would you have any objections?'

'None that come to mind immediately,' Blackstone admitted. 'But I can't see any real need for a change of venue, either. Couldn't you do just as good a job of it here?'

'Ah, but that's the point, you see. If the autopsy were to be at UCH, I wouldn't be the one in charge.'

'Then who would?'

Donaldson put his hands in his trouser pockets, and shifted his weight from one foot to the other. 'I've got a brilliant young student who's very interested in the science of criminal forensics,' he said.

'Criminal forensics? I didn't even know there *was* such a science,' Blackstone confessed.

'There isn't, really,' Donaldson admitted. 'Or, at least, there is one, but it's still in its infancy. But this young ... this student ... of mine is very eager to help put it on a more rigorous and disciplined footing. Only, in order to do that, this student needs a few bodies to work on, you see.'

'You keep saying, "this student",' Blackstone pointed out. 'Is that to hide the fact that he's not actually a qualified doctor yet?'

'Oh no,' Donaldson said, almost scandalized. 'I would never

61

ask you to hand one of your stiffs over to someone who is unqualified. Dr Carr – that's the name of this particular student of mine – is a fully-fledged physician – and a very good one, in my opinion.'

There was still something not quite right about the conversation, Blackstone thought, but he couldn't quite put his finger on it.

'So I'm not likely to lose out by handing my corpse over to this student of yours?' he asked.

'Far from it,' Donaldson assured him. 'Dr Carr has far more free time than I do, and, that being so, might well uncover things which I, in my haste, might have overlooked.'

'What's in it for you?' Blackstone asked.

Given the doctor's complexion, it was hard to be definite about it, but Blackstone was *almost* certain that he blushed.

'There's nothing in it for me,' Donaldson said. 'Nothing at all, save – naturally – knowing that I have, in some small way, facilitated the advancement of medical science.'

Blackstone smiled. 'You're full of shit,' he said.

Donaldson returned his smile. 'We all are,' he said. 'You'd know that yourself – if you'd cut up as many bodies as I have.'

The Minister of War had requested – and been granted – an urgent meeting with the Prime Minister. Now the two men sat facing each other across an inlaid teak coffee table in the Prime Minister's study.

'I've come to urge you, Prime Minister, to pay this ransom without further delay,' the Minister of War said.

'The whole Cabinet were against it,' Lord Salisbury pointed out. 'You saw that for yourself. And not just against it, but *strongly* against it. There were very few who had even half a mind to vote in favour.'

'There are very few of them who have half a mind *at all*,' the Minister of War said.

'That's really a bit uncalled for, don't you think, my dear fellow?' the Prime minister protested, though he secretly agreed with the minister's assessment of his colleagues.

'You could swing them around, if you had a mind to, Prime Minister,' Lansdowne said.

'I probably could,' Lord Salisbury agreed. 'But I'm not sure that I *want* to do that.'

'The traffic in the Thames was in chaos this morning,' Lansdowne pointed out.

'But not for long,' the Prime Minister countered. 'There was some disruption, I'll grant you, but it certainly wasn't a *hundred thousand pounds* worth of disruption.'

'But it could have been,' the Minister of War argued strongly. 'It so easily *could* have been. And who is to say what will happen the next time that this arsonist strikes?'

'If there *is* a next time,' the Prime Minister countered. 'As I understand it, there were two men involved in fire-bombing the sloop, and one of them is now dead. Perhaps his partner will lose heart, and give up.'

'I promise you that he won't.'

'I don't see how you could possibly make such a promise.'

'I can make it because these men are not common criminals,' the Minister of War said.

'Are they not?' the Prime Minister asked, raising one eyebrow.

'They are not *ordinary* criminals,' Lansdowne said, correcting himself. 'They're not interested in doing damage, only in getting their money.'

'And what brings you to that conclusion?'

'Their targets, you blood— Their targets, Prime Minister. They were specifically selected to warn us that they are serious, but not to cause us any really major problems.'

'An interesting interpretation of the facts,' the Prime Minister said, enigmatically.

'But if we continue to ignore them, they will hit us where it really hurts,' Lansdowne ploughed on. 'They'll be forced to, in order to get us to react. And who knows what their next target might be? The Royal Naval Dockyard at Chatham? The Government Armoury?' Lansdowne paused to catch his breath. 'If we lose this war in Southern Africa, Prime Minister, we will also lose office. And we may not regain it again for twenty or thirty years. We may *never* regain it. Think of that, Prime Minister. Do you want to go down in history as the man who destroyed your party?'

'Rather that than go down in history as the man who gave way to blackmail,' the Prime Minister said sternly. 'But I'm sure you're worrying unnecessarily, Lansdowne. You said yourself that not too much damage has been done this time. Probably the same will be true if the arsonists strike again. You should not overestimate the powers of imagination of the criminal mind.'

'And with respect, you should not *under*estimate it,' the Minister for War said. 'We are dealing with very clever and ruthless men here, and even if you refuse to accept that now, you will have no choice but to grant that I am right about them after the next attack.'

'You sound almost as if you knew what the next attack – if it comes – will be,' the Prime Minister said.

'A clever man rarely has difficulty getting into the minds of other clever men,' Lansdowne said. 'It is only the dull man who flounders when faced with the unknown.'

'And when you talk of dull men, are you talking of me?' the Prime Minister demanded, angrily.

'Of course not,' Lansdowne said soothingly. 'How could you ever think such a thing, Prime Minister?'

Twelve

The Dutch captain was standing on the jetty – watching what was left of the *Golden Tulip* being laboriously pulled away by two tug boats – when the plump young man approached him.

'Are you Captain van Diemen, by any chance?' the plump man asked, almost diffidently.

'Yes, I am. And what is that to you?'

'I'm . . . er . . . I'm Sergeant Patterson, from Scotland Yard. I was wondering whether you could answer a few questions for me.'

The Dutchman scowled. 'I have already been questioned – several times,' he said.

Patterson took his notebook out of his pocket, and made a show of consulting it.

'Yes, that's true, you have,' he admitted. 'But the people you've talked to before have either been firemen or uniformed constables, and the detective branch likes to take its own statements, you see.'

'I do not see the necessity—' the Dutchman began.

'Of course, I wouldn't want to do it out here in the open,' Patterson interrupted. 'It's far too noisy. And there's a bit of a wind blowing up, which could making writing difficult. However, there is, by some happy chance, a pub called the Crown and Anchor just round the corner, and I thought we could go there. And since you'll be helping the police, I can see no reason why the police, for our part, shouldn't pay for whatever you drink while we're talking.'

'Very well, let us go to this pub of yours,' the Dutchman said graciously.

*   *   *

65

Sitting in the lounge bar of the Crown and Anchor, Captain van Diemen could see no reason why he should feel worried by the presence of the plump man he was sharing the table with. True, Patterson claimed to be a detective sergeant – and the captain had no reason to doubt that claim – but it was still hard to take him seriously. He looked so young – so innocent – a million miles from the hardened dockyard police and customs officials the captain was used to dealing with.

A waiter came across to the table. 'I think I'll just have a glass of lemonade, if you don't mind,' the Sergeant said.

He didn't even drink hard liquor, the captain thought. This was going to be a cakewalk.

'My owners will be very angry that the London police have allowed their ship to be destroyed right in the heart of the city,' van Diemen said. 'They may even decide to sue your government.'

Patterson looked suitably worried. 'Our job isn't always easy, you know,' he said.

'Neither is mine,' van Diemen countered. 'But my owners would not excuse any failure on my part, so I can see no reason why they should feel inclined to excuse one on yours.'

'I suppose not,' Patterson said miserably.

The waiter came across with the drinks. The captain took a healthy slug of his Dutch gin, while Patterson, despite his girth, did no more than sip girlishly at his lemonade.

'It was lucky you were up on deck of the *Golden Tulip* when it all happened,' the Sergeant said. 'If you hadn't been, the consequences might have been even more disastrous.'

'Indeed they might,' the Dutchman agreed.

'Why *were* you on deck?' Patterson asked.

'I was having a smoke before going to bed. Didn't any of the other policemen tell you that?'

Patterson consulted his notebook again. 'No,' he admitted. 'They don't seem to have done.'

'It looks to me that there is very little organization or discipline in the way the London police go about their investigations,' Captain van Diemen said, almost contemptuously.

'We do sometimes get into rather a muddle,' Patterson

conceded. 'It is rather complicated being a detective, you know.'

'Complicated!' van Diemen repeated witheringly.

Patterson squinted at his notes again. The man couldn't even see straight, the captain thought.

'Wasn't it rather late for you to be still awake?' the Sergeant asked.

'Late?'

'I mean, late considering that you were due to start unloading in only a few hours.'

'Only the lily-livered need much sleep,' van Diemen told him. 'We captains are made of much stronger stuff.'

'Of course you are,' Patterson agreed, looking a little shame-faced. 'But perhaps, even so, you were a *little* sleepy last night, and might have dozed off for just a short time?'

'I was once caught in a storm so fierce that I had to stay awake for three days, in order to save my ship from it,' the captain said boastfully. 'It was no problem for a man like me.'

'Then you *weren't* asleep last night?'

'No, I most certainly was not.'

'So you saw the skiffs approaching your ship?'

'I did.'

'And you recognized them for what they were? You didn't think that they were some other kind of vessel – a barge, a tug or a small paddle steamer, for example.'

The captain laughed scornfully. 'You might have made such a mistake, but do you really think a man of my great experience would be unable to tell the difference?'

'Of course not,' Patterson said. 'So what did you think?'

'Think?' van Diemen echoed.

'Think,' Patterson repeated.

'I thought nothing.'

'Now that is strange,' Patterson said reflectively. 'A "man of your great experience" must surely have been aware that, in the Port of London, skiffs are only licensed to carry passengers.'

'Well, yes,' van Diemen answered, suddenly starting to feel a little less at ease than he had earlier.

'And that it was most unlikely that there would be any passengers travelling across the river at that time of night?'

'I suppose so.'

'Yet you weren't the least concerned when you saw the skiffs approaching your craft?'

'I ... er ... I may have dozed off after all,' van Diemen said. 'Yes, I think I must have done.'

'Interesting,' Patterson said. 'And what has led you to that conclusion, Captain?'

'I saw the skiffs leave the shore, but the next thing I remember is one of the watermen hammering something into the side of my ship. So I must have been asleep between those two events, mustn't I, Sergeant? There is no other possible explanation.'

'Oh, I think you'll find there is,' Patterson said easily. 'Do you often use this pub?'

'Why should you wish to know that?'

'Just curious.'

I should never have come here – here of *all* places – with this detective, van Diemen thought.

He drained his glass. 'No, I do not think that I have ever been here before,' he said.

'Even though it's easily the most convenient pub for you from where you're anchored?'

'There are other public houses just as convenient.'

'Really?' Patterson asked. 'Well, I certainly can't think of one, off-hand. And the reason I thought you might be a regular, you see, is that the waiter asked me what I wanted to drink.'

'So? That is what waiters do. The man is not a mind-reader.'

'That's true,' Patterson conceded. 'But he didn't see any need to ask you, did he?'

'I am obviously a Dutch seaman,' van Diemen said. 'And Dutch seamen always drink Dutch gin.'

'Yes, that probably explains it,' Patterson agreed.

He summoned the waiter again, and when the man arrived at the table, he held up his warrant card.

'What's ... what's wrong?' the man asked, worriedly.

'A great deal,' Patterson said severely. 'We expect very

high standards from those who we entrust with the dispensing of alcohol, and it doesn't take much of a deviation from those standards for a pub to be declared a disorderly house and closed down, you know!'

'But . . . but I don't understand.'

'I'll bet you don't,' Patterson said, giving van Diemen a knowing look which was quite unlike any expression the Dutchman had seen on his face before. 'This gentleman, who you see sitting beside me, claims he was robbed the last time he was here.'

'That's impossible!' the waiter protested.

'Is it now?' Patterson asked, nodding his head sagely. 'I take it you're not going to pretend you've never seen this gentleman before?'

'No,' the waiter protested. 'He was in here, all right, but he wasn't—'

'Where was he sitting?' Patterson interrupted.

'Over there,' said the waiter, pointing to a table in the corner.

'And was he alone?'

'No, he had another man with him.'

Patterson nodded again, reached into his pocket, and produced a photograph. 'Was this the man?'

The waiter studied it. 'He doesn't look very well, does he?' he said dubiously.

'He looks *dead*,' Patterson told him. 'Which is exactly what he is. But I didn't show you his picture so we could talk about his health. I want to know if you've seen him before.'

'No, I don't think so.'

Patterson nodded, put the photograph away, and produced the sketch the police artist had made. 'How about him? Is *he* the man you saw drinking with my friend?'

'Well, yes, I'm almost sure he is.'

'Good,' Patterson said. 'Then he was probably the thief, which means that he came in with my friend, so you've nothing more to worry about.'

The waiter breathed a sigh of relief. 'Thank you, Sergeant.'

Patterson drained his lemonade glass. 'We appear to need some more drinks,' he said.

'Of course, Sergeant,' the waiter said gushingly. 'Another gin, and another lemonade?'

'Another gin, certainly,' Patterson agreed. 'But I rather think I'll have a whisky this time.'

Yes, Sergeant. Right away.'

'And make it your good whisky, mind.'

'But of course. We only serve—'

'I don't want any of your normal rot-gut. Mine's to be poured from the bottle you keep hidden away at the back of the top shelf for your special customers. Understood?'

'Understood,' the waiter agreed, scurrying away.

Van Diemen's shoulders had slumped. 'I'm in trouble, aren't I?' he asked miserably.

'That depends,' Patterson said.

'On what?'

'On whether you actively assisted with the arson attack on your own ship . . .'

'I swear I didn't.'

' . . . or were doing no more than trying to make a little bit of money on the side.'

'And if it is the second thing?'

'We're not interested in your little fiddles. Good God, man, we're trying to catch a dangerous arsonist!'

'Then it *is* the second thing,' the Dutchman confessed.

'How did it happen?'

'The man came up to me while I was having a drink and—'

'The man in the picture?'

The Dutchman studied the sketch. 'Yes, that is him. He said that the owners of my ship would never notice if a little of the cargo went missing, and he had it all set up with some costermongers he knew to quickly get rid of the eels. It seemed a very good plan.'

'He was the only man you saw?' Patterson asked. 'He didn't have anyone else with him?'

'No, he was alone.'

'And how much did he offer you?'

'Two pounds.'

A good figure to choose, Patterson thought. Enough to get the captain interested, but not enough to make him suspicious.

'What else can you tell me about this man?' he asked.

'He looked exactly as he does in the sketch.'

Patterson sighed heavily. 'If you're to be let off the hook, you have to tell me more than that,' he said.

'The . . . the man did not talk with a London accent.'

'You're saying he was a foreigner?'

'No, I . . . I think he was from the north of your country – or, more likely – from Scotland.'

'How would you recognize a Scottish accent?'

'I have sometimes sailed to Scotland with my cargo.'

Patterson nodded. 'So we'll assume he's probably Scottish,' he said. 'Now this Scot told you that he and his accomplice would row out to your boat at two o'clock in the morning, did he?'

'Yes.'

'And that is exactly what they did?'

'Yes.'

'But we now know that they didn't want to buy eels from you at all. That their plan was to set your sloop on fire.'

'I know,' van Diemen moaned. 'But I swear to you on my mother's grave that I had no idea—'

'So why did they need you at all?'

'I don't understand.'

'You were a necessary part of the plan if they were going to steal some of your cargo. But if all they wanted to do was set fire to your sloop, what did they need *you* for? Wouldn't it have been better, from their point of view, if there'd been no witnesses?'

'Yes,' van Diemen said. 'Yes, I suppose it would.'

'So why go to the trouble – and the risk – of contacting you at all? What did they hope to gain from it?'

'I don't know,' van Diemen said helplessly.

And neither do I, Patterson thought.

71

Thirteen

Blackstone stood in the open doorway, and looked in on the morgue of the University College Hospital. It was bigger than the police morgue, he thought, but other than that it was pretty much the same. It, too, had white tiled walls, It, too, had sinks, dissection tables and refrigeration drawers for the cadavers. And it, too – unfortunately – stank of formaldehyde and other obnoxious chemicals the Inspector didn't even know the names of.

On the other hand, the doctor – who at that moment was bending over a corpse which Blackstone recognized as his – appeared to be as different from the police doctor as chalk is from cheese.

Dr Donaldson was a powerful man who looked capable of taking a corpse apart with only his bare hands, though perhaps – with a particularly tough body – he'd also have to resort to using his teeth. This bloke was so slight it seemed as if he'd have trouble *lifting* a surgical saw, let alone cutting through a diaphragm with it. Still there was no doubting his enthusiasm – he couldn't have had the corpse in his possession for more than a few minutes, and already he was hard at work on it.

Blackstone knocked lightly on the door, then stepped into the room. The doctor, still absorbed by his work, did not even look up.

'Excuse me!' the Inspector said.

The doctor continued to ignore him.

Why did doctors always behave as if the normal rules of polite society didn't apply to them? Blackstone wondered.

Who gave them the right to act as if they were God Almighty?

We do, he thought answering his own question. We don't talk to them as if they were normal people at all. There's always a deference in our voices – whether we intend it or not.

'I'm Inspector Blackstone from Scotland Yard,' he said, louder and more authoritatively this time. 'I'm here to see if you've got any questions that you'd like to ask me about the body.'

The figure bent over the corpse turned round to face him, and Blackstone's jaw dropped in surprise.

'*You're* not Dr Carr!' he said accusingly.

The woman, who was a brunette, about five feet one inch tall, and seemed to be in her middle-to-late twenties, smiled at him.

'I said you're not Dr Carr,' Blackstone repeated.

'Ain't I?' the woman asked.

'Well, no,' Blackstone said, wondering – briefly – where his earlier resolution had gone.

The woman laughed. 'Course I ain't Dr Carr,' she said. ''Ow the bloody 'ell could I be? Dr Carr's a bloke, ain't 'e?' She pulled her smock down deliberately, so that it clung to her small, well-rounded breasts. 'An' in case you 'aven't noticed, I definitely ain't.'

'That's true,' Blackstone admitted, running his eyes – involuntarily – up and down her slim shapely body.

'Seen enough?' the woman asked.

Not really, Blackstone thought. Nowhere near enough.

But aloud, he contented himself with saying, 'So who are you, and what are you are doing with my body?'

'Your body?' the woman said. 'I thought you was *wearin'* your body.'

'You know what I mean,' Blackstone said crossly.

'Suppose I do,' the woman admitted. 'Well, I'm the cleaner, ain't I?'

Of course she was, Blackstone thought. Her accent was clearly East End. What else could she be but a cleaner?

'Fing is,' the woman continued, 'the doctor doesn't like to get 'is hands dirty, so I fort I'd spruce this poor bloke up a bit before 'e gets to see 'im.'

'You thought you'd do *what*?' Blackstone asked, outraged.

73

'Spruce 'im up. 'E's been in the river, you see, an' 'e's covered in filth. So I fort I'd give 'im a good scrubbin'.'

'A good scrubbing?' Blackstone repeated.

'Yeah, a touch of the old rub-a-dub-dub. An' just to make 'im look tidy, I pulled that bit of old iron out of 'is chest an' frew it away.'

'But that was—' Blackstone began.

'Evidence?' the woman interrupted him. 'A vital part of the forensic pathology.'

'That's right,' Blackstone agreed, 'but how did you . . .?'

But he'd already guessed the answer, because as the woman stepped aside he could see that, despite what she'd just said, there was no evidence of a scrubbing brush, and the 'bit of old iron' she claimed to have thrown out was still clearly embedded in the corpse's chest.

'You're . . . you're Dr Carr,' he said.

'That's right, me ole cock sparrer,' the woman confirmed.

Blackstone found that he was suddenly – and, he recognized, unreasonably – angry. 'Well, if you really are Dr Carr, why don't you drop that phoney accent?' he demanded.

'There's nuffink phoney about this accent. Oh, I can talk posh enough when I 'ave to,' the woman – Dr Carr – said. 'When, for example, I'm meeting with my colleagues from the Royal College of Surgeons, I speak like this. But don't make no mistake about it, Inspector Blackstone,' she continued, reverting to her East End patois, 'this is the real me – little Ellie Carr from the Whitechapel Road.'

'But you really *are* a doctor?' Blackstone asked, still not quite able to come to terms with the situation.

'That's right,' the woman said. 'An' a very clever doctor, to boot, don't you think? Because you 'ave to be extra smart to travel from where I've come from to where I am now.'

'So why pretend to be a cleaner?' Blackstone asked.

'You was the one wot told me I *wasn't* a doctor,' the woman reminded him. 'And you was the one wot seemed more than willin' to accept I was nuffink but a drudge.'

Blackstone lowered his head in what was – undoubtedly – shame, then lifted it and said, 'Shall we start again?'

Dr Carr smiled. 'Why not?' she asked. 'You seem like you

might be a reasonable sort of bloke, once you've pushed your preconceptions and prejudices to one side.'

Some sort of enlightenment was beginning to dawn, and Blackstone grinned. 'Do you make everybody you meet for the first time jump through the same hoops you've just made me jump through?' he asked.

The doctor returned the grin. 'Pretty much,' she admitted. 'After that first meeting they never dare to patronize me again.'

Blackstone offered Dr Carr a cigarette and took one himself. 'It might have helped avoid embarrassment if Dr Donaldson had told me you were a woman,' he said, as he lit both cigarettes up.

'It might,' Ellie Carr agreed. 'But Clive Donaldson was probably afraid that if he told you the truth, you'd have kicked up a fuss about me getting my hands on the stiff. And can you honestly say that wouldn't have?'

'So he omitted to tell the whole truth for the best of motives,' Blackstone said, avoiding the question. 'He did it because he really thought you could contribute something significant to my investigation.'

'The reason Clive *lied* was because he knew I'd be delighted to get my hands on the cadaver,' Dr Carr said. 'It would be like sending a bunch of flowers to another woman.'

'I'm not sure I'm quite following you,' Blackstone admitted.

'I don't see why not,' said Ellie Carr. 'It's perfectly simple.'

'Then perhaps you could expl—'

'Clive's great ambition is to get inside my knickers, and his working theory is that the more he does things to please me, the better the chances of me letting him have his way.'

'I see,' Blackstone said, slightly worriedly.

'But even allowing for Clive's ignoble motives, things have worked out for the best,' Dr Carr continued. 'Because the simple fact of the matter is that you couldn't have anyone better examining your cadaver than me.'

'You're a little short on modesty,' Blackstone said.

'I have little to be modest about,' the doctor retorted.

'So what can you tell me about my stiff?' Blackstone asked.

'He's dead,' the doctor replied.

'But what killed him?'

'The short answer is that he stopped breathing.'

'And what's the long one?'

'The long one will take some time,' the doctor said. 'That's what "long" means.'

'Dr Donaldson said he was almost certain it was the chunk of metal which did it.'

'Dr Donaldson is paid per body. So the more of them he gets through, the better off he is. Accuracy's not particularly important to him. Why should it be? The dead can't contradict him, and the quick – who have the greatest respect for a medical man – see no reason to. I, on the other hand, am a research scientist.'

'And that makes a difference, does it?'

'A world of difference. If I can't tell you more about your body than Clive Donaldson could have done if he'd devoted a lifetime to it, then I'll give up dissecting cadavers for a living, and take a job cutting up cloth in a sweat shop in Whitechapel – which is what all the people in my old neighbourhood thought I'd end up doing anyway.'

'So you're saying Donaldson's wrong about the wound from the piece of metal killing him?'

'No, I'm not saying that at all. What I'm actually saying is I don't know *what* killed him. Yet.'

'And when do you think you *will* know?'

Dr Carr took a deep drag on her cigarette. 'It's very hard to tell in these cases. But rest assured, Inspector Blackstone, when I have got something to report, you'll be the first one I'll report it to.'

She was a formidable woman, Blackstone thought, and he could have stayed talking to her for ever. The problem was, he couldn't think of anything to say that wouldn't end up making him look foolish.

He hesitated for a few seconds more, then tipped his hat in her general direction. 'I'll bid you good morning and leave you to your work, then, Dr Carr,' he said.

Ellie Carr, too, hesitated for a moment. Then she gave him a mock curtsey. 'Gawd bless yer, sir,' she said. 'Gawd bless yer for makin' the time to come an' see a poor woman like me.'

Fourteen

A late spring evening fog descended on Soho. It was cold, clammy – and all-pervasive. It shrouded the coughing, hacking prostitutes, who were waiting – always hopeful and desperate – on street corners. It offered both ambush-cover and an escape route for the pickpockets and purse snatchers who swarmed on to the street in the wake of its arrival. It swirled and thickened, turning even the most innocent passer-by into a dark and sinister figure. And if the firebug was planning a third attack, Blackstone thought as he approached the door of the Austro-Hungary Club, he probably couldn't have asked for a better night for it.

The door to the club was a solid one – undoubtedly solid *enough* to defy a police battering ram just long enough for those on the other side of it to get rid of any incriminating evidence. There was a sliding grille at eye level, and, as Blackstone had expected, it slid open when he rapped on the door with his cane.

'What do you want?' a voice on the other side of the door demanded aggressively.

'A little entertainment,' Blackstone replied.

'What kind of entertainment?'

'What kind have you got on offer?'

There was a slight pause, then the doorman said, 'You're not from the police, are you?'

'Do I look as if I'm from the police?' Blackstone countered.

He certainly shouldn't, he told himself. The evening suit he was wearing had been the best that Moss Bros. of Covent Garden had for hire, and his cane – so the manager had informed him – was tipped with solid silver.

'This is a members only club,' the doorman informed him.

'Then make *me* a member,' Blackstone suggested.

'It'll cost you a quid,' the doorman pointed out.

Blackstone reached into his inside pocket, and produced a thick wad of bank notes.

'Do you think that will bother me particularly?' he asked airily, waving the wad in front of the grille.

There was another pause, followed by the sound of bolts being drawn. The door swung open, and the doorman said, 'Inside! Quick!'

Blackstone stepped through the gap, and the doorman immediately slammed the door closed behind him. He was standing in a foyer, expensively carpeted, but furnished with only a table and two chairs. A corridor ran off the foyer, and down that corridor drifted the sounds of loud laughter and even louder piano music.

The doorman – who was a professional brute if Blackstone had ever seen one – gave the new arrival a quick, though thorough, inspection.

'Where have you come from?' he demanded.

'What do you mean exactly?' Blackstone asked lazily. 'Where have I come from tonight? Or where have I come from previously?'

'Both,' the doorman said.

'Tonight I've come from the Ritz, where I have engaged a suite for a fortnight,' Blackstone told him. 'Previously, I came from the Dominion of Canada, which is where I happen to live.'

'You don't sound like a toff,' the doorman complained.

'I'm not,' Blackstone agreed. 'But I am *very* rich, and I've found that's usually as useful a key as good breeding when it comes to gaining entry into most social circles.'

The doorman thought for a moment. 'Wait here,' he said, before disappearing down the corridor.

He returned with two new men. One was around fifty, very solid, and with a ruddy face which could have been the result of a healthy outdoor life – or might have been brought on by a wholly *un*healthy excess of booze. The second man was younger, leaner, and had dark calculating eyes.

'The commissionaire tells me that you wish to become a member of this club,' the florid man said.

He was a foreigner from his accent, Blackstone decided. Perhaps Dutch. Or perhaps German.

'I don't particularly want to join, no,' Blackstone replied.

'But he said—'

'I wish to *gamble*,' the Inspector interrupted. 'But if, in order to do that, I must join your club, then I certainly have no objections.'

'Jack says you're from Canada,' the second, leaner, man said.

American, Blackstone thought. Definitely American. 'That's right, I am,' he agreed.

'Don't sound like a Canadian to me.'

'I didn't say I was *born* in Canada,' Blackstone pointed out. 'It's merely the place where I live now.'

'And how d'you happen to be rich?' the American wondered.

'Jack told you that, as well, did he?'

'If he hadn't, we wouldn't be having this conversation now.'

'I made my money in lumber,' Blackstone said. 'Lots of it. Whole forests of it.'

The American and the Dutch/German exchanged quick, searching, glances, then the American said, 'If you wish to join the club, we can see no objection to it. My friend here will propose you as a member, and I will second you. The membership fee is five pounds.'

'Your man said it was only one pound,' Blackstone said.

The American shrugged. 'One pound! Five pounds! Does it really make any difference to a man of your wealth?'

No, Blackstone thought, because he *had* no wealth.

But it would certainly make a difference to Sir Roderick Todd, when he found out how little of the money from the special fund – which he'd allowed the Inspector to draw on – would actually be returned.

'Well?' the American asked.

'It makes no difference at all,' Blackstone said. 'So why don't we call it *ten* pounds?'

The American looked satisfied. 'Five pounds will be just

fine and dandy,' he said. 'You want to hand it over to Jack, here?'

Blackstone reached into his pocket again, and produced the wad of notes – or rather the *few* notes, supplemented by many equally sized pieces of blank paper. He peeled off a five pound note, and handed it to the doorman.

'Great,' the American said. 'Now if you'll just sign our register, Mr Smith, the fun can begin.'

'How did you know my name was Smith?' Blackstone asked.

The American chuckled. 'Most of our clients are called Smith – and usually have John as their given name,' he said.

Fifteen

There were three doors leading off the corridor of the Austro-Hungary Club. From one came the sound of the piano that Blackstone had heard earlier, from the second the incessant click of ivory billiard balls. But it was the third, the one which led to the gambling room, through which the Inspector was shepherded.

In one corner of this room there was a bar. It was tended by a man who looked as if he had been selected more for his muscle than for his cheery attitude or ability to mix drinks. There were several customers sitting around the bar on high stools. Most of them were women, and were dressed in such a way as to indicate that while they would probably be prepared to surrender their virtue without a fight, they would certainly not give it up without some cash changing hands.

But it was the baccarat table, located in the middle of the room, towards which most people's interest was directed. There were six people sitting around the table – the banker and five players – but perhaps three times as many others standing and watching.

Blackstone took them all in with a sweeping gaze. He recognized none of the people as individuals, though most of them were clearly instantly identifiable as types. There were three or four men who were obviously 'something in the City' – stockbrokers or bankers – and several who looked like prosperous merchants or manufacturers on a visit to London from the provinces. Half a dozen men were wearing military dress uniform, though only three of the uniforms belonged to the *British* Army. It was an impressive gathering, by any standards, and Blackstone was a little surprised that he had been admitted to it – even with his disguise of a hired suit and fake wad of money.

'The guy who's running the bank is in real trouble,' said a voice just behind him.

Blackstone looked around, to see the American who had signed him in, standing there.

'He doesn't seem to be in trouble to me,' Blackstone said.

'That's because you're not a regular, and don't know what signs to look for,' the American said easily. 'Half an hour ago, he was making a stack of money and he was as cool as a cucumber. Now his luck's turned, his money's running out, and he's starting to sweat like pig. Another five minutes, and he's gone. Want to buy the bank when he leaves?'

It wasn't a casual question, Blackstone decided. It was a test to see just how rich – and how reckless – he was.

'What's the house's take of the bank?' he asked.

The American laughed. 'A miserable seven percent,' he said. 'I keep telling the management they should raise it, but they won't listen. They're fools to themselves.'

'So you're not one of the management yourself, then, Mr ...?' Blackstone asked.

'Smith,' the American said. 'My name's Smith, just like yours.'

'So maybe we're distant cousins,' Blackstone suggested.

'Could be,' the American said indifferently. 'Why should you think I was part of the management?'

'You signed me in.'

'Look on that as a courtesy from one punter to another,' the American said. 'But you still haven't told me whether you might consider buying the bank when the current banker withdraws,' he continued, his voice hardening.

'No, I won't,' Blackstone said firmly.

'I thought you said you'd come here for a bit of excitement,' the American said, his tone now almost inquisitorial.

'I did,' Blackstone agreed. 'I even came here willing to lose money. But I didn't come prepared to *throw* it away.'

'I'm not sure I know what you mean,' the American said.

'It's a game of both percentages and odds, and the one affects the other,' Blackstone explained. 'If the house took four or five percent, which would be reasonable, I'd have a good chance of coming out ahead, and I might take the bank. But seven percent is just greedy.'

'I thought you were a businessman, not a professional gambler,' the American said suspiciously.

'I'm sure there's a difference between the two, but I've never been able to work out what it is,' Blackstone said.

The American laughed and slapped him on the shoulder. 'So if you're not going to gamble, why don't you come over to the bar?' he suggested. 'There's somebody I'd like for you to meet.'

'My name's Sophia,' the woman said.

'John,' Blackstone told her.

'John Smith?'

'That's right.'

The woman giggled girlishly. 'We get *a lot* of John Smiths in here, most nights.'

That was probably the house joke, Blackstone thought, and laughed, since it was obviously expected of him.

He gave the woman an appraising look which she – missing the policeman's eyes lurking behind the man's – would probably consider to be one of frank admiration. She was twenty-four or twenty-five, he guessed, though she would no doubt pretend to be older – or younger – when the situation called for it. She had a pretty face, though heavily enhanced by make-up, and a good figure which was more than adequately revealed by her tight-fitting, low-cut gown. And if she really *was* called Sophia, he was a Chinaman.

'It was very nice of Robert to bring you over, don't you think?' the woman said.

'Robert?' Blackstone repeated.

'Robert Mouldoon. The American gentleman.'

'Yes, it was nice of him,' Blackstone agreed.

'Because otherwise I might not have had the chance to talk to you, and I can already tell that you're a fascinating man.'

There was a pause, during which he was obviously expected to come back with some kind of compliment of his own, but when it became plain he wasn't going to do any such thing,

Sophia said, 'You wouldn't, by any chance, like to buy a lady a drink, would you?'

'Of course,' Blackstone said. 'What's it to be? Champagne?'

Sophia giggled again. 'Champagne! That's my favourite drink. You must be a mind-reader.'

'Yes, I must be, mustn't I?' Blackstone agreed, signalling to the bruiser behind the bar, and pulling out his wad of money.

'Why don't you tell me a little bit about yourself?' Sophia suggested, flickering her eyelashes at him.

'Why don't we talk about you, instead?' Blackstone countered.

Sophia ran her index finger down the top of her cleavage and batted her eyelashes again. 'Me?' she said.

'Yes, you,' Blackstone replied. 'I'm sure that you're much more interesting than a boring old millionaire.'

Sitting in a cab across the street from the Austro-Hungary Club, Sergeant Patterson lit a cigarette and, while the match was still burning, checked the time on his pocket watch.

Blackstone had been inside the club for over an hour, he noted. He wished the Inspector had allowed him to go too, but the other man had been adamant that it wouldn't work.

'You'd have to pretend to be either a gambler or a lady's man, Sergeant,' Blackstone had said. 'And, to be honest with you, I doubt if you could carry off either of those roles.'

It had hurt at the time Blackstone had said it, but thinking about it, Patterson had been forced to conclude that his boss had been right. He looked, he had to admit, like a plump detective sergeant who was walking out with a very nice girl whom he eventually hoped to marry – which, by some strange quirk of fate, was exactly what he was.

Still, there were compensations in that. He was *almost* certain that he would end up happy – or, at least, reasonably content. Blackstone, on the other hand, was never destined to achieve either of those states. The Inspector was a driven man who would never rest – would never settle for anything that was less than perfect, even though he knew perfection was totally unattainable.

Patterson glanced across at the club door again, and just at that moment, the door itself swung open and two figures stepped out into the thick fog. One of them, Patterson saw immediately, was Blackstone – there was no mistaking that tall, almost-gaunt figure – and the other was smaller, and appeared to be a woman.

As Patterson watched, the two walked over to his cab, and Blackstone opened the door.

'I told you we'd get a hansom, even in the fog,' Patterson heard Blackstone say.

'But there's already somebody in it,' the woman told him.

'Of course there is,' Blackstone answered. 'That's my secretary – Mr Patterson. I never travel anywhere without him. Get into the cab.'

'I'm not sure about this,' the woman said doubtfully. 'It isn't what we agreed at all.'

'What we agreed on – and what you seemed most interested in – was twenty pounds,' Blackstone reminded. 'Now get in the cab – or I'll go back to the Austro-Hungary Club, and find another young lady who will.'

The woman climbed into the cab, and sat at the opposite end of the seat to Patterson. 'I'll go along with this, but I want to make one thing clear from the start,' she said.

'And what might that be?' Blackstone asked, sliding deftly into the space next to her.

'My arrangement was with you,' the woman said. 'If I have to do him as well, it's extra. An' if I have to do both of you at one an' the same time – as I know some gentlemen likes – then it'll be *a lot* extra.'

'I'm not sure my secretary knows what you mean when you say "do",' Blackstone said.

'Then he must be pretty thick,' the woman said.

'He is,' Blackstone agreed. 'If he had brains, I'd be the secretary and he'd be the millionaire. So would you mind spelling it out for him?'

Sophia sighed. 'I mean that if you're both goin' to get your ends away with me – if I'm takin' you both for a ride in the woods – it's not goin' to be the same price as if there was just one of you.'

'I still don't understand,' Patterson said, in a bemused mumble.

'For Gawd's sake, ain't it obvious?' Sophia demanded. 'I'm talkin' about sex! Is that clear enough for you?'

'Perfectly,' Blackstone said. 'Would you be so good as to strike a match, Patterson?'

The Sergeant did as he'd been instructed, and in the light of it Blackstone held out his warrant card.

' 'Ere, what's goin' on?' Sophia asked.

'Ain't it obvious?' Blackstone asked, imitating her earlier comment. 'You, my girl, are nicked.'

Sixteen

Though the dead were strangely unaffected by it, the living who worked in the morgue at University College Hospital viewed the descending fog with something like mild alarm. They knew, from previous experience, that a good fog could completely shut London down – that omnibuses ceased to run, and that hansom cabs would be notoriously hard to find. Thus it was that the doctors and researchers who had been loudly proclaiming the urgency of their work only minutes earlier suddenly discovered that this same research could easily wait till morning after all, and, grabbing their coats, rushed out into the ever-increasing murkiness.

Dr Ellie Carr did not join the mass exodus. This was in part due to her obsession with her work, and in part because her soulless lodgings were not somewhere she felt inclined to run home to.

Ellie circled the dissection table for perhaps the twentieth time, wondering if her unease was the result of her *wanting* something to be wrong, or whether things were not, in fact, as simple as they appeared.

'Thought you'd have had him well and truly gutted by now,' said a voice from the doorway.

Ellie turned. The speaker was a man in his early forties, who had managed to keep his hard body in shape, but was rapidly losing the battle to retain his hair. As he walked into the room, he moved with grace and authority. A watcher might have guessed he was a policeman, and the watcher would have been half-right. Jed Trent had served with the Metropolitan Police for twenty years. He was now employed as a general factotum in the morgue, though, in his head, he had already decided that he was really a special assistant to Dr Ellie Carr.

Trent reached the dissecting table, came to a halt, and looked down at the dead body. 'You normally can't wait to start digging,' he said. 'Why the delay this time?'

'There's more to criminal pathology than simply cutting the cadavers open,' Ellie Carr said.

Trent smiled affectionately. 'If you say so.'

'The way I see it, my job is to be half doctor and half detective,' Ellie continued.

'And have you informed our employers of this fact?' Trent asked, his smile broadening.

'What we're doing here is breaking new ground,' Ellie said, side-stepping the question.

'What *we're* doing here?' Trent asked.

'Of course. I'd never get anywhere without your help, Jed.'

'Call me Trent,' the ex-policeman said.

'Why should I do that?'

'I get worried when you call me by my first name, because it's usually a sign that you're going to ask me to do something that could get both of us into trouble.'

'This won't get us into trouble,' Ellie Carr said airily.

'So there *is* something?'

'One small favour – so small that it's really hardly worth calling it a favour at all.'

'And what would this one small favour entail?'

'You must know some soldiers from your days working in the Met,' Ellie said.

'A few,' Trent agreed reluctantly.

'And you're such a kind-hearted, helpful man that these soldiers you know must owe you a few favours.'

'What is it you want?' Trent demanded.

'A field gun.'

'*A field gun!*' Trent repeated incredulously.

Ellie Carr frowned. 'Or should I have called it a cannon?' she asked. 'You men are so much more knowledgeable about these things than we mere women could ever be.'

'*A field gun!*' Trent said for a second time.

'Only a little one,' Ellie said reasonably. 'The smallest

they've got. And, of course, we'll need somewhere to fire it. And a couple of soldiers to fire it for us, because I'm sure we'd be too frightened to fire it ourselves.'

'Not to mention the fact that neither of us would know one end of the weapon from the other,' Trent said.

'Quite,' Ellie Carr agreed.

'But I still don't see why you want it,' Trent said.

'It's because I'm . . .'

'I know! I know! It's because you're half doctor and half detective.'

'Exactly,' Ellie said. 'I knew you'd understand, Jed.'

The fog seemed to be thickening by the hour. The police were on patrol – as was their duty whatever the weather – but they were patrolling empty streets and protecting absent citizens. The buses had stopped running long ago. Now even the last of the cab drivers had given up – for what was the point of searching for customers when there were no customers to be found? Had a foreign army chosen to invade the capital that night, it would have met with no resistance – but how could foreigners have been expected to find their way, when even the natives could get lost in the swirling maze the fog had created?

The two men with the heavy canvas bags were not worried about losing their way. Why would they have been, when the barge on which they had been waiting all afternoon was so close to their target? For them, the fog was not an inconvenience but an ally – a friendly act of nature which would enable them to do their work without fear of interruption.

They stepped off the barge, and made their way to the two towers which loomed massively – but indistinctly – in the near distance.

It had taken eight years to complete this bridge, and it had been opened to massive public acclaim. Londoners had pronounced it one of the wonders of the modern world – and there were few people anywhere who would disagree with them. But even a wonder such as this was not immune to the other wonder which the men carried in their bags – a wonder which had been developed by a Swedish chemist, and went by the name of dynamite.

It took the men less than five minutes to reach the northern end of the bridge and another two to cover the distance between it and the nearest of the two towers.

Once there, they automatically checked over their shoulders. There was no need. The fog had not miraculously cleared behind them, nor had a troop of policemen suddenly appeared to catch them in the act.

The men put their bags on the ground, and then opened them. Each one worked independently. They did not speak because they did not need to – because they had practised this action so many times that they could have done it blindfolded and gagged.

The whole operation was over in less time than it would have taken to strip and wash a corpse. The fog was now so thick that, even standing a few feet apart, the men could not really see each other's faces, so instead of smiling, as they might otherwise have done, they merely nodded their heads. Then they turned and walked back the way they had come. It would have been too dangerous to return to the barge, but they did not need to – they had already arranged for another bolt hole which was almost as convenient.

Seventeen

The woman looked very frightened, but given the situation she now found herself in, that was hardly surprising. She must have known that common prostitutes who were picked up by the police were dealt with at the nearest station, rather than taken to Scotland Yard. And as for *un*common prostitutes like herself – prostitutes who could ask for, and *get*, twenty pounds for a single night's work – well, they were hardly ever arrested *at all*.

'Name!' Blackstone said, looking at her across the table in the interview room.

'I told you that when you first asked me in the club. It's Sophia – Sophia de Vere.'

Blackstone slammed his hand down hard on the table. 'Stop wasting my time, and tell me your real name!'

The woman looked down at her hands. 'It is my real name,' she said in an insistent mumble. 'But,' she conceded, 'I was *born* Molly Scruggs.'

'Well, Molly . . .' Blackstone began. He paused, 'I can *call* you Molly, can't I?' he continued.

'Suppose so.'

'Well, Molly, you're in real trouble.'

'I can pay the fine.'

'Is that a fact?' Blackstone asked sceptically.

'Or, at least, I know somebody who can,' Molly amended.

'Yes, that sounds closer to the truth,' Blackstone said. 'We'll come back to who that "somebody" might be later, but for the moment I just want you to realize how serious your situation is. You attempted to solicit a senior policeman while he was in the course of going about his duties and—'

'I never knew you were a copper,' Molly protested.

'Ignorance is no excuse,' Blackstone said, 'and I'll thank you not to interrupt me again.'

'Sorry,' Molly mumbled.

'As I was about to say, there are special regulations to cover what you've done.' Blackstone turned to Patterson. 'Remind me what those regulations are, Sergeant.'

'Regulation 673/2 and 673/3 of the Criminal Code of 1896,' Patterson said, making it up as he went along, but still sounding convincing.

Blackstone frowned. 'Haven't you left one out?' he asked.

Patterson looked abashed. 'Sorry, sir, there's also Regulation 731, subsections 5 and 7,' he said.

Blackstone nodded, as if satisfied. 'And what are the penalties for breaching those regulations, Sergeant?'

Patterson pretended to be searching his mind for an answer. 'A minimum of three – and a maximum of six – years imprisonment,' he said finally.

'Correct!' Blackstone agreed.

'My guess is, she'll get the maximum,' Patterson added.

The pantomime was all too convincing – and all too much – for Molly. She bowed her head, and began to cry.

Blackstone tried his damnedest to harden his heart, but – as always when he was dealing with those he considered to be the victims of society – he was only partially successful in his attempt. Still, he had a job to do, and he steeled himself to do it.

'Crying won't do you any good, my girl,' he said harshly.

'Do you need to be so rough on her, sir?' Patterson asked.

'She's going down, and she might as well get used to it,' Blackstone told him.

'But she doesn't *have* to go down, does she, sir?'

'Doesn't she?' Blackstone asked, noting that while Molly was still crying, she was also listening intently.

'Aren't we empowered to make exceptions – to show mercy – if the miscreant is exceptionally co-operative?' Patterson asked.

'Yes, but this one isn't going to be, is she?' Blackstone said aggressively. 'You can see, just by looking at her, that she'd rather do hard time in prison than tell us what we want to know.'

Molly was still sniffling, but the tears had stopped flowing. 'What *is* it you want to know?' she asked.

'She won't tell you anything useful,' Blackstone told Patterson. 'This is just a stalling tactic. I've seen it a hundred times before. You might as well book her now, and save yourself the effort.'

'I'd like to give it just one try, if you don't mind, sir,' Patterson said diffidently.

Blackstone shrugged. 'Why not? If you don't make your own mistakes, you'll never learn.'

Patterson leant across the table, so he was closer to Molly. 'How long have you been working at the Austro-Hungary Club?'

'I don't work there. I was just visiting and—'

'See what I mean?' Blackstone said fiercely.

'Molly!' Patterson pleaded. 'Help me, won't you? It's the only way you can help yourself.'

'I've been there for about six months,' the woman told him.

'And who, *exactly*, do you work for?' Patterson asked.

'Mr Mouldoon.'

'He's a Yank,' Blackstone explained. 'I thought he was a pimp the moment I met him.'

'What can you tell me about this Mr Mouldoon?' Patterson asked solicitously. 'Do you like him, Molly?'

The woman shrugged. 'I've known worse. He doesn't slap us about, and he lets us keep two pounds from every job.'

Two pounds! Blackstone thought. Ten percent! The miserable Yankee bastard!

'I'm going to show you a drawing and photograph, Molly,' Patterson said. 'And I want you to tell me if you recognize either of the men.'

He slid the two articles across the table, and Molly looked at them. 'If I do recognize them, will it help me?' she asked.

'It certainly won't help you if you only *pretend* to recognize them,' Blackstone snarled. 'If you lie, it will only make things worse for you.'

'I *do* know them,' Molly told Patterson. 'I'm not just saying it, I really do. I haven't seen either of them recently, but until last week they were both regulars at the club.'

'What can you tell me about them?' Patterson asked.

'The one in the drawing's called Peter, and the other one's William.' Molly examined the photograph again. 'William doesn't look well.'

'No, he's feeling a little under the weather at the moment,' Blackstone said curtly. 'Did William and Peter come to the club together, or did they come separately?'

'Together,' Molly said firmly. 'And they always had Lord Moneybags with them.'

'Lord Moneybags?' Blackstone repeated.

'His real name's Henry,' Molly explained. 'Lord Moneybags was just what us girls called him among ourselves.'

'Describe him.'

'He was older than the other two.'

'How much older?'

'I'd say he was in his middle-to-late fifties.'

'And where did the nickname come from?'

Despite the seriousness of her situation, Molly laughed. 'Oh that! The "lord" bit came from the way he carried himself, and from the way he spoke. You know, as if he was somebody really important.'

'And the other half of the nickname?'

'Moneybags? That's because he has a lot of money, of course. Tons and tons of it.'

'Do you know that for a fact?' Blackstone demanded. 'Did he show you his bank book?'

'No, but . . .'

'So you're only guessing.'

'He certainly gambles as if he has a lot of money,' Molly said defensively. 'One night last week, Friday, I think it was, he lost four thousand pounds – and he didn't even blink.'

'Do other people lose a lot of money?' Blackstone asked.

'Yes – but not like him.'

'Who runs the club?'

'Mr Rilke.'

'First name?'

'We call him Frank, behind his back, but I think his real name is something like Fritz.'

'Is he the big man with the red face who signed me in?'

'Sounds like him. Probably *is* him, since he's the one who signs in most of the new members.'

'And where's he from?'

'Come again?'

'Is he German? Dutch?'

'Dunno. But he's definitely some kind of foreigner.'

'I want you to describe this "Lord Moneybags" to the police sketch artist,' Patterson said.

'And then can I go?' Molly asked hopefully.

Patterson checked with Blackstone, who nodded.

'And there'll be no charges?' Molly asked.

'There'll be no charges,' Patterson assured her.

Molly hesitated before she spoke again. 'So can I . . . er . . . go back to the club?'

'We *want* you to go back to the club,' Blackstone said.

'You do?' Molly asked, surprised.

'We do,' Blackstone confirmed. 'But for your own protection, I suggest you don't tell Mr Mouldoon what happened tonight.'

'How do you mean?'

'If Mouldoon learns you've been talking to the police, he could turn nasty. And let me tell you, you wouldn't want that. I've seen pimps turn like that before, and like as not he'd slash your face with a cut-throat razor.'

'You're joking!' Molly said.

'Tell her, Sergeant,' Blackstone said.

'Happens all the time,' Patterson confirmed.

Molly's face hardened. 'In that case, I'll need twenty quid,' she said.

'What for?' Patterson asked.

'Because if she's to conceal the fact she's been talking to the police, she'll have to pretend she's been with a client,' Blackstone said. 'And the client would have paid her twenty pounds. Isn't that right, Molly?'

'Yeah. So can I have it?'

Blackstone reached into his pocket, and peeled off four of the remaining five-pound notes from his wad of false ones. Sir Roderick Todd wasn't going to like this at all, he thought.

95

Eighteen

Milkmen, by the very nature of their trade, are tradition-ally early risers, so it was not at all surprising that it should be a milkman who first encountered the latest example of the firebug's work.

The milkman in question was called Dick Todd, but, despite sharing his surname with Sir Roderick, he was no relation – not even a distant one – of the Assistant Commissioner. He lived in Southwark, and would have been fairly happy – or at least as happy as his grumpy nature allowed – to continue living there, had it not been for the distance between his home and Paddington Station.

'The milkmen wot live norf of the river have it easy,' he would tell anyone in the Goldsmiths' Arms who was willing to listen. 'They get up in the mornin', stick the old 'orse between the shafts of their carts, an' they're in Paddin'ton before they know it. It's a diff'rent matter for me. I got to cross the river, ain't I? 'Cos if I don't, I don't get me churns of country milk wot come in on the first train. An' if I 'aven't got me churns, I've got nuffink to sell.'

It was on his second journey across Tower Bridge that morning – on his return to Southwark with his rattling churns of milk – that he noticed the infernal device resting against the side of the first tower he reached. He did not at first appreciate its nature, and rather than seeing it as a danger, he considered it something of an opportunity.

'If somebody's left it lyin' there like that, it must mean that they don't want it,' he told his horse as he reined her in. 'An' if they don't want it, well then, it's mine.'

He applied the brake, climbed down from his cart, and approached the object – or rather collection of objects.

'Now just what 'ave we got 'ere, Snowdrop?' he called to his horse over his shoulder.

But the horse made no answer, and he was left to work it out for himself.

There was an alarm clock, which he could clearly hear was ticking happily away. There was a small wooden box, the contents of which he had yet to identify. And there were a number of sticks of wood – except that they looked too regular to be *ordinary* sticks.

A sudden breeze blew up, caught a piece of wrapping paper which had been nestling between the sticks, and blew it in the milkman's direction. Todd bent down and picked it up.

'Danger!' he read. 'Dynamite! Highly Explosive!'

'Gawd Almighty!' the milkman exclaimed.

He had no memory of dropping the piece of paper or of climbing back on to his cart. He remembered nothing more, in fact, until he became aware that he had crossed Tower Bridge and the nag between the shafts of his cart was running like a racehorse.

Ellie Carr looked across the firing range, at the field gun and the two men standing next to it.

'You did very well to fix things up at such short notice, Jed,' she said to her assistant, who was standing next to her and was in the process of manoeuvring a hastily constructed dummy on to a small chair.

Trent's only response was to mumble something to himself.

'Really well!' Ellie Carr said. 'My only complaint is that it would have been nice if you could have arranged it for just a *little* later, so we could have snatched a couple of hours sleep before we came out here. The thing about experiments, you see, is that I find I'm much better at observing them when I'm awake.'

'So it's early in the morning!' Trent said, dismissively.

'Or, more accurately speaking, it's the crack of dawn,' Ellie said, almost to herself.

'And when else did you expect the Army to turn their artillery range into your personal playground?' Trent asked. 'They have got a couple of other little jobs to do, you know – like defending the country.'

'Nonsense! Nobody's tried to invade us since Napoleon,' Ellie told him. 'And even he got no further than Calais.'

She stepped back, and gave the dummy a quick critical examination. It really was rather crude, she thought. The legs looked more like sausages than limbs, the head like a badly filled bag of potatoes. Still, she'd got the weight distribution about right. And it was sewn together beautifully – as it should have been, considering how many corpses she'd had to stitch up in her time.

Trent had finally got the dummy into place, and was now tying it firmly to the chair.

'He's supposed to be sitting in a rowing boat,' Ellie said. 'Are you sure he'd be that far out of the water?'

Jed Trent sighed heavily. 'Do I look like a complete amateur to you?' he demanded.

'No, but . . .'

'While you were stitching the dummy up, did you even notice I wasn't there?'

'Yes, I noticed you weren't there. I thought you'd gone off for a cup of tea or something.'

'A cup of tea or something!' Trent said contemptuously. 'What I, in fact, did was go round to the house of one of my mates and drag him out of bed.'

'Why would you have done that?'

'Because I'm working for a bloody perfectionist, that's why. Thing is, this mate of mine's just about the same size as your stiff. So I took him down to the river, didn't I? And when we got there, I told him to sit in a skiff. And once he was in the skiff, I measured him. So when I put the dummy in this position, you can be sure it's the *right* position,'

'You're very thorough,' Ellie Carr said admiringly.

'Thorough I might be – but I'm rapidly running out of friends,' Trent complained.

'You'll always have me,' Ellie told him. 'Now I really do think it's time I went and talked to those soldiers.'

The gunnery sergeant, and the private who was assisting him, watched with interest – and not a little admiration – as Ellie Carr covered the hundred yards between the dummy in the chair and the point at which they were standing.

'Didn't even know there were such things as women doctors, Sarge,' the private said. 'And I certainly never imagined that if such things *did* actually exist, they'd be involved in anyfink as strange as this.'

'A woman's place is in the home,' the sergeant said firmly. 'Always has been an' always will be. If they start allowin' women doctors, then what's next? Women *lawyers*? Women *soldiers*?'

The private chuckled. 'Women soldiers!' he repeated. 'Now that's something that *will* never happen.'

Ellie Carr had drawn level with them. 'Good morning,' she said pleasantly. 'You know what you're supposed to do, don't you?'

The sergeant shook his head. 'We were just told to bring the gun here and wait for instructions.'

'You see the dummy in the chair?' Ellie asked.

'Couldn't really miss him.'

'I'm glad about that,' Ellie said.

'Glad about what?'

'That you couldn't really miss him. Because I'd like you to shoot him square in the centre of his chest.'

'Why?' the sergeant asked.

'Because that's what I want,' Ellie said, her voice hardening. 'And because your officer has agreed that's what you'll do.'

'What's it stuffed with, this dummy of yours?' the sergeant asked. 'Is it sand?'

'Sand's certainly part of it,' Ellie Carr said. 'But there are other things as well.'

'Like what?'

'Well, ribs for a start.'

'Cow's ribs?'

'Human ribs,' Ellie said, and wondered what the people in the Anatomy Department at UCH would say when they realized one of their skeletons had gone missing.

'If it had been tightly packed sand, it might just have survived the impact,' the sergeant said dubiously. 'If it's anything else, a shell will blow it to pieces at this range.'

'I don't want you to use a shell,' Ellie said, reaching into

99

the carpetbag she'd brought with her. 'I want you to use this.'

She produced the piece of metal she had dug out of the chest of the corpse in the morgue, and held it out for inspection.

'Tricky,' the sergeant said, as his questioning-obstructionist side all but fell away, and his professional interest took over.

'What's the problem?' Ellie asked. 'Can't you fire it?'

'Oh, we can fire it, all right,' the sergeant said. 'It's getting it where you want it to go that's the problem. It's not shaped like most projectiles, you see. I'm not sure we can make it fly true.'

'Maybe if we centred it, and then gave it some padding,' the private suggested.

'That might work,' the sergeant conceded. 'But even so, when it hits the dummy at high velocity, it'll be like hitting an egg with a hammer – bits of it will fly everywhere. Is that what you want?'

Ellie shook her head, reached into her carpetbag again, and produced a photograph of the dead man in the morgue. 'That's how I'd like it to look,' she said. 'I want the piece of iron embedded in its chest.'

The two soldiers glanced at each other questioningly.

'I suppose if we used a light charge, we might just be able to do that,' the private said.

'We'll give it a try, anyway,' said the sergeant, who was now becoming quite enthusiastic about the challenge.

'I appreciate your help,' Ellie told him.

The uniformed inspector – who had been the first man with any real authority to arrive on the scene – had quickly deployed his men at both ends of Tower Bridge. Now he stood watching, at a safe distance, as an Army officer with a cut-glass accent and a lieutenant's pips on his shoulder examined the infernal device.

'Rather him than me. *Much* rather him than me,' the inspector murmured – and found himself wondering why a man like the lieutenant, who obviously had all the right connections, should actually *choose* to go in for this line of work.

The lieutenant stood up, and waved what the inspector took to be the 'all-clear' signal. The inspector, not without some misgivings, began to walk towards the tower.

The lieutenant smiled as the inspector approached. It was the fresh-faced smile of a fresh-faced young man who looked as if he really didn't have a care in the world.

'Quite an intricate piece of work,' the lieutenant said, as if he were talking about some common household object, rather than a bomb which could have blown him to Kingdom Come.

'It's safe now, is it?' the inspector asked nervously.

'Oh, quite safe,' the lieutenant assured him. 'In point of fact, it was never in any real danger of going off.'

'So it was a dud?'

'I didn't quite say that.'

'Then I don't understand what you *did* say,' the inspector admitted.

The lieutenant reached into his jacket pocket, and produced a packet of expensive-looking cigarettes. He extracted one, flicked it into the air, caught it in his mouth, lit up, and inhaled with obvious pleasure.

'When would you say the bomb was actually set up?' he asked.

'That's almost impossible to say,' the inspector admitted. 'That milkman didn't notice it the first time he crossed over the bridge, but that doesn't necessarily mean it wasn't here then. It was still foggy at that time, and he could easily have missed it.'

'If I were a betting man – which, of course, I am – I'd be willing to wager it was placed here at around two o'clock,' the lieutenant said.

'That's very precise,' the inspector said.

'Precision is my watchword,' the lieutenant replied. 'It's the clock which tipped me off. It was supposed to be the timer for the bomb. It's an alarm clock, you see.'

'It'd certainly alarm *me*,' the inspector said.

The lieutenant did not seem to notice the joke. 'When the alarm goes off, the hammer, instead of hitting the bell, makes contact with this wire here, and the bomb is detonated,' he said.

'So what went wrong?'

'The bombers got confused about the time – probably because they were working in thick fog.'

'How do you mean? Confused?'

'The bomb was set to go off at two o'clock, when, presumably, the bombers themselves would be well clear. But they must have actually set it *after* two o'clock. In other words, instead of it going off when they wanted it to, it was actually timed to go off at two o'clock *this afternoon.*'

'So you were never in any danger?'

'None at all.'

'You must have been relieved when you realized that.'

The lieutenant shrugged. 'Not really. Made the whole job rather boring, as a matter of fact.'

'I'm sure it did,' the inspector said, thinking, as he spoke, that the lieutenant didn't *look* like a lunatic.

'By the way, I found this among all the gubbins,' the lieutenant said, holding out a brown envelope. 'It seems to be addressed to one of your people.'

The inspector took the envelope from him, and saw that 'Inspektor Blackstone, Scotland Yard' was written on it.

The first shot the two artillerymen fired missed the dummy by a good twenty yards. The second – after adjustments to the padding had been made – missed by ten.

The third – after further adjustments – was more or less on target. The dummy, still tied to the chair, was lifted into the air and deposited several feet from its original position.

'Well?' Jed Trent demanded when Ellie Carr had walked over and examined the results.

'Encouraging,' Ellie said.

'And what, exactly, does that mean?'

'It means that it's a close enough result to what I suspected to indicate that I might be on the right lines . . .'

'Well, thank Gawd for that!'

'. . . but not so close that it absolutely confirms my theory.'

'So you're saying we're going to have to do it again?'

'I'm afraid so,' Ellie Carr said. 'But we can't use dummies any more.'

'Then what will we use?'

'Bodies.'

'What!'

'Bodies, Jed!' Ellie said sweetly. 'Corpses! Cadavers! Stiffs! Surely you've been working in the morgue long enough to know what I'm talking about by now.'

Nineteen

There used to be only two groups of people who wished to have their portrait painted, Marcus Leighton thought, as he busied himself with charcoal and paper that early morning in Blackstone's office.

The first group had been like Oliver Cromwell – the man who had once been the virtual dictator of Great Britain, and who had instructed the artist who painted him to depict him as he really was – 'Warts and all'.

Then there had been the second – much larger – group. They wished to be painted as they *thought* they were – or as they would *like* to be – and they did not appreciate the warts in the least. These people were worse than criminals in Leighton's eyes. They were cultural philistines. They were to art what Genghis Khan had been to market gardening. They had made it almost impossible for any artist with integrity – and he considered he had integrity enough to sink a ship – to scrape even the meanest of livings.

The scarcity of the first group and preponderance of the second had almost driven him to despair. Then his talents had been called on by the Metropolitan Police – the wonderful, wonderful Metropolitan Police – which wished his art to reflect life as closely as possible. The Met had enough murderers and robbers on its hands to keep him in work for ever, and whilst he would have preferred his work to hang in a gallery, he took some pride in knowing that instead it hung on every police notice board in London – and was studied with an intensity that most gallery patrons could rarely muster.

Leighton finished the sketch, and handed it across the desk to Blackstone. 'Is that all right?' he asked.

'It's perfect,' Blackstone replied. 'You've caught the very essence of the man.'

Leighton smiled – perhaps he even smirked. 'And is that the last one?' he said.

'That's the last one,' Blackstone agreed.

Leighton yawned. 'Then I'll get back to the bed from which you unkindly ripped me in the middle of the night.'

'You do that,' Blackstone said. 'And you won't forget to send us your bill, will you?'

'Would Leonardo da Vinci have forgotten to put in a bill for the *Mona Lisa*?' Leighton asked rhetorically. 'Would Michelangelo have neglected to collect his rightful recompense for his work on the statue of David?'

'Probably not,' Blackstone admitted.

Leighton grinned. 'Then neither will I,' he said.

When the police artist had gone, Blackstone spread the results of his labours out on the desk in front of him.

There were five sketches in all. Three had been drawn from Molly's descriptions: one of the man she called 'Lord Moneybags' and the others of his companions, whom Blackstone had started to think of as the Dead Man and the Workhouse Man. The remaining two, of Mouldoon and Rilke, had been drawn from Blackstone's own descriptions.

'Molly's got a good eye,' the Inspector said approvingly. 'Her impressions of the Workhouse Man pretty well match up with the other descriptions we have of him. As for the Dead Man, we've only seen him on a slab, but I can well imagine he did look like this before he got a rowlock through his chest. So if she's right about the two of them, there's a more than even chance that her description of Lord Moneybags is spot on, too.'

'And that's important, because this "Lord Moneybags" bloke is our man,' Patterson said firmly.

'You sound very confident about that,' Blackstone said.

'I am. He's the one.'

'And what brings you to that conclusion?'

'The application of my logical thought processes to the problem,' Patterson said, perhaps a little pompously.

'Anything else?'

'And, of course, my instinctive grasp of detective work.'

Blackstone remembered Patterson as he had been four years earlier – newly promoted and very unsure of himself – and found it almost impossible to suppress a smile.

'So would you like to tell me where your "natural instincts" and "logical processes" have led you?' the Inspector asked.

'Certainly, I will,' Patterson agreed. 'We know for a fact that this Lord Moneybags's two closest associates were both involved in the arson attacks, don't we, sir?'

'Yes, we do.'

'So it'd be nothing short of a bloody miracle if Moneybags wasn't involved as well.'

'Perhaps,' Blackstone said cautiously. 'And what, in your opinion, caused him to become involved in the attacks?'

'Gambling debts!' Patterson told him. 'A man who loses money as heavily as Lord Moneybags does is bound to end up heavily in debt sooner or later, however rich he was to start with. And in his case, I think it's more a question of "sooner". Four thousand pounds is a hell of a lot of money for *any* man to lose in a single night's gambling.'

'True,' Blackstone agreed.

'I think he's hugely in debt to the Austro-Hungary Club, which is almost the same as saying he's hugely in debt to Rilke and Mouldoon. And how's he ever going to pay it back? By blackmailing the British Government out of one hundred thousand pounds!'

'Yes, that would certainly be a solution to his dilemma,' Blackstone said. 'Given the size of his debt, it's possibly the *only* solution which he feels is open to him.'

'So now we pull in Rilke and Mouldoon for questioning, do we?' Patterson asked enthusiastically.

Blackstone shook his head. 'I don't think so.'

'Why not? Once we have them down in the cells, we'll soon sweat Lord Moneybags's real name out of them.'

'I think you're wrong about that,' Blackstone told him. 'There are men who crack like an egg once the questioning's started, and men you need a sledgehammer to break open. From what I've already seen of them, those two are going to need a sledgehammer – and even then, it'll take time.'

106

'That's all right,' Patterson said cheerfully. 'I like a good long interrogation. Who needs a week in Southend-on-Sea, when you could be spending your time locked up in a small, sweaty room with two gutter-snipes instead?'

Blackstone grinned. 'I applaud your enthusiasm,' he said. 'But we can't hold them for a week. Without charging them, we can only hold them for seventy-two hours.'

'Then, by all means, let's charge them.'

'With what?'

'With running an illegal gambling club.'

'And we can prove that, can we?' Blackstone asked.

'Well, not actually *prove* it, in so many words,' Patterson admitted.

'Not actually prove it *at all*,' Blackstone countered. 'If we pull them in, it will only alert them to the fact that we're on to Lord Moneybags, and the moment we release them – and we *will* have to release them – they'll tell him just that.'

'So we just let them go on about their nasty business as if they were as pure as the driven snow?' Patterson asked, disapprovingly.

'I didn't say that,' Blackstone pointed out. 'We *will* pull them in eventually. But *before* we do, I want to find out more about them. What I really need is some kind of leverage I can use to make them open up.'

'And where are you planning to get this leverage from?'

'From my doggedly determined Sergeant, of course. I'd like you to collect as much information as you can on the pair of them.'

'From where, exactly?'

'You could try the American and German Consulates first. And once you've done that, you could send telegrams to the police in both of those countries, to see if either Rilke or Mouldoon has a criminal record.'

'Well, I am going to be busy, aren't I?' Patterson said. 'Is there anything else you'd like me to do, sir? Clean your spare pair of boots for you? Discover a cure for the common cold?'

'I don't think you'll have time to do either of those things,' Blackstone said, mildly. 'But there is one further task you might turn your hand to, if you've got a little extra time.'

'And what might that be?'

'I'd also like you to try and establish the identity of our corpse. If we know who he is, it might give us a lead on Lord Moneybags.'

'Simple stuff. Consider it done,' Patterson said sarcastically. 'And while I'm running round like a blue-arsed fly, what exactly will you be doing with your time, sir?'

'I shall be going back to St Saviour's Workhouse.'

'Why would you want to do that?'

I *don't* want to do it, Blackstone thought. I *hate* the idea of doing it. But it has to done.

'I think I rather hurried the investigation the first time I was there,' he admitted aloud.

And who wouldn't hurry it? Who wouldn't get away from that dreadful place as quickly as he could?

'What do you mean – you *hurried* it?' Patterson asked.

'Workhouse Man had to have had a reason for getting himself admitted to St Saviour's. We know that for a fact because, from what we've seen of the way they operate so far, this gang doesn't do *anything* without a reason.'

'True.'

'So what I'll be trying to find out is why Workhouse Man was willing to devote two days to going through the indignity and discomfort of pretending to be a pauper.'

There was an urgent knock on the door, and a uniformed constable entered the room.

'Yes?' Blackstone said.

'Sorry to disturb you, sir, but there's been another attack. They used dynamite this time. On Tower Bridge. But fortunately, the bomb didn't go off.'

'And why should you think this attack had anything to do with our arsonist?' Blackstone asked, sounding slightly irritated. 'It could just have easily been the Fenians, striking what they see as a blow for Irish independence.'

'The Fenians wouldn't have left a note addressed to you personally, sir,' the constable said, placing the letter on Blackstone's desk.

Blackstone opened the envelope.

'SEE HOW VERSATILE WE ARE, MR BLACKSTONE?'

the note taunted. 'WHY DON'T YOU TELL YOUR BOSSES TO STOP BEING SUCH BLOODY FOOLS AND GET THEM TO PAY UP BEFORE IT'S TOO LATE?'

'When did all this happen?' Blackstone asked.

'The bomb was discovered a couple of hours ago, sir.'

'And why wasn't I informed immediately?'

'Like you, everybody thought it was the work of the Fenians at first. Then the bomb was defused and the soldier in charge found the note.'

'Who was there when the note came to light?' Blackstone asked.

'Let me see. There was Inspector Walker, Sergeant Watts, half a dozen constables and—'

Blackstone sighed. 'Thank you, you can go,' he told the constable.

He read the note once more, then slipped it across the desk to his assistant.

'Doesn't tell us anything we couldn't already have worked out for ourselves,' the Inspector said gloomily when the Sergeant had finished reading it. 'We know our arsonists are determined, and we know they're resourceful. And we know there's as much chance of the Government giving in to their threats as there is of the Queen dancing the cancan in Piccadilly Circus.'

Patterson grinned. 'Now that's a sight I'd pay money *not* to see,' he said. 'So what do we do now?' he continued, growing more serious. 'Should we go down to Tower Bridge and examine the scene of the crime?'

'What would be the point of that?' Blackstone asked. 'Our firebugs are far too clever to leave behind anything that might lead us to them. And if they had made a mistake, what's the chances any clue would have survived the combined assault of half a dozen uniformed bobbies trampling all over it with their big flat feet?'

'Virtually nil,' Patterson agreed. 'So we stick to our previous plan, do we? I go to the German and American Consulates, and you—'

'And I go back to St Saviour's Workhouse,' Blackstone said, shuddering again.

109

'We could swap jobs, if you'd prefer it, sir,' Patterson said, sympathetically.

And what would be the point of that? Blackstone wondered. When had any man ever overcome his fear by running away from it?

'*I'll* go to the workhouse,' he said firmly.

'Good luck, sir,' Patterson said, as if he had some little inkling of what was going on in his boss's mind.

'You should wish us *both* good luck,' Blackstone told him. 'Because we're both going to bloody well need it.'

Twenty

Blackstone looked out of the window of the Workhouse Master's office and down on to the courtyard below. It seemed to be as much like a prison as anything he had ever seen.

'That's the men's exercise yard,' the Master said, following his gaze. 'We're not like some of the workhouses you may have heard of, which keep their inmates inside all the time. We're progressive here. We believe that those placed in our charge should get a breath of fresh air now and again.'

Fresh air? Blackstone repeated in his mind. *Fresh* air?

Just how fresh was the air supposed to be, in a courtyard surrounded by such high, imposing, walls?

'Would the "casual" I'm interested in have had access to that exercise yard?' he asked – because he was now wondering if the reason the firebug had entered the workhouse in the first place could have been because he desperately needed to contact someone who was already there.

The Master laughed. 'A casual! Have access to the men's exercise yard?' he said in a tone which suggested it was the most ridiculous idea he had ever heard. 'Oh dear me, no, Inspector. Certainly not!'

'Why not?'

'The workhouse operates on a principle of division and classification,' the Master said, lowering his voice as if he were revealing a closely guarded trade secret. 'Our regular inmates are split into three groups – men, women and children – and each group is housed in a different section of the building. They are not normally allowed to meet, although sometimes – on purely compassionate grounds – we will permit a mother to visit her children.'

'Very good of you,' Blackstone said dryly. 'But I was asking about the casuals.'

'The casuals are another category entirely – or rather, two categories, since they are both men and women. They have their own blocks.'

'You still haven't explained why the casual men are not allowed to mix with the regular male inmates,' Blackstone pointed out.

'I should have thought that was obvious,' the Master said. 'The casuals we admit are, on the whole, a pretty rough lot. They take what they're given readily enough, but they don't always appreciate how lucky they are to get it. Some of them have even been known to complain.'

'Scandalous!' Blackstone said.

'It is indeed,' the Master replied, nodding his head sagely. 'So you can see why we don't want them mixing with our regular inmates, can't you?'

'Because they'd spread discontent?'

'Exactly! Or, at least, they would try to.'

'Only *try* to?'

'They would meet with absolutely no success. The regulars are quite happy with their lot. They're grateful for their three square meals a day and a warm, dry place to sleep at night. They have no wish to be reminded that on the outside a man may rise and go to bed at what hour he wishes, whereas in here he must get up at six in the morning and be abed – with his candle extinguished – by eight in the evening. It is no longer of any interest to them that a man with money in his pocket may – if he chooses to squander it in such a manner – purchase strong drink. They have completely abandoned their baser instincts, too, and would be shocked to hear about the amorous exploits of the lascivious men who have just come in off the street.'

And quite right, too, Blackstone thought. For who, in his right mind, would ever want to drink and spend the night in the arms of a woman when he could, instead, reside in this paradise on earth?

'So, just to be clear on the point, the casuals are kept completely separate from the normal inmates,' Blackstone said.

'Precisely!'

112

Then that was that, Blackstone thought. Whatever the reason the firebug had had for seeking admission to the workhouse, it couldn't have been to talk to one of the inmates, because he must have known he would never be allowed to.

And yet . . . and yet . . . for all their boasting, the men in charge rarely knew everything that was going on in the institutions they administered.

'Would you mind if I talked to some of your staff?' he asked.

'I can see no reason why you shouldn't,' the Master said. 'But you won't learn anything more than I've already told you. There are strict rules – and they are scrupulously obeyed. We run a tight ship here.'

Yes indeed, Blackstone thought – a tight *prison* ship!

Located as it was – on St Helen's Place, and but a short walk from both the London Stock Exchange and Liverpool Street Station – the American Consulate was a convenient stop for men with either commerce or travel on their minds.

When Patterson arrived, it was already full, almost to bursting point, with both: on one side of the room, the American tourists with their guidebooks; on the other, British business-men shuffling stacks of invoices which needed an official stamp before they could begin to ship their goods to the United States. None of those waiting were exactly pleased to see the plump young man – who didn't look as if he were in any way important – ushered straight into the Consul-General's office.

The Consul-General was most welcoming. 'We always like to co-operate with the police in any way we can,' he said, shaking Patterson's hand, 'and if any of our own bad apples have found their way over here, we're more than willing to help you weed them out.'

Do you really 'weed out' bad apples? Patterson found himself wondering. But since he couldn't come up with any better image himself – and since, even if he could have, it was probably unwise to correct a senior diplomat – he contented himself with nodding and agreeing that bad apples were, indeed, his business.

'I believe that you keep a register of American citizens who are in London, do you not, sir?' he asked, when he'd accepted the Consul-General's invitation to sit down.

'Yes, but it probably isn't as inclusive as you might wish,' the Consul-General cautioned him. 'You see, it's not a record of all Americans in London, but only a record of those who *choose* to register.'

'I understand that, sir,' Patterson said, 'but I'd still be very grateful if you'd check through your books and see if one of those who *chose* to register was called Mouldoon.'

'Why, certainly,' the Consul-General said. There was a bookcase to the left of his desk and, reaching across to it, he extracted a leather-bound volume. 'What's the first name of the man you're interested in?'

'Robert.'

'And how long has he been in this country?'

'I don't know.'

The Consul-General sighed. 'It would have been much easier if you did,' he said. 'Do you at least know what profession this Mr Robert Mouldoon of yours is following?'

Yes, Patterson thought. He's a pimp – and I wouldn't be surprised if he was a part-owner of a gambling club, as well. But I'm certainly not going to tell *you* that until we have a clearer picture of the man.

'Sorry, I can't supply that information,' he said.

'You really don't seem to know much about your business,' the Consul-General said, sounding – for the first time – slightly disapproving. 'I would have expected a more professional approach from an old-established force like the Metropolitan Police.'

But he opened the ledger, and began to flick through it anyway.

'I've gone back three years, and there's no record of anyone called Mouldoon registering,' he said, after several minutes had passed.

That was only to be expected, Patterson thought. He reached into his pocket and produced the sketch which the police artist had made, based on Blackstone's description. 'This is the man,' he said. 'Do you recognize him?'

The Consul-General studied the sketch for quite some time.

114

'It's certainly a striking face,' he said, 'and a vaguely familiar one, too. But I don't know this man from any dealings I might have had with him in London.'

'But you *do* know him from somewhere else?'

'It's difficult to say,' the Consul-General admitted. 'This is a very good sketch indeed – please convey my congratulations to the artist – but it *is* still only a sketch. Now if you had a photograph . . .'

'Despite the fact that it's only a sketch, you do think you recognize him?' Patterson pressed.

'Yes, I must admit that I think I do.'

'Could you put a name to the face?'

'Not at the moment.'

'Then where do you think you might have seen him?'

'Somewhere in the States. Possibly in New York.'

Maybe you saw him when you were visiting your favourite New York brothel, Patterson thought, but realized he would have to find some way to rephrase it before he actually put it into words.

'Perhaps he's involved in the entertainment business,' he suggested.

'The entertainment business?' the Consul-General echoed. 'Doing what, exactly?'

The evil goblin who seemed to have crawled through Patterson's ear and into his brain had several suggestions, including one that Mouldoon might have been handing out whips in the brothel lobby and pouring fountains of champagne over naked prostitutes. The Sergeant decided to ignore the goblin altogether.

'I don't know exactly what he might have been doing,' he admitted. 'Perhaps he was the head waiter in your favourite restaurant. Or the manager of your dining club.'

'No,' the Consul-General said. 'If that had been the case, I think I would have recognized him instantly.' He considered the problem for a few seconds more. 'I get the distinct impression that I may have met him – though only briefly – on a more equal footing.'

'You mean that he might have been some kind of diplomat, much like yourself?'

115

'No, definitely not that,' the Consul-General said. 'I think . . . I think we must have come across each other at some sort of reception. Perhaps he's a businessman or a theatre producer.'

So we're back to the brothels, Patterson thought.

'Anything you tell me is completely confidential,' he said, trying to sound both worldly-wise and discreet.

'I'd assumed confidentiality from the very beginning,' the Consul-General told him. 'What's your point?'

A difficult point, Patterson thought. A *very* difficult point.

'That if you had not met him in the most salubrious of surroundings—' he began.

'What on earth are you talking about?'

'If . . . er . . . for example, you'd happened to stray – purely by accident – into a house of ill-repute . . .'

The Consul-General laughed. 'You think I might have met him in a cat house?'

'I . . . er . . .' Patterson said, lost for words.

'If I patronized such establishments, I would feel no embarrassment in telling you about it, but – trust me – I do not,' the Consul-General said, looking Patterson straight in the eye.

'I believe you, sir,' Patterson said, and was *almost* certain that he was speaking the truth.

'Are there any other copies of this sketch available?' the Consul-General asked.

'Yes, there are,' Patterson said. 'We're very up-to-date at the Met, and we have the very latest in reproductive—'

'I don't want a lecture on how Britain is not as backward as it sometimes seems,' the Consul-General said. 'I was merely enquiring as to whether I can keep this particular sketch, so that I can study it at leisure.'

'Well, yes, I suppose you can,' Patterson said, feeling more-than-somewhat deflated.

The Consul-General nodded. 'Good. And if you do manage to obtain a *photograph* of this man, why don't you have that sent over to me too?'

'I'll do that,' the Sergeant promised.

They shook hands, and Patterson was nearly at the door when the Consul-General said, 'It almost came to me then!'

'What did, sir?'

'Where I'd seen him before. I had a picture in my mind of crystal chandeliers, a polished wood floor, and some kind of musical entertainment. And before you're impertinent enough to ask the question, Sergeant, yes, I'm absolutely sure it wasn't a brothel.'

Patterson grinned. 'It had never occurred to me to think that it might be, sir,' he lied.

Twenty-One

While the senior warder was examining the sketch of the suspected firebug, Blackstone took the opportunity of examining *him*. He was one of those men who thought a little authority lifted them well above the common herd, the Inspector quickly decided – one of those men who likes to listen to nothing so much as the sound of his own voice.

'Oh yes, I remember this bugger, all right,' the warder said. 'I didn't like his attitude from the very start.'

'Oh?' Blackstone said, noncommittally.

'He was the sort of bloke who doesn't seem to realize just how lucky he's been to be taken in.'

'You mean, he was a bit like a dog which bites the hand that feeds it, rather than one that will even lick your boots to show how grateful it is?' Blackstone suggested.

'Exactly,' the warder agreed, pleased that the Inspector seemed to have grasped the point. 'Anyway, given this attitude of his, I wasn't the least bit surprised when he went off the rails.'

'*How* did he go off the rails?'

'He went missing, didn't he? What, in the Army, you would call going absent without leave.'

'When was this?'

'Let me see,' the warder said, self-importantly stroking his chin. 'It would have been the second morning he was here.'

'In other words, less than twenty-four hours before he was due to be discharged.'

'That's right.'

'Why don't you tell me exactly what happened?' Blackstone said.

'Be glad to. I'd set all the casuals to work picking oakum, and I went off for a smoke,' the warder said. 'Speaking of which,' he looked meaningfully at Blackstone, 'you don't happen to have any fags on you, do you?'

'Of course,' Blackstone replied, offering the warder a cigarette – and almost hating himself for doing it.

The warder lit up the cigarette, and inhaled greedily. 'When I got back to the workroom, there didn't seem to be as many of the casuals as there'd been when I left,' he continued, 'so I did a quick head count, and sure enough one of them was missing. Well, it didn't take me long to work out *which* one it was, did it? Like I told you, I'd had that cocky sod's card marked right from the start.'

'So you went looking for him?'

'Indeed I did. Can't have the casuals wandering around as if they own the place.'

'And where did you find him?'

'That kind of thing's happened before – not often, but it *has* happened – so I pretty much knew what to do,' the warder said, refusing to come directly to the point and thus ruin a good story in which he would undoubtedly feature as the hero. 'The first place I looked was in the women's section. Some of these women haven't seen a man for years, you know, and I thought that he'd probably figure they'd be gasping for a bit of how's-your-father and wouldn't be too particular about who they took the tumble with.'

'But he wasn't there?'

'No, he wasn't. The matrons hadn't seen hide nor hair of the blighter. So the next place I checked was the infirmary. They keep surgical alcohol there, you see, and even though it tastes foul, some of these blokes are so desperate they'll drink anything.'

'But he wasn't there, either?'

'No, he wasn't.'

'So where *did* you find him?' Blackstone asked, suppressing his natural urge to shake the man until his teeth rattled.

'Believe it or believe it not, I found him standing outside the old couples' apartments.'

'The old couples' apartments?' Blackstone repeated. 'I

thought it was the policy of this institution to keep the men and women completely separated from one another.'

'Then you've got it wrong,' the warder said. 'The *policy* is to stop them from enjoying themselves.'

'I don't understand,' Blackstone admitted.

'If you allowed a youngish couple to live together, they'd be jumping on each other all night. Going at it hammer and tongs. Humping till the cows come home. Making the—'

'I get the point,' Blackstone interrupted.

'*Enjoying* themselves,' the warder summed up. 'And we can't have that. But once they get to the stage where all that unhealthy passion's drained away, they can apply to the Board of Guardians to live together. And if the Board thinks they're suitable – which is the same as saying they're so dried up there's absolutely no chance of reigniting the fire – well, then they're given a room in the block where the other old couples live.'

Dear God! Blackstone thought.

'How did the man react when you caught him outside the old couples' block?' he asked.

'Didn't seem to mind at all,' the warder said, the disappointment he must have felt at the time still evident in his voice now. 'In fact, he was better behaved at that point than at any time since he'd been admitted. He didn't even object when I informed him that, as his punishment for his misbehaviour, he'd only get bread and water for his supper.'

Of course he didn't object, Blackstone thought. He didn't object because he'd already achieved his aim – whatever that was!

'When you caught him, did you notice anything unusual about him?' the Inspector wondered.

'How do you mean?'

'Did he look any different to the way he had when you'd last seen him in the workroom?'

'I noticed he'd ripped his jacket, if that's what you're asking.'

'Tell me more,' Blackstone coaxed.

'The regular inmates get issued with a uniform,' the warder said, 'but since the casuals are only here for a couple of days, they wear their own clothes. Now this particular bloke was wearing what must once have been a good jacket – tweed, if my memory serves me well – but sometime between him disappearing from the work room and me finding him again, he'd managed to rip it.'

'Exactly *how* had he ripped it?' Blackstone asked. 'Had he torn the sleeve or the lapel?'

'No,' the warder said. 'It was the lining which had got torn. It was hanging down below the edge of the jacket.'

Of course it was, Blackstone thought.

The German Consul-General had a heavily waxed moustache, a monocle firmly wedged in his left eye, and cuts on his cheeks which Patterson could only assume were duelling scars. He wore his severe dark suit as if it were a uniform, and had an air of brisk efficiency about him.

'How can I be of assistance to you, Sergeant?' he asked, in heavily accented English.

'I was wondering if you had some information on a German we're interested in who is living in London,' Patterson said.

'Yes, of course I have,' the Consul-General replied without hesitation.

'But . . . but how can you say that when I haven't even told you his name yet?' Patterson exclaimed.

'We are an orderly people,' the Consul-General said. 'If he is here, I will know about him.'

'Are you telling me that you have files on every single German citizen in London?'

The Consul-General shook his head. 'We do not run a police state, any more than you do,' he said, with a slightly rebuking tone in his voice. 'It would be wrong of us to keep files on our citizens.'

'Well, then . . .?'

'But we do have *records* of them.'

'And how do you go about collecting these "records"?' Patterson asked, fascinated that any organization could – apparently – be so efficient.

'Our citizens provide them themselves,' the Consul-General said, as if it were so obvious a point it was hardly worth making.

'They do? How?'

'Take, for example, our young men who come here to work

or to study. They know they will eventually be called up to perform their military service, so naturally they provide us with an address at which they can be contacted.'

'And what if they don't?' Patterson asked.

'If they *don't*?' the Consul-General repeated, mystified. 'But it would never occur to them not to register. It is their duty.'

'What about the ones who don't *need* to register for military service?' Patterson asked. 'How do you keep in touch with them?'

'Through the various organizations to which they belong,' the Consul-General said, again as though explaining the obvious. 'Those who have served in the Army will join a *Militarverein.*'

'That would be a military something-or-other,' Patterson guessed.

'Exactly,' the Consul-General agreed.

'And *verein* means?'

'It is hard to explain in English. It is neither a club nor a union, as you would understand those terms, yet it is both – and much more besides. It is said that wherever a dozen Germans meet, there is bound to be a *verein* of some sort. Take, for example, the *Deutscher Gewerbe und Theatre Verein* – the German Industrial and Theatre Club. It holds dances, concerts and dramatic recitations every week, but it is also the base for the *vereins* of typographers, bicyclists and chess players. It is a drinking and dining club. It is also a benefit society which provides for the sick and out-of-work, and for the burial of the dead. It has many members—'

'It would have,' Patterson interrupted.

'. . . and all its members are registered with both the *verein* and with the Consulate. Then there are the *heims* – homes, if you like. They provide subsidized food and accommodation for the poorer German workers. The Kaiser himself makes a generous donation towards their maintenance. They are very popular, and all the men who use them are, of course, properly registered.'

'It all seems highly organized,' Patterson said.

'We are an organized nation,' the Consul-General said. 'We

would never consider being anything else.' He paused for a second. 'So tell me, Sergeant, which of my compatriots are you interested in?'

'The man's name is Rilke,' Patterson said.

'You have a first name for him?' the Consul-General asked.

'My informant said his first name was Fritz, but I'm not sure how much we can rely on that,' Patterson admitted.

'It doesn't matter,' the Consul-General told him, off-handedly. 'Rilke is not a common name. There cannot be more than a few of them residing in London, and it will not take us long to narrow down the shortlist to the one you are particularly interested in.'

The American Consul-General had had one ledger from which to consult. The German had at least a dozen to choose from, but seemed to know exactly which one to select.

'I told you there would probably only be a few Rilkes,' he said, after he had scanned the ledger. 'In fact, there is just one Friedrich Rilke – Fritz is a shortened version, so he is registered as Friedrich.'

The Germans really knew how to run things, Patterson thought admiringly. 'I'd like any details you have on Rilke,' he said. 'And if you could also supply me with his address, that would be a bonus.'

'Naturally, I can supply you with an address,' the Consul-General said. 'He lives in Kensington – with his mother!'

'With his mother?' Patterson repeated, dumbfounded.

The Consul-General closed the ledger, carefully but firmly. 'Would you mind telling exactly why you are interested in this Fritz Rilke?' he asked.

'He runs a gambling club in Soho.'

'Does he, indeed?'

'And we suspect that he may also be involved in several other criminal activities – possibly even prostitution.'

Unexpectedly, the Consul-General began to chuckle, and then the chuckle turned into a full-bellied laugh.

'That is extraordinary,' he said, when he'd eventually calmed down. 'Who would ever have thought that a five-year-old boy could become involved in such things?'

*   *   *

123

The 'private apartments' that the workhouse offered were no great shakes in their own right, Blackstone thought – but in comparison to the rest of the grim institution they looked almost like little palaces. Each apartment consisted of only one room, but the rooms were brightly painted, and these inmates – unlike the younger, more vigorous ones – were permitted to have a few personal possessions like photographs and knick-knacks.

'I never dreamed we'd ever be lucky enough to end up in a place like this,' said the wizened old man sitting at the table. 'See, we've got our own chest of drawers!'

'Very nice,' Blackstone said.

'And there's a room at the end of the block where we eat our meals,' the old woman sitting next to him chipped in. *'That's* very nice as well.'

'I'm sure it is,' Blackstone agreed. 'You remember I said I'm a policeman, don't you?'

'Detective Inspector, you said,' the old man replied.

'That's right.'

'We used to know some of the local coppers on the beat when we lived on the outside,' the old man told him. 'Nice enough geezers to pass the time of day with, they were, but – you know – just ordinary. Not like you. We've never talked to a *detective inspector* before.'

Dear God, what is it about authority which impresses people so, thought Blackstone – who had never suffered from that particular failing himself.

'Would you like to know why I'm here?' he asked.

'We don't get many visitors,' the old man said. 'I can't remember the last one we had.'

'Yes, you can,' his wife said. 'It was just the other—'

She stopped suddenly, and put her hand to her mouth.

'Why don't you tell me about this visitor you had the other day,' Blackstone suggested.

'Don't listen to her. She doesn't know what she's talking about,' the old man said, in a harsh, yet squeaky, voice. 'Her mind wanders a bit, you know. It does, when you get to our age.'

Blackstone produced the sketch from his pocket and held it out. 'Is this the man?' he asked.

'Never seen him before,' the old man said, not even looking.

'You don't recognize him from your life outside?'

'I told you, we never saw him,' the old man protested.

'Why was he here? Did he want you to give him something?' Blackstone persisted.

'What could he have wanted from us?' the old man asked. 'We don't have nothing more than what you can see for yourself.'

Then it was just as Blackstone had suspected. 'Ah, then if he didn't want to *take* something, he wanted to *leave* something,' he said. 'Was it a package? A *thin* package?'

Thin enough to have been stored between the outer cloth of his jacket and the lining. Thin enough to have escaped detection when the porter searched him at the main gate.

'He said it would be all right,' the old woman said.

'Shut up, Betty, you fool!' the old man said, in a panic. 'You'll get us into trouble!'

'There'll be no trouble,' Blackstone promised. 'None at all. Just tell me what happened.'

'He came knocking on the door in the middle of the morning. He said he had something he wanted kept safe,' the old man admitted.

'Why do you think he came to you, rather than anybody else?' Blackstone asked.

'He said he'd been asking around, and everybody he'd talked to thought that we were the most reliable couple in the whole workhouse,' the old man replied, with a certain pride.

And the meekest, Blackstone thought – the most easily intimidated, the most easily persuaded.

'I'm sure your visitor made the right choice,' he told the old man. 'If I had a package that I needed looking after, you'd be the first people I'd come to.'

'And it'd be as safe as houses,' the old man told him.

'But I'll still need to look at it,' Blackstone said gently.

'We promised him,' the old man whined. 'We gave him our word that we'd keep it safe.'

'There's no shame in breaking your promise when there's no choice in the matter,' Blackstone said. 'Not when a *detective inspector* asks you for it. Besides, I have reason to believe this man to be a criminal. It's your duty to hand over whatever he gave you.'

'What if he comes back?' the old man asked worriedly. 'What if he comes back and asks us for it?'

'He won't come back,' Blackstone said. 'With the help you're about to give me, he'll probably be safely behind bars a few hours from now.'

The old man thought for a moment – Blackstone could read the indecision on his face – then, with an effort, raised himself from the table and hobbled over to his precious chest of drawers. He slid the top drawer open, put his hand inside, and withdrew the package.

'This is it,' he said, placing it on the table with great care.

It was long and thin – as Blackstone had suspected it would have to be in order to be smuggled in – and was wrapped up in oilskin material.

'He said it was very valuable,' the old man said.

'I'm sure it is,' Blackstone replied, picking the package up and slipping it into his pocket. 'So valuable, in fact, that it may well save the Government a hundred thousand pounds.'

Twenty-Two

The Blackstone whom Patterson found sitting behind his desk at the Yard – and gazing down at his ink blotter as though he thought he'd find some message hidden in it – was a very different one to the man the Sergeant had seen only a few hours earlier. This Blackstone seemed distracted, Patterson thought – this Blackstone seemed positively *worried*.

'Is anything the matter, sir?' he asked.

His words startled the Inspector out of his trance.

'What?'

'I asked if anything was the matter?'

'Yes, there is,' Blackstone said heavily. 'I don't like the direction that the evidence we're uncovering is pointing us in. I don't like it all.'

'Is the problem something you found out at the workhouse?' Patterson guessed.

Blackstone nodded gravely. 'But before we get to that, let's hear what you've got to report,' he said, sounding a little more like his old self.

'I don't know what Mouldoon and Rilke's real names are, but unless the German's much younger than he looks, they're not Mouldoon and Rilke,' Patterson said, sitting down opposite his boss. 'And men rarely use aliases unless they've got something to hide.'

He told Blackstone about his visits to the two consulates – about how the American Consul-General had said that Mouldoon looked familiar, and the German Consul-General had said that the only Rilke in London was a child.

When he'd finished, Blackstone nodded again, then said, 'We'd better have the Austro-Hungary Club watched.'

127

'It's already under observation,' Patterson said. 'I assigned two of our best men to it half an hour ago.'

'Good,' Blackstone said.

'Now do you want to tell me what's bothering you, sir?' Patterson asked softly.

The workhouse was bothering him, Blackstone thought. The idea of ending his days in a place where the only emotion he would be allowed to express was gratitude was bothering him. And the knowledge that the evidence he'd discovered could cost him his job – and take him one step closer to the workhouse – was bothering him most of all.

'Sir?' Patterson said worriedly.

Blackstone sighed, and laid the oilskin-wrapped parcel which he'd taken from the old couple on the desk. 'Have a look at this,' he said.

Patterson unrolled the package. Inside it – and wrapped up in a thick sheet of plain white paper – were some bank notes and an official-looking document.

The Sergeant wet his finger and quickly counted the notes. 'There's five hundred pounds here!' he exclaimed.

'That's right,' Blackstone agreed.

Patterson picked up the document. 'And this is a passport,' he said.

'Probably a fake.'

'So what we seem to have here, sir, is "running away" money,' Patterson said.

'That's exactly what it is. If things started to go badly wrong, our firebug planned to take shelter in the workhouse for a couple of days – and who'd think of looking for him there? Then, when things had cooled off a bit, he'd simply retrieve his package, and leave the country.'

None of which explained Blackstone's dark mood, Patterson thought. The package wasn't a major step forward in the investigation, but it was *a* step forward – so why was the Inspector looking so gloomy?

'You've missed something,' Blackstone said.

'Sorry, sir?'

'When you were looking at what I retrieved from the workhouse, you missed something.'

'I did? What?'

'Whoever gave the firebug the money and the passport wrapped it up in that sheet of paper.'

'So?'

'What you're looking at is the *back* of the paper. Why don't you see what's on the other side?'

Patterson turned the piece of paper over, and smoothed it out. It was standard – if expensive – writing paper. There was nothing actually written on it, but there was a crest embossed at the top of it – the crest of the House of Lords.

'Jesus!' Patterson said.

'Jesus!' Blackstone agreed.

The Minister of War had requested yet another urgent meeting with the Prime Minister at ten o'clock that morning, but it was not until early afternoon that Salisbury agreed to see him.

It was a stormy meeting from the start. Lansdowne burst – rather than walked – into the Prime Minister's office, and though he was invited to sit down, he chose to pace the floor instead.

'Do you realize the amount of damage that would have been done if that bomb had actually gone off as it was intended to?' Lansdowne asked the Prime Minister.

'I imagine it would certainly have meant closing the bridge for a time,' the other man replied.

'Closing the bridge!' Lansdowne repeated. 'Closing the bridge. That bomb could have demolished the bloody bridge! Or, at least, one end of it.'

'I remember watching that bridge being built,' the Prime Minister said, attempting to sound sanguine. 'It was an immense project – a miracle of engineering. It took eight years to build, I need not remind you, and a huge amount of concrete and steel was used in the construction. I doubt that any bomb, however large, could have actually demolished it.'

'I did not know you were an expert in such matters, Prime Minister,' Lansdowne said witheringly, continuing to pace the floor.

'Nor I, you,' Salisbury countered.

'I'm not. But I've seen the preliminary report.'

'And which report might that be?'

'The report of the Army bomb-disposal experts.'

'Which is more than I have,' the Prime Minister said. 'That report should have gone first to the Home Secretary. How did you manage to get your hands on it so quickly?'

'Does that matter now?' Lansdowne asked exasperatedly. 'The point is that the effect of the bomb – had it gone off as intended – would have been devastating. And it would not only have done physical damage to our war effort, it would have done great *psychological* damage as well.'

'To whom?'

'To our troops fighting in Southern Africa! Can you imagine what effect it would have had on their morale to learn that the centre of the very Empire they are fighting for is under attack? And what about the Boers? Can you even begin to conceive of what the news might have done for *their* morale? Until now they have thought themselves alone, fighting the mighty British Army. If they learned they had an ally – even an ally who is only working for his own greedy ends – it would greatly strengthen their resolve. It could have put the whole campaign back months. It might even have damaged it irrevocably.'

'*You* are the Minister of War, yet *I* seem to be the one who has the greatest faith in the courage and resolution of the British fighting man,' the Prime Minister said rebukingly.

'The British fighting man!' Lansdowne said, with scarcely veiled contempt. 'We're not discussing knights in shining armour, squaring up to each other on a small battlefield, Prime Minister. What we have here is a modern war. Such wars are not won by acts of individual courage, but by well-oiled military machines. And these attacks are throwing a spanner in the works of our particular machine. For God's sake, pay these people off, Robert – pay them while you still have the chance!'

Lord Salisbury shook his head gravely. 'I will not go against the wishes of the Cabinet in this matter,' he said.

'If we were not at war with the Boers, I'd tender my resignation,' Lansdowne said hotly.

'And if we were not at war with the Boers, I'd accept it,' the Prime Minister replied.

Patterson put down the telephone. 'I've just been talking to a mate of mine who works for the House of Lords,' he said. 'He tells me that they're very careful with their control of stationery supplies, because they don't want any of them falling into the wrong hands.'

Of course they didn't, Blackstone thought. A House of Lords letterhead would be an absolute gift to a con-man who was pretending to be a member of the aristocracy.

'But however careful they are, no system's perfect,' Patterson said, trying his best to sound optimistic. 'A clerk or a secretary might have been able to steal a sheet or two.'

But where would the clerk or secretary get the five hundred pounds which was wrapped up in it? Blackstone wondered.

Whichever way he looked at it – however much he tried to explain the evidence away, he was forced back to the conclusion that Lord Moneybags was, in fact, a real lord.

And real lords were rarely punished for their crimes, however heinous. Rather it was the little man who tried to bring them to justice who suffered – because what happened to him didn't matter a damn.

There was still a chance to extricate himself from the situation, Blackstone told himself. All he had to do was discard the evidence he had found in the workhouse. Of course, that would mean he'd fail to solve the case, but his career could possibly withstand that. And even if it didn't, even if he was thrown out on his ear, he would still have the five hundred pounds – because nobody was going to try to claim that back.

But he knew, even as he was holding this debate in his head, that he could never do it. Most of the general public looked down on orphans – were not the least surprised when they fell from grace. It had been a hard battle to convince this same general public that it was wrong, but up to that moment he had always been able to point to himself as just one example of the many orphans who hadn't fallen. But what if he now *did* go off the rails? Even if his fall went generally undiscovered, *he* would know about it – *he* would feel he had betrayed all those children he helped to keep alive with his donations.

The phone rang, and Patterson answered. 'It's the lads I've got watching the Austro-Hungary Club,' he said. 'They thought we might like to know that Mouldoon and Rilke have just arrived.'

Perhaps he still might have a chance of coming out of this whole bloody mess in one piece, Blackstone thought. Perhaps he could advance the investigation without having to deal directly himself with the rogue peer in the House of Lords. Perhaps – just perhaps – one of his superiors would take over when it became clear that an important man was involved.

'What do you want me to tell the lads, sir?' Patterson asked.

'Tell them to arrest Rilke and Mouldoon, and bring them down to the Yard,' Blackstone said.

Twenty-Three

There was a spy-hole set in the door, and by putting his eye against it, Blackstone could observe the man sitting at the table in what was officially called the Interview Room, but which both of them knew was, in truth, the *Interrogation Room*.

It didn't look good, he told himself. The very act of being arrested should have shaken the man inside. The period he had already spent in this forbidding room – with no company but his own thoughts – should have further unnerved him. Yet Mouldoon seemed as calm as if he were simply waiting for a train to arrive.

Blackstone opened the door and stepped heavily into the room. Mouldoon, for his part, looked up with what could almost have been called a wry smile playing on his lips.

'I know what's going through your mind,' Blackstone warned him.

'Do you really?' Mouldoon replied.

'Yes, I most certainly do. At the moment you're congratulating yourself on how well you're standing up to your ordeal. But the feeling won't last, you know. Believe me, it *never* lasts. And what will replace it? Well, I think I'll leave that to you to find out for yourself.'

'You have no right to treat me in this manner, you know,' Mouldoon said, almost conversationally. 'I'm not a criminal.'

His response was a bad sign, Blackstone thought. It was far too relaxed – far too complacent. A *good* sign – a sign that he might eventually break – would have been a defiant response, an insistence that, despite what his captor had just said, he could take whatever was dished out to him.

Blackstone sat down opposite his prisoner. 'So you don't

think you're a criminal,' he said. 'That's funny, because I could have sworn I'd seen you in an illegal gaming club.'

Mouldoon grinned. 'I could have sworn I'd seen you there, too.' He held up his hands to forestall anything Blackstone might say. 'I know! I know! You were pursuing an inquiry.'

'That's right.'

'And I was there to gamble. OK, I admit it. I'll sign a statement to that effect, if it will keep you happy. But what will be the consequences of my "illegal" action? A fine? Then why don't we save some time? Just tell me how much this fine of yours is likely to be, and I'll pay it right now.'

'Gambling's not the only reason you're here,' Blackstone said. 'I could also charge you with living off immoral earnings.'

'With what?' the American asked.

'I have reason to believe that you run a string of prostitutes out of the Austro-Hungary Club.'

'I certainly do no such thing.'

'You introduced *me* to one of them.'

'I introduced you to a *young lady*,' Mouldoon corrected him.

'And why should you have done that?'

'I was being no more than polite to a fellow guest at the club. I had no idea the woman in question was a professional – and you'll never be able to prove that I did.'

'We have her signed statement in which she swears that she was working for you.'

'So it's my word against hers. The whore versus the well-dressed, soft-spoken American gentleman. So tell me, Inspector, which one of us do you think the magistrate's more likely to believe?'

'It'll be more than just *her* word when we've interviewed the other whores,' Blackstone said.

Mouldoon leaned back in his chair. 'Well, I sure wish you luck in finding them,' he drawled. 'I don't recall seeing any of the young ladies around since the night before last.'

So whatever she'd promised, Molly the prostitute had warned Mouldoon off, Blackstone thought. He shouldn't be surprised by that, he supposed. In fact, he should have been *expecting* it.

'Maybe I won't be able to make the charges stick at the end of the day,' he said, changing tack. 'But I'll certainly try my damnedest to. And *while* I'm trying, you'll be locked up in a prison, where some very nasty people will want to get at you – especially if they're given some sort of encouragement.'

Mouldoon smiled. 'Is that a threat?'

'You tell me! I'd certainly think that it was, if I were on the receiving end of it.'

Mouldoon nodded thoughtfully. 'You're not truly interested in locking me up for running a few hookers out of a gaming club,' he said. 'What is it you're really after?'

Blackstone took the sketch of 'Lord Moneybags' out of his pocket, and slid it across the table. 'Tell me about him,' he said. 'Or are you going to pretend that you don't recognize him?'

'Oh, I recognize him, right enough. He's a customer at the Austro-Hungary Club.'

'And what's his name?'

'He signed in the register as Mr Smith.'

'But we both know that's not his real name.'

'Of course we do. No more than it is yours. But I don't happen to know what his true name is.'

'Did he ever show an interest in any of your girls?'

'They're not *my* girls.'

'Did he show any interest in *the* girls, then?'

'No. He didn't appear to care for women.'

'So it's *boys* he likes?'

'Nor boys, either. His vice is gambling.'

'Did he gamble heavily?'

'Not excessively.'

'I heard that on one night alone he lost four thousand pounds at the baccarat table.'

'Did he indeed? Well, that's easy enough to do, if you're facing an unlucky run of cards. But since I didn't see it for myself, I really couldn't say whether that's true or not.'

'You're not being very helpful, Mr Mouldoon.'

'You may well be right, Inspector Blackstone,' the American agreed easily, 'but perhaps the reason for that isn't because I *won't* be, but rather because I *can't* be.'

'Need I remind you that you could have some very nasty experiences down in the cells?' Blackstone said, shaking his head mournfully. 'Some *very* nasty experiences. I don't want to go into any of the unpleasant details, but I should think you could pretty much imagine them for yourself.'

Mouldoon smiled again. 'Let me give you a piece of advice, Inspector,' he suggested. 'Never make a threat you can't keep.'

'And what's that supposed to mean?' Blackstone demanded.

'It means that I regard myself as a pretty good judge of character. And this is the way I read yours – you'd like a confession of some sort from me, but there's certain means you wouldn't employ, however badly you needed it.'

He was right to think he'd be as safe in the cells as he would be in his own home, Blackstone thought. He was right to assume that the man who was locking him up would see to that personally – because that was just his way.

The Inspector sighed and turned to the constable who was standing in the doorway. 'Take Mr Mouldoon down, will you, please?' he said. 'Find him a nice quiet cell on his own.'

Rilke was quite as relaxed as Mouldoon had been, but in a stiffer, more Germanic manner.

'Tell me about this man,' Blackstone said, showing him the same sketch he had shown to Mouldoon only minutes earlier.

'I believe his name is Smith.'

'And he's a heavy gambler?'

'He certainly *likes* to gamble. Most people who go to gambling clubs do. That is why they go there.'

'I don't think you quite appreciate your own position, Mr Rilke,' Blackstone said. 'You're in a great deal of trouble.'

'Am I?'

'You most certainly are. As the owner of the Austro-Hungary Club—'

'But I am *not* the owner,' Rilke interrupted.

'As the manager, then.'

'I am not the manager, either.'

'Then who is?'

'The manager, as I understand it, is a man called Jones.'

'And where might I find him?'

136

'I am afraid I cannot help you there, Inspector. I haven't seen him for several days.'

'So, in his absence, the club's been running itself, has it?' Blackstone asked sceptically.

'Any institution which has been established with care and precision is perfectly capable of running itself for some quite considerable time,' Rilke said. 'That is something we Germans have learned – and something you English could learn *from* us.'

'According to the German Consul-General, the only Rilke in England at the moment is five years old.'

Rilke shrugged. 'The German Consul-General is wrong,' he said. 'I am the living proof of that.'

'But can you prove your real name is Rilke?'

'No.'

'You can't? You don't have any documents? A passport, for example? Or an identity card?'

'No.'

'I thought that you Germans prided yourselves on the extent of your documentation.'

'And so we do. But, unfortunately, all such documents were stolen from me a week ago.'

'Did you report the theft?'

'No.'

'Why not?'

'There seemed no point in doing so. I have very little confidence in the English police.'

'You do understand your position, don't you?' Blackstone asked. 'You do *know* you could go to gaol?'

'For what?' Rilke responded. 'You will find no evidence to tie me in with the club.'

'In that case, we'll just have to deport you as an undesirable alien, won't we?'

'I wish you would. I am already bored with this wet little country of yours, and would welcome the chance to travel back to the Fatherland at the expense of your government.'

The pub seemed much more subdued than it normally did. Or maybe it was just he, himself, who was subdued, Blackstone thought, as he drew patterns in the beer some earlier customer had spilled on the table. Probably it was just him – he certainly had reason enough.

Patterson returned from the bar with two pints of best bitter. Blackstone examined his for a moment – as if he were not quite sure what it was – then downed half of it in a single gulp.

'Does that make the world look any better, sir?' Patterson asked, his voice edged with concern.

'We can't hold them, you know,' Blackstone said moodily, ignoring the question. 'At least, we can't hold them for *long*. Rilke took great pleasure in informing me that we'll never tie him to ownership of the Austro-Hungary Club, and he sounded so confident about it that I'm inclined to believe him.'

'What about Mouldoon?'

'The same with him. We'll never make the charge of procurement stick – not if he's been as careful as I think he's been. Besides, when all's said and done, neither of them is *directly* involved in the crime we're actually investigating.'

'You don't think they have anything at all to do with the arson attacks?' Patterson asked.

'Why should they have? Why get their own hands dirty when there's absolutely no need for them to do so?'

'If they want the money . . .'

'It's Lord Moneybags – or whatever the bugger's real name is – who *owes* the money. And it's Lord Moneybags who has to find some way of raising it. All they have to do – as the people who are no more than his creditors – is to sit back and wait for him to hand it over.'

'Do you think they know who he really is?'

'Of course they do! If he's that much in debt to them, they just have to know his real name, and where he lives. But if they tell us his identity, we'll arrest him – and he'll never be able to clear his debt to them. So it's in their interest to keep quiet, even if keeping quiet involves them spending a little time in gaol.'

'And you don't think gaol will soften them up at all?'

'Not a chance. It's . . .' Blackstone waved his hands helplessly in the smoke-filled air, '. . . it's almost as if they'd known this very thing was going to happen all along, and had been mentally preparing themselves for it.'

'I know just what you mean,' Patterson said. 'So what's your next move, sir?'

'I've been thinking about it, and there is only one move *I* can make,' Blackstone told him. 'I'm going to have to take everything we've got so far, and lay it on the desk of Sir Roderick-bloody-Todd.'

Patterson was taking a sip of his pint, and when he heard what Blackstone had said, he almost choked on it.

'You're going to take it to the Assistant Commissioner?!' he said, when he could finally speak again.

'Yes.'

'But you know Todd as well as I do, sir. Probably better!'

'True,' Blackstone agreed.

'If you went to him with cast-iron proof of our theories, then he might – and I say just *might* – be prepared to put all his personal prejudices aside for one moment, and listen to what you had to say. But we haven't got cast-iron proof, have we? What we do have is a piece of House of Lords notepaper, and the opinion of a common prostitute that one of the clients at the Austro-Hungary Club acted as if he *were* actually a lord.'

'And the sketch Molly provided us with,' Blackstone pointed out. 'Don't forget the sketch.'

'Normally I'd say that what we've got is no more than circumstantial – but I'm not even feeling that optimistic at the moment,' Patterson said. 'You can't go and see Todd, sir. He's never going to stand for you accusing a member of the House of Lords – a peer of the realm – of arson. Not on our evidence!' He paused, and, for the first time since they'd been working together, put his hand on his boss's shoulder. 'Don't do it, sir. He'll blow his stack. He'll have your balls for breakfast.'

'Possibly he will,' Blackstone agreed. 'But as I said earlier, there's really nothing else I *can* do.'

Twenty-Four

Sir Roderick Todd did not ask the Inspector to take a seat. But then, Blackstone thought, that scarcely came as a surprise. He had never been asked to sit down on any previous occasion, either – and if such a possibility had been offered to him now, his first thought would have been that the chair in question must be strategically placed over a trapdoor.

Todd glared at him for several seconds, then said, 'You're going to tell me something I'd rather not hear, aren't you?'

'Why should you think that, sir?' Blackstone asked.

'Because you've come to see me voluntarily, rather than waiting to be summoned. And you only do that when you have something particularly unpleasant to impart. Am I right, Inspector?'

'Yes, sir,' Blackstone said, because it was – after all – the truth.

'Tell me the worst, then,' Sir Roderick said, resignedly.

Blackstone took a deep breath. 'I have reason to believe that the mastermind behind the spate of recent arson attacks is a person of some significance, sir,' he said in a rush.

Todd frowned. 'A person of some significance? What are we talking about here? A barrister, perhaps? Or a doctor?'

'No, sir. A lord.'

Todd shook his head, almost despairingly. 'I should have expected something like this. You simply never tire of trying to bring your betters down, do you, Blackstone?'

'I have proof, sir.'

The Assistant Commissioner sighed. 'Well, now you're here, I suppose I might as well hear it,' he said ungraciously.

Blackstone told Sir Roderick about the visit he had made to the Austro-Hungary Club, the package he had found in the workhouse, and the interview he had conducted with Molly.

'So a common prostitute – a woman of the streets – believes that one of her clients acted as though he were a lord,' Sir Roderick said, almost echoing Patterson's earlier comments.

'He wasn't—' Blackstone began.

'Well, that's almost crushingly convincing, isn't it?' Sir Roderick interrupted, cuttingly.

Blackstone tried again. 'He *wasn't* one of her clients, sir.'

'So he chose one of the other whores instead of her. That would explain why she's out to get him.'

'He wasn't interested in any of the prostitutes. He was there to gamble – and he lost heavily.'

'And that's what makes him a lord, is it? That he lost heavily? Don't you find it strange that though you will have come across the phrase, "As drunk as a lord", often enough, there doesn't seem to be one which refers to their addiction to gambling?'

Patterson had been right, Blackstone thought. Todd wouldn't see what he didn't want to see. He hadn't even bothered to listen closely to what evidence there was.

'What ties the arson attacks in with a lord is not what the prostitute said,' he explained, as patiently as he was able. 'The link is the sheet of House of Lords notepaper.'

'So why mention the prostitute at all?'

The Assistant Commissioner had turned obstructionism into an art form, Blackstone thought.

'I mentioned her because, once we've found out through other means who this lord is, she'll be able to identify him,' he said.

'But why resort to other means at all?' Sir Roderick said. 'Why not go straight to the heart of the matter?'

'I don't understand, sir.'

'Then I'll explain it to you, Blackstone. This is what we'll do. Tomorrow morning, we'll herd every lord in the country – however important he happens to be – into the most dilapidated police station we can find, and—'

'Sir, we—'

'Perhaps, on reflection, we won't even bother to use a police

141

station at all. Perhaps we'll make them line up along the Old Kent Road. And once we've got them there, we'll ask this *common prostitute* to walk up and down the line and see if she can identify one of them. Would *that* suit you, Inspector?'

'That won't be necessary, sir,' Blackstone replied.

'Good! I'm *so* pleased to hear that. And *why* won't it be necessary, pray tell, Inspector?'

'Because we have a police artist's sketch of the man.'

'You do? Then would it be too much of an imposition to ask you to show it to me?'

'Of course not, sir,' Blackstone said, taking the sketch out of his pocket and placing it on the desk.

In his current obstructionist mood, there were several ways Todd could react to the sketch, Blackstone thought.

He might choose to belittle it by saying it was a very poor sketch indeed – that it could as easily be of a horse as of a person. He might attempt to undermine its value by claiming it reminded him of his coalman or his baker. He might even simply pronounce it a waste of time, and throw it on the floor.

Todd chose none of these courses. Instead, he gazed down at the sketch with a growing look of horror on his face.

'Is . . . is this some kind of joke?' Todd demanded. 'Because if you think I'll find it amusing, Blackstone, I can assure you that you're entirely wrong.'

'It's no joke, sir.'

'But you surely know who this is, don't you?'

'I'm afraid I don't.'

'Good God, man, don't you read the papers?'

'Not if I can help it, sir.'

'The man in this sketch is – without a shadow of a doubt – Lord Lansdowne himself.'

Blackstone felt as if the back of his head had been struck hard by a brick. He had thought it likely that the man might be moderately well known or moderately powerful. He had been prepared to learn that he was a personal friend of Sir Roderick Todd's. But he had never – never – even considered the possibility that Lord Moneybags could be someone *so* important.

'The . . . the Minister of War!' he gasped.

142

'The Minister of War,' the Assistant Commissioner agreed. 'The ex-Governor-General of Canada! The ex-Viceroy of India! And are you seriously trying to tell me that a man of his stature would allow himself to become involved in a scheme to blackmail the Government of which he himself is a part?'

Blackstone's head was still reeling from what he had just learned, but he was already starting to pull himself together again.

'All men have weaknesses,' he said, 'even important ones like Lord Lansdowne. Gambling's an obsession. And having blue blood running through your veins doesn't automatically make you immune to it.'

'But the man's a member of the Cabinet. He has a fine house in town, and a country estate.'

'Then he has more to lose than most people,' Blackstone said, regaining a little more of his shattered confidence. 'And even for someone like him, a gambling debt of one hundred thousand pounds must be a considerable strain.'

'It's ludicrous!' Sir Roderick said. 'Simply insane. I won't even entertain the idea.'

But despite Todd's reaction, the more Blackstone thought about it himself, the more it made sense.

'Look at the facts,' the Inspector said. 'We know he gambled heavily at the Austro-Hungary Club – and that he lost. We know that one of the two men who he went to the club with was killed when the *Golden Tulip* was set on fire. And we know that the arsonist has been an *unwilling* firebug at best.'

'Unwilling?' Sir Roderick said.

'*Very* unwilling. Why did he start such a small fire on Tooley Street, and do it at a time when the river was so high that the Fire Brigade would find it easy to draw water? Why did he arrange for the captain of the *Golden Tulip* to be on deck when he set the sloop on fire? And why did he make certain that the bomb he left on Tower Bridge would never go off?'

'You're wrong on that last point, at least,' Sir Roderick said. 'The reason the bomb on Tower Bridge didn't explode was because the bomber had set the timer incorrectly.'

Blackstone shook his head. 'No, sir. It didn't go off because he didn't *want* it to.'

'And how can you possibly be so sure of that?'

'Because of the note he left me.'

'I've read that note myself,' Todd said. 'There's absolutely nothing in it to suggest he didn't expect the bomb to explode.'

'He left it on the bridge,' Blackstone said patiently.

'And just what does that prove?'

'If the bomb had gone off, it would have destroyed the note, so there would have been no point in leaving it in that particular spot. The very fact that he *did* leave it there proves my point.'

Sir Roderick turned the idea over in his mind for a few seconds. 'I suppose there may be some truth in what you claim,' he said grudgingly.

'Put yourself in Lord Lansdowne's place,' Blackstone argued. 'He has probably convinced himself that he is the best person to conduct the war against the Boers and—'

'He *is* the best person,' Sir Roderick interrupted.

'. . . and so he sees it as his duty to remain in office for the duration of the hostilities. But, at the same time, he has this crushing gambling debt which he knows could bring about his downfall. So what does he do? He persuades himself that, for the good of the country, he will embark on a course of action that he would never normally consider. He will black-mail the Government because, in the long term, he is doing it to benefit the Empire.'

'I'm not sure I want to listen to any more of this—' Sir Roderick Todd interjected.

'But he can fool himself so far, and no further,' Blackstone pressed on. 'If he actually impedes the war effort – and the war effort is the only real justification for these criminal activ-ities of his – then his delusion that he is acting unselfishly collapses. If he impedes the Southern African campaign in any way, then he reveals himself, *to* himself, for what he really is – a man desperate merely to salvage his own reputation.'

'That's ludicrous,' Sir Roderick said – but he didn't sound convincing, even to himself.

'We need to bring him in for questioning,' Blackstone said.

'You might be able to bring a dustman in for questioning on the evidence you've got – or even a tea merchant or a book-keeper – but it's certainly not strong enough to bring in a Minister of the Crown,' Sir Roderick scoffed.

'So you admit there is *some* evidence?' Blackstone asked, pouncing on his inadvertent admission.

'Yes,' Sir Roderick said heavily, and as he spoke he took his handkerchief out of his pocket and mopped his perspiring brow. 'There is, perhaps, the possibility of *some* evidence.'

'So how do you intend to act on it?'

'We'll talk to Lord Lansdowne, you and I—'

'Talk to him!'

'*Talk* to him. That is what I said, and that is what I meant. We will not drag him down to a police station, as you seem to be so crudely suggesting we should. This is a matter of some delicacy, and calls for a much lighter touch.'

'And what kind of "lighter touch" did you have in mind?'

'We will make an appointment with His Lordship, and see him in his office at the Ministry of War.'

'How very civilized,' Blackstone said. 'How very civilized – and how totally bloody useless.'

'You came to me for help, Inspector Blackstone, did you not?' Sir Roderick said sternly.

'Yes, but—'

'And this is the help that I am offering you. We either go to see Lord Lansdowne in his office, or we do not see Lord Lansdowne at all. Which of those is it to be?'

'So it's one law for the rich, and another for the poor,' Blackstone said bitterly.

'It was *always* one law for the rich and another for the poor. I thought that a man in your position would have come to appreciate that long ago,' Sir Roderick said. 'But you have still not answered my question. I've given you two clear alter-natives. Which one will you choose?'

'We'll go and see Lord Lansdowne in his office at the Ministry of War,' Blackstone said, forcing the words out of his mouth.

Sir Roderick permitted himself a slight smirk. 'I thought that would be your answer,' he said.

Twenty-Five

Standing at his office window and watching the river flowing past below, Blackstone remembered the night, three years earlier, when he had felt the urge to walk down the nearest steps – and keep on walking until the water covered his head and he drowned. If Vladimir, the Russian secret policeman, hadn't suddenly appeared, he was convinced he would have done just that. But Vladimir *had* appeared, and – in a way Blackstone still didn't quite understand – had restored his will to keep on fighting against the odds, to keep on striving towards goals he knew deep inside himself that he could never achieve.

Not once since that night had he again contemplated drowning himself, but that did not mean the urge was buried for ever – didn't mean it wasn't just in hiding, waiting for the moment when it could re-emerge and absorb him completely.

'I've seen dozens of magicians in the music halls, but they're nothing but bumbling amateurs compared to you, sir,' said a voice behind him.

Blackstone, not quite sure if someone else had actually spoken or if he had merely been hearing one of the numerous voices which seemed – from time to time – to inhabit his brain, slowly turned round.

'Did you say something, Sergeant?' he asked Patterson.

'Yes, sir. I said that you could knock spots off most of the magicians I've ever seen.'

'And what's brought on this sudden enthusiasm for my powers of wizardry?' Blackstone wondered.

'I should have thought it was obvious, sir. You go to the Assistant Commissioner with evidence so flimsy you could see light through it, yet he still agrees to allow you to talk to Lord Lansdowne.'

Blackstone sighed. 'There are times when I wish I could see the world through your eyes, Patterson,' he said. 'But if you're ever going to rise above the rank of sergeant, you're going to have to start seeing it through mine.'

'What do you mean, sir?' Patterson asked, puzzled.

'Todd's not allowing me to meet Lansdowne because he thinks it will give me the opportunity to build up my case against him.'

'Isn't he?'

'No, he bloody isn't. The meeting's being held for Lansdowne's benefit, not mine. It's intended to scare him off.'

'Pardon?'

'Sir Roderick's pretty much accepted that Lansdowne is behind the arson attacks . . .'

'Well, then?'

'. . . but a member of the Government can't possibly be punished for his crimes, as he would be if he was an ordinary bloke like you or me. *That's* why we're going to see him.'

'I don't understand,' Patterson confessed.

'The meeting has no other purpose than to let him know that we're on to him. It's a way of saying that he'll have to find another way to solve his financial problems – because if he continues with these arson attacks, he'll reach a stage at which even his influential friends won't be able to protect him any longer.'

'So if you go to see Lansdowne, you'll be helping Sir Roderick in his attempt to prevent the guilty from being punished?'

'That's right.'

'And you're still going along with it?'

'Yes. Because it just might be possible to play Todd's game *and* play one of my own.'

'You've lost me again,' Patterson admitted.

'If Lansdowne refuses to see us at all, then he's won,' Blackstone said. 'If he agrees to see us, but throws us out of his office as soon as we start asking questions, then he's also won. But I don't think he'll do either of those things, because he's a very clever man.'

'But from what you've just said, the cleverest thing he could do would be to have nothing to do with you,' Patterson protested.

'And clever men always think they're in control,' Blackstone continued, as if his assistant had never spoken. 'Clever men believe they can handle any situation they find themselves in, and so it becomes a point of pride with them to meet trouble head on. That's what I think Lansdowne will do.'

'I still don't see how that will get you anywhere.'

'The more he says, the more chance I have of catching him out in a lie. And once I've done that, we're into a different kind of game entirely.'

'That's all very well, but do you know enough about the intricacies of the whole affair to be able to *appreciate* when he's lying and when he's telling the truth?' Patterson wondered.

'Not yet,' Blackstone said. 'But I will by the time I meet him.'

It had been three years since Blackstone had last visited the house on Park Lane which was the Montcliffe family's London home. Then, as now, the visit had been to do with a body found floating in the Thames, and then, as now, he did not enter the house through the front door, but by way of the basement servants' entrance.

A maid – one of the dozens who seemed to occupy the area below the family's spacious quarters – led him along the maze of corridors to the butler's private parlour.

'Mr Hoskins is expecting you, sir,' she said, then gave him a quick curtsey and disappeared.

Blackstone knocked on the door. When the butler answered, he seemed genuinely pleased to see the Inspector, and shook his hand warmly.

'Please, do come inside, Mr Blackstone,' he said.

Blackstone stepped into a room which was furnished with family cast-offs, but was still luxurious in comparison to what he was used to himself.

'A glass of port, Mr Blackstone?' the butler enquired. 'I have a bottle of the '56, which I'm sure you'll find more than palatable.'

'I'm sure I will,' Blackstone agreed.

Mr Hoskins poured the drinks, then sat down opposite Blackstone. 'I remember the first time you came to this house,' he said. 'I was, I think we could say, a little unwilling to co-operate with you.'

'We *could* say you treated me as if I were an enemy soldier, approaching with fixed bayonet,' Blackstone said.

Mr Hoskins looked as if he were a little unsure how to react for a moment. Then he laughed.

'Yes, we could say that,' he admitted. 'I felt it my duty, as I always do, to protect the family from the intrusion of a hostile, outside world. I did not think a policeman in a . . . in a . . .'

'In an obviously second-hand suit?' Blackstone supplied.

'Thank you,' Mr Hoskins said. 'I did not think a man from your background would have the finesse to deal with the delicate situations which inevitably exist in a house of this nature – and in a family of this nature.' He paused. 'What is your opinion of the port, Mr Blackstone?'

'It's very good,' said Blackstone, who would rather have had a pint of best bitter in his hand than this delicate, crystal glass.

'It's very kind of you to say so,' the butler acknowledged. 'Now where was I?'

'You thought I'd rampage through this house like a wild bull in a china shop?'

'Indeed I did. But I was wrong about you, Mr Blackstone. You are a sensitive man, and you handled yourself – and the whole affair – with the greatest of discretion. I think it is fair to say that the family's reputation could have been severely damaged by that rather unpleasant and regrettable incident, and the fact that it was not is largely due to you.'

'I think you rather overrate the part I played, Mr Hoskins,' Blackstone said modestly.

'I do not,' Hoskins insisted. 'I will go even further in my praise of you. Had you chosen to enter service instead of the police force, I am convinced you would eventually have risen to be a very fine butler indeed.'

'Thank you,' Blackstone said.

'But you are not here to reminisce, are you? No one ever comes to see a butler unless they have a problem which needs solving. What is your problem, Mr Blackstone?'

'I'm pleased you recall your first reaction to me,' Blackstone said. 'I also understand – and sympathize with – the thinking behind it. And that is where my current problem really begins. Whenever a case brings me into contact with a butler I have not met before, I must convince him that his preconceived notions are wrong. That takes time. And time, as you will readily appreciate, is in somewhat short supply during a criminal investigation.'

Mr Hoskins took a long, thoughtful sip of his port. 'You want an introduction to another butler,' he said finally.

'Yes.'

'Am I acquainted with the butler in question?'

'I don't know.'

'Because if I am not, I fail to see what purpose an introduction from me will serve.'

Blackstone did no more than chuckle.

'I was not aware I was being amusing,' Mr Hoskins said.

'It doesn't really matter whether you know him or not,' Blackstone said. 'He will be aware of your reputation, and that will give your introduction all the weight it needs.'

'You're flattering me,' Mr Hoskins said.

'Am I?' Blackstone asked, noncommittally.

Mr Hoskins laughed. 'But even if it is flattery, it is also the truth,' he conceded. 'Appending my name to a document does give that document a certain gravity.' He paused again. 'Who is it you wish to speak to?'

'Lord Lansdowne's butler.'

The pause was even longer this time. 'Lord Lansdowne is in the Government,' he said finally.

'I'm well aware of that,' Blackstone replied. 'So was your master, the last time we met.'

'Am I to take it, then, that this is a matter of national importance?' Mr Hoskins asked.

'It is a matter which has already involved the death of one man, and may yet involve more. Whether or not that makes it a matter of national importance, I wouldn't like to say – but

150

it is certainly important *enough* for me to ask for your help, and for you to be willing to give it.'

The butler nodded slowly. 'I will write you your letter, Mr Blackstone,' he said.

'Thank you, Mr Hoskins,' Blackstone replied.

Twenty-Six

Mr Chalmers's sitting room was almost identical to the one occupied by Mr Hoskins, and – like his fellow butler – Chalmers carried with him all the weightiness of a prime minister.

'I would not normally have consented to this meeting, Inspector,' the butler said.

In his younger days, Blackstone would have been outraged by such a comment.

'Consented!' he would have demanded. 'For God's sake, who needs your consent? I'm a police officer, going about my lawful duty, and I don't need the *consent* of anyone!'

He didn't say that now. The intervening years had taught him a good deal, and whilst he didn't like the way the system worked, he had long ago decided that given the choice of working within it, or not working at all, he would extract from it all that he could.

'It is only because you brought with you a letter of introduction from the estimable Mr Hoskins that I ever contemplated seeing you,' the butler continued, 'and even so, if I think that your questions prejudice my master's interests in any way, I will be forced to refrain from answering them.'

'That is completely understood,' Blackstone said, 'but since all I wish you to do is to attempt to identify two people for me, I cannot imagine your master's interests would be in the least endangered.'

'We will see about that,' the butler said, ever cautious. 'Would you be so good as to show me your pictures?'

The first sketch which Blackstone showed the butler was the one of Workhouse Man.

'Do you know him?' he asked.

Mr Chalmers studied the sketch for some moments. 'It certainly looks like Mr McClusky,' he conceded.

'And who is Mr McClusky?' Blackstone asked.

'He is the manager of His Lordship's country estate.'

'How do you happen to know him? Do you serve His Lordship both here *and* at the estate?'

The butler grimaced, as if Blackstone had struck a nerve. 'It would be well within my capabilities to do so,' he said, 'but His Lordship insists – for what, I am sure, are perfectly valid reasons – on having one butler for London and one for the estate.'

'So it's in London where you've seen this McClusky?'

'Yes.'

'In this house?'

'Yes.'

It was like pulling wisdom teeth, Blackstone thought grimly. 'And what was McClusky doing here?' he asked.

The butler seemed at a loss as to how to answer. 'He has been here as a guest,' he said finally.

'A guest?'

'Mr McClusky is not perhaps quite a gentleman in the strictest interpretation of the word, but he is certainly considered good enough to attend some of His Lordship's less prestigious dinner parties.'

'When did you last see him?'

'He was up in town last week.'

Just about the time that 'Lord Moneybags' and his friends made their last visit to the Austro-Hungary Club, Blackstone noted.

'And this man?' the Inspector asked, producing the sketch of the other man who accompanied Moneybags to the club.

'It could be the Honourable Charles Davenport,' the butler said. 'In fact, I'm sure it is.'

'And is this the same man?' Blackstone asked, producing the photograph of the corpse which had been fished out of the river.

'Yes, but . . . but in the photograph, he looks dead.'

'And so he is,' Blackstone said.

'How did he . . .? Whatever could have . . .?'

153

'And what can you tell me about him?' Blackstone demanded.

'Very little,' Mr Chalmers said unconvincingly.

Blackstone sighed. 'Has he been a guest at this house?'

'On occasions.'

'But not recently?'

'No, not recently.'

'And what is the reason for that?'

The butler's face froze, as if an iron grille had suddenly descended over it. 'On reflection, I have decided that it is not my place to discuss my master's guests with you,' he said.

'What are you holding back from telling me?' Blackstone prodded. 'Has Davenport done something wrong?'

'I think we have spent quite enough time discussing the subject,' the butler said. He reached for the bell pull. 'The scullery maid will be here in a moment, to escort you to the door.'

'Mr Chalmers . . .' Blackstone began.

'Good day, Inspector Blackstone,' the butler said resolutely.

Sergeant Patterson considered the telephone to be the greatest invention of the nineteenth century, and possibly the greatest thing that would – or could – *ever* be invented. He often treated it as if it had been created solely for him and, watching him use it, Blackstone was almost convinced that it had been.

Patterson, Blackstone had long ago learned, had a gift for making contacts. He was on first-name terms with newspaper reporters and middle-level civil servants, but also with circus performers, costermongers and shoe-shine boys. It was virtually impossible to take him to a place where he *didn't* know someone, and the telephone only added to his reach and his influence.

He had been on the phone ever since Blackstone had returned to Scotland Yard, and it was only now, after more than an hour had passed, that he finally hung it up again.

'Who do you want to know about first?' he asked his boss. 'McClusky or Davenport?'

'McClusky,' Blackstone said.

154

'I talked to some people who work at Bowood House, which, as you know, is Lord Lansdowne's country estate,' Patterson said.

'I didn't know, as a matter of fact,' Blackstone said.

'Didn't you?' asked Patterson, as if mystified that Blackstone should be missing such a vital piece of knowledge.

'And how does it come about that you know someone there?' the Inspector asked, intrigued, despite himself.

'Ah, that's a very interesting story,' Patterson said. 'I have a friend who used to be involved in the smoked bacon industry and—'

'Forget it,' Blackstone said.

He should have known better than to ask, he told himself. Patterson's web was so complex and intricate that even an expert in logic would have had trouble following it.

'Anyway, the butler's wrong about McClusky. He's not the estate manager, only an *assistant* estate manager.'

'So how does someone so lowly get to dine with Lord Lansdowne?' Blackstone wondered.

'Ah, that's because of the fishing.'

'The fishing?'

'Lord Lansdowne's almost fanatical about salmon fishing. Apparently, he acquired a taste for it when he was Governor-General of Canada. And McClusky's reputed to be one of the best salmon fishermen around. Comes from being brought up in Scotland, I suppose.'

'So that connection's explained,' Blackstone said.

'And here's another connection,' Patterson said, looking immensely proud of himself. 'Before he went to work for Lord Lansdowne, McClusky was in the Army. And guess what particular branch of the Army.'

'The Royal Engineers,' Blackstone said.

Patterson looked a little disappointed. 'That's right, the Royal Engineers,' he admitted. 'So making the kind of explosive device which destroyed the *Golden Tulip* would have been an absolute doddle to him. And he'd have been perfectly capable of designing a bomb which looked as if it was intended to go off, while in fact making certain that it wouldn't.'

155

'Where's McClusky now?' Blackstone asked.

'That's the thing,' Patterson told him. 'He got an urgent phone call from Scotland last week. Whoever it was who called said his mother was dying. McClusky told the estate manager that he had to leave for home right away.'

'And is that what he *really* did?'

'No, it isn't! A couple of days after he'd left, his mother called the estate manager's office. Far from having been seriously ill, she said she was as fit as a fiddle.'

'Tell me about Davenport,' Blackstone said.

'He's a different kettle of fish altogether,' Patterson said. He chuckled. 'Different kettle of fish! That's rather good, what with McClusky and Lansdowne being fishermen.'

'Get on with it!' Blackstone said.

'He used to be quite a good friend of Lord Lansdowne's until the scandal broke.'

Blackstone sighed. '*What* scandal?'

'According to Edward Totterington, who works for a brokerage firm in the City, and who I know because—'

'I think we can skip that bit,' Blackstone said.

'It's very interesting,' Patterson protested.

'And will it help us to solve this case?'

'Well, not exactly.'

'Then let's move on.'

Patterson tried not to look offended. 'According to Totterington, Davenport comes from quite a good family – the sort of family that's likely to be invited into the Royal Enclosure at Ascot.'

'I get the picture,' Blackstone said.

'Well, it turns out the Honourable Charles has always been a bit of a black sheep. He's been a gambler of sorts for most of his life, but over the last few years he's become more and more addicted to the gaming tables. He was left a small fortune by his grandfather, but he pretty much exhausted that, and a few months ago he started dipping into the coffers of the rest of the family. There was a frightful stink about it, when it all came out. His people were furious, but of course none of the relatives actually wanted to see him go to gaol. Family name and all that.'

'Of course,' Blackstone said dryly.

'Anyway, Lord Lansdowne distanced himself from Davenport as soon as the whole thing broke. Couldn't *afford* to be associated with a scandal – what with being in the Cabinet and everything.'

'Naturally,' Blackstone said.

'The Davenport family decided that the best thing to do with the Honourable Charles was to send him abroad. They gave him a small allowance, and packed him off to Italy. As far as they're concerned – and this according to Edward Totterington again – he's still there, wandering round ancient ruins and doing his best to keep out of trouble.'

'But we know he isn't still there,' Blackstone said. 'He returned to England and re-established his relationship with Lord Lansdowne. Then the two of them teamed up with McClusky – the salmon fishing expert – and they began visiting at least one gambling club, and possibly more.'

'And found themselves in a deep hole,' Patterson suggested. 'So deep that the only way they saw of getting themselves out of it was to blackmail the Government.'

'Exactly,' Blackstone agreed. 'And they were the perfect team, because each of them had something to offer. McClusky had the expertise to start the fires, Davenport had a nature reckless enough to agree to join him.'

'And Lansdowne?'

'Lansdowne was their spy, at the very centre of government. He could keep them informed as to just how the establishment – and especially the Cabinet – was taking their demands.'

'It's incredible that a man like Lord Lansdowne, with so much too lose, would ever allow himself to get in that sort of situation in the first place,' Patterson said.

'Never underestimate human weakness,' Blackstone said. 'As a driving force, it makes all those modern engines you so admire look like the work of a bumbling amateur.'

Twenty-Seven

It was a misty morning out on the firing range, but the mist was not quite so thick that the two artillerymen, positioned behind their field gun, did not have a clear view of Dr Ellie Carr, her assistant, and all the paraphernalia they'd just unloaded from their cart.

'This ain't right,' the private complained. 'I didn't join the Army to be dragged out of my bed at some god-awful hour of the morning and fire my gun for the benefit of civilians.'

'No, you didn't,' his sergeant agreed.

'I mean to say—'

'You joined the Army to obey orders. If you're told to drop your pants and paint your arse canary yellow, that's just what you do.'

'I know, but—'

'And if you're told to help a doctor – even a *woman* doctor – with some kind of lunatic experiment, then you'd better bloody do it without question.'

'She must have a lot of influence with somebody,' the private muttered moodily.

'It's the bloke with her who's got the influence,' the sergeant informed him. 'From what I've heard, he's an old drinkin' mate of the RSM.'

Which meant he sat on the right hand of God, the private thought – and shuddered.

'What's them things they've got with them?' he asked.

'The thing with the three stick-legs is a camera of some sort,' the sergeant said.

'I know that. I mean the *other* things.'

He was referring to three handcarts which looked as if they had closed cucumber frames on top of them.

'Ah, they're what you call "police ambulances",' the sergeant said.

'And what are they used for?'

'They're used for carrying corpses.'

'You mean we're going to be firing at dead people?'

'That'd be my guess.'

'But we can't do that!'

'Oh, really?' the sergeant asked. 'So will you tell the RSM we're about to mutiny, or shall I?'

Ellie Carr looked at the three police ambulances standing side by side. 'I'd have been a lot happier if we'd had four or five cadavers to conduct our experiments on,' she said.

'Four or five!' Jed Trent exploded. 'Four or bloody five! Don't you have any idea just how difficult it was to get even *three* corpses of the same height and weight at the same time?'

'I'm sorry, I didn't mean to—' Ellie Carr began.

But Jed Trent hadn't finished. 'Can you even imagine the number of favours I've had to call in? Not to mention the number of arms I've had to twist? Don't you understand how much credit we've used up to get even *three*?'

'Of course I do,' Ellie Carr said contritely. 'You've done a wonderful job, Jed.'

'And if you're expecting any more stiffs to be available for your little experiments in the next few months, you can think again,' Trent said. 'If it was money rather than bodies that we were talking about, we'd both already be in a debtors' prison.'

'I *have* ruffled your feathers, haven't I?' Ellie Carr said.

'Damn right you have!'

'Well, never mind that now,' Ellie Carr said, as if the matter had been dealt with to everyone's complete satisfaction. 'Let's get on with the main job in hand, shall we?'

Trent thought of saying more, then realizing that Ellie Carr would find some way to disarm him *whatever* he said, he walked over to the nearest police ambulance and extracted the corpse from it.

'God, he stinks, this bugger,' Trent said, as he carried the body over to the chair.

159

'He was a tramp,' Ellie Carr said lightly. 'It'd be a miracle if he *didn't* stink.'

Carrying the body had presented no problem to a big man like Jed Trent. Seating it in the chair, however, was an entirely different matter.

'He's still in rigor,' Trent said. 'We'll just have to wait until it starts to wear off.'

'What about them?' Ellie Carr asked, pointing in the direction of the gunners. 'Will *they* be prepared to wait?'

'Probably not,' Trent admitted. 'Probably can't, even if they were willing to. They're due on the parade ground in a little more than an hour, and my mate, the RSM, will blow his top if they're not there. So it looks like we'll just have to come back again tomorrow.'

The longer this particular experiment continued, the greater the chance there was that others – *disapproving* others – would find out about it, Ellie Carr thought. And she couldn't have that.

'I'm going to have to cut a few corners,' she announced.

She'd brought her big carpet bag with her, and now she took a large hammer out of it.

'You're never going to break the poor bloke's legs for him, are you?' Trent asked.

'Why ever not?' Ellie replied. 'We'll have done a lot worse to him by the time we've finished, won't we?'

'Yes, but . . .'

'And it's not as if he's going to feel it, is he?'

Ellie swung the hammer, and the sound of cracking bone reverberated across the range like a rifle shot. Satisfied with the result, she directed her efforts to the other knee, with a similar result.

'Try it now,' she said.

Trent lifted the corpse again, and this time the legs swung as freely as those on a ventriloquist's dummy. Holding the body in place with one hand, he strapped it to the chair with the other.

'All this buggering about!' he grumbled, as he worked. 'It's the bloody limit, that's what it is.'

Ellie grinned. 'You'd never make a scientist, you know, Jed. You just haven't got the patience for it.'

160

'Maybe not,' Trent agreed. 'I'd certainly never make a *mad* bloody scientist. That's for sure.'

'All scientists are a *little* bit mad,' Ellie Carr pointed out. 'We wouldn't be much good at our job if we weren't.'

'Is that the excuse that you'll give when we're arrested?' Trent asked. 'Will your defence be based on the fact that you only did it because the voices in your head were telling you to? Because I have to remind you, Doctor, that didn't work for Joan of Arc.'

'Why should we be arrested?' Ellie Carr said innocently.

'I don't know,' Trent replied, stroking his chin in mock-thoughtfulness. 'It couldn't possibly be because what we're doing out here is in the nature of being highly illegal, could it?'

'Illegal!' Ellie Carr scoffed. 'How *can it* be illegal? I'm a doctor. I'm licensed to cut dead bodies open.'

'But *cutting* it open isn't exactly what you've got in mind,' Trent reminded her.

'It's an incision,' Ellie Carr countered. 'I'm just not using an entirely orthodox tool.'

Trent shook his head. 'You'll end up being the ruin of both of us, Dr Carr,' he said.

'Possibly you're right,' Ellie Carr agreed, picking up her carpetbag and turning in the direction of the artillerymen and their field gun. 'But at least we'll have gone down having fun.'

'One of us will, anyway,' Trent said.

The first time they'd been through this procedure, the sergeant and his assistant had had to make several adjustments between shots before they actually hit the dummy. Now, using their previous experience as a guide, they were bang on target the first time.

The corpse, and the chair it was attached to, were lifted high into the air and then deposited on the ground again some yards from their original position with a resounding thud.

'Most satisfactory,' Ellie Carr said.

'I'm pleased you're happy,' Jed Trent said dryly.

Ellie picked up the camera, took it over to where the corpse

161

had landed, and spent several minutes photographing it from all possible angles.

Watching her work – and taking the occasional guilty glance over his shoulder – Jed Trent found himself wondering just how many laws they'd broken, and whether his fascination with Ellie was actually worth spending the rest of his life behind bars for.

'You can put this one back in the ambulance, and set the next one up,' Ellie Carr called to him.

Why not? Jed thought. Having come this far, he might as well get hanged for a sheep as a lamb.

The experiment was repeated twice more, and twice more Ellie photographed the results before Jed returned the corpses to the ambulances.

'I still would have liked a couple more cadavers to work on, just to be sure I was right,' Ellie Carr said, as her assistant was sliding the last body back into its police ambulance.

'What was that?' Trent demanded.

'Nothing, Jed,' Ellie Carr said sweetly.

'Well, it certainly sounded like something to me,' Trent countered. 'A complaint, maybe.'

'For heaven's sake, don't be so sensitive, Jed,' Ellie said. 'I was just musing. That's all.'

'You can muse all you like, but you'll have to patch this lot up before I return them to the people I've borrowed them from,' Trent said.

'Don't worry about that,' Ellie Carr replied. 'By the time I've finished with them, they'll be as good as new.'

'Apart from the broken legs and the whopping great holes that have been blown in their chests,' Jed Trent said.

'Yes,' Ellie Carr agreed. 'Apart from that.'

Twenty-Eight

There were times when Blackstone truly despised butlers as a class. They were – as he saw it at such times – men who had willingly sold themselves into bondage; men prepared to devote their every waking hour to the service of masters who, they must surely very soon come to appreciate, were not worthy to lick their boot-straps.

There were other occasions however, when – despite his natural inclination – he found that he had a sneaking admiration for those who chose to follow a career in buttling. And meeting Chalmers again, at the front door of Lord Lansdowne's town house, was one of those occasions.

The butler favoured Todd with a slight bow – as a baronet, he did not merit more, and both men knew it – and gave no indication that he had seen Blackstone at all.

'His Lordship wishes me to thank you for agreeing to meet him here, rather than in his office in the Ministry,' Chalmers said to Sir Roderick. 'He is feeling a little under the weather this morning, and we both thought it would be wise for him to avoid the dank air.'

It's more likely that, in a tricky situation like this one, he decided he'd rather meet us on his home ground, Blackstone thought to himself.

'His Lordship is awaiting you in his study, Sir Roderick,' the butler continued. 'If you will follow me, I will announce you.'

'That's very kind of you, Chalmers,' said Sir Roderick, who prided himself on his ability to treat the lower orders humanely.

'May I enquire if your man will be accompanying you to the meeting, sir?' the butler asked.

'Yes, he will,' Sir Roderick confirmed.

'And in what way should I announce *him*, sir?'

'Announce him as Inspector Blackstone,' Sir Roderick said.

'Inspector Blackstone,' Chalmers repeated, to all appearances committing the name to memory. 'Very good, sir.'

It was as if they'd never met before, Blackstone thought – as if the butler hadn't almost ordered him out of his parlour the day before. And so well did Chalmers play his lack of recognition that, for a moment, the Inspector almost doubted that they *had* met.

Mr Chalmers led the two policemen up a gently curving staircase and along a wide corridor. He came to a halt at an impressively solid door, opened it, and announced the visitors. That done, he opened the door wider, and then stepped smoothly to one side.

Surely a man like Chalmers could think of a more worthwhile use for his obvious talents than this, Blackstone thought. But then perhaps he already had. Perhaps he calculated that a lifetime of servitude was a small price to pay in order to avoid having the shadow of the workhouse hanging over him – as it hung over most other working men.

Lord Lansdowne was sitting at his desk. He first blew his nose into a large silk handkerchief, then rose to his feet and shook Todd's already outstretched hand. That done, he hesitated for scarcely more than a heartbeat before offering the same hand to Blackstone.

'Sit down, gentlemen,' he said, indicating two chairs which had been laid out with almost military precision in front of his desk. 'I must apologize, as I expect Chalmers has already done on my behalf, for asking you to meet me here. I have a slight head cold, and, given the vital nature of my work at the moment, thought it best to avoid letting it get any worse.'

Nicely done, Blackstone thought. In one sentence the minister had established both that he was ill and that he was important.

The Minister for War sat down himself, and closed his eyes for a second. 'Blackstone,' he murmured quietly. 'Blackstone? Weren't you the officer involved in that case in Russia last year?'

'That's right, My Lord,' Blackstone replied.

'You did rather well in the matter, if my memory serves me,' Lansdowne said.

'Blackstone was really no more than a courier,' Sir Roderick said in a voice which was almost a growl. 'The resolution of the investigation fell into his hands, and he merely brought it back to London.'

Lansdowne looked thoughtful. 'Well, you're his superior, Roderick, and if you say that's how it was, then I suppose that must be the case – but I did have the impression there was more to it than that. What do you have to say about the matter, Inspector Blackstone?'

'I was no more than a courier,' Blackstone lied.

'It appears I must have been misinformed, then,' Lansdowne said. He turned his attention to Todd. 'You were very vague about the purpose of this meeting, Roderick. Now that you're here, would you care to put a little more flesh on the bones?'

Todd coughed uncomfortably. 'We are, as you know, currently investigating the case of this damned arsonist.'

'Yes?'

'And our enquiries have led us to an establishment in the West End which goes by the name of the Austro-Hungary Club.'

'Yes?' Lansdowne said again.

He was good at giving the impression of ignorance, Blackstone thought – almost as good as his butler had been.

'Some of the people we interviewed led us to believe that you were a regular patron of the club,' Todd said awkwardly.

'What!' Lansdowne asked.

'It's been suggested that, as a totally understandable relief from all the pressure you have been under these last few months, you might have visited the club from time to time,' Todd ploughed on.

'Well, I haven't,' Lansdowne said firmly. 'I have excellent recall, and if I'd ever been to this establishment, even once, I'm sure I would remember it.' He paused for a second, as though a thought had just struck him. 'But why are you asking these questions at all?'

165

'Well, I . . . er . . .' Todd said, as if he were suddenly finding it difficult to breathe.

'Do you think the firebug might have been a patron of this club?' Lansdowne asked, rescuing him from his dilemma. 'Is it supposed that if I *had* attended this establishment, I might have seen this miserable wretch there?'

'Exactly,' Sir Roderick said, with some relief. 'But since, as you've just explained, you've never even heard of this club, such an event could never have occurred.' He stood up. 'And now that that matter's been dealt with, we won't trouble you—'

'I have a couple of questions I'd like to put to His Lordship, if you don't mind, sir,' Blackstone said.

The look of loathing that his remark elicited made it clear to Blackstone that Sir Roderick *did* mind, but nonetheless the Assistant Commissioner sank back into his chair again, saying no more than, 'Make it quick, Blackstone. His Lordship is a very busy man.'

Blackstone produced the sketch of McClusky. 'Do you recognize this man, My Lord?'

Lansdowne gave the picture no more than a cursory examination. 'Can't say I do. Should I be able to?'

'It doesn't look like anyone who works for you?'

'One of my civil servants, do you mean?'

'I was thinking more of someone who has worked for you in a personal capacity.'

Lansdowne looked at the sketch again, more carefully this time. 'I suppose it does look vaguely like one of the ground-staff I employ at Bowood House,' he conceded.

'A man by the name of McClusky?' Blackstone suggested.

'Yes, but how did you . . .?'

'How about this one, sir?' Blackstone asked, showing him the sketch of Davenport.

'Since you expect me to recognize him, I suppose I probably do. Is it, by any chance, Charlie Davenport?'

'And would you say that this is the *same* man?' Blackstone asked, producing the photograph.

'Well, yes, it . . . But wait a moment, it can't be Charlie. This man looks dead!'

166

'He is,' Blackstone agreed.

'Then it clearly isn't Davenport.'

'What makes you say that?'

'Because he's in Italy at the moment.'

'Do you know that for a fact, sir?'

'Of course I don't. I've had absolutely no contact with Charlie since the matter of the . . .' Lansdowne paused again. 'Why are you asking me these questions, Inspector?'

'Yes, why are you?' Sir Roderick Todd demanded. 'It was certainly not what we agreed on before we arrived.' The Assistant Commissioner stood up determinedly. 'It's time we left, My Lord. Truth to tell, we should have left quite some time ago. Come on, Blackstone.'

'If I may just—' Blackstone began.

'You may do *nothing* except obey a direct order from your superior,' Todd snapped. 'And that order is that you should remove yourself from these premises immediately.'

Todd waited until they were out on the street again before he launched his attack on Blackstone.

'You never told me you'd identified the two men involved in the arson attacks!' he said furiously. '*Why* didn't you tell me?'

Blackstone shrugged. 'It didn't come up in the course of our conversation, sir.'

'Don't play me for the fool, Blackstone,' Sir Roderick said. 'I want the truth.'

'I didn't tell you because, if I had, you'd have stopped me doing what I just did,' Blackstone admitted.

'And what exactly *did* you just do?'

'I gave Lord Lansdowne the opportunity to lie – and he grabbed at it with both hands.'

'Gave him the opportunity to lie! *I* never heard him lie! When, according to you, *did* he lie?'

'When he said he didn't know the man in the sketch.'

'Perhaps he didn't.'

'It was a sketch of his assistant estate manager, sir. They often go fishing together.'

'Perhaps it doesn't really look like the assistant estate manager. Perhaps it *isn't* him.'

'The butler had no difficulty identifying him.'

'You've . . . you've spoken to the butler? To Chalmers? Without my permission?'

'Yes, sir.'

'And when did this outrage take place?'

'Last night.'

'We'll deal with your insubordination later,' Sir Roderick said. 'For the moment, it should be sufficient to point out that I am certainly not surprised that the butler recognized the man while His Lordship didn't.'

'Indeed?' Blackstone said.

'Indeed!' Todd repeated. 'Butlers are *trained* to look closely at faces. For a man like Lord Lansdowne, on the other hand, studying the lower orders would be a complete waste of his valuable time.'

'Is that right?' Blackstone asked.

'You should *know* it is. They are not his friends. They are not even his associates. Their function in life is to smooth his passage for him, as he goes about his important business. Good servants should be almost invisible. They should be grateful, of course, if their master deigns to notice them – but they should certainly not expect it.'

'It's just as I thought,' Blackstone said, finding he too was experiencing a rising anger which it was impossible to contain. 'We weren't there to question Lansdowne at all. We were just there to warn him off.'

'Have you completely lost your sanity?' Sir Roderick Todd demanded.

'I thought I might be able to change your mind if I managed to trip him up,' Blackstone said, ignoring the comment. 'But that was never really on the cards, was it?'

'If you wish to drag Lord Lansdowne's name into this sordid affair, there's a very easy way to do it, isn't there?' Todd said unexpectedly.

'Is there?'

'Of course there is. If you believe that Lansdowne's working with McClusky, then catch McClusky. A few hours in the cells should have him singing like a canary – especially if you're not too gentle with your questioning – and if

Lansdowne's involved, McClusky will implicate him, won't he?'

'Even if he did, you'd never take his word against that of a member of the Cabinet,' Blackstone said.

'You don't know that,' Todd countered. 'You *can't* know that until you've interrogated him – and you can't interrogate him until you've caught him. So I suggest you forget all about Lord Lansdowne for the moment, and concentrate on the job you're paid to do!'

Twenty-Nine

Blackstone followed the constable along the long corridor in which the monotony of the walls was broken up by heavy steel doors.

'This is the one, sir,' the constable said, coming to a halt. 'Holding Cell Number 17.'

Blackstone slid back the shutter over the peephole and looked inside. Mouldoon was sitting on his small, hard prison bed, and when he heard metal scrape against metal he looked up and raised his hand in the air.

The Inspector stepped away in disgust.

'Did he smile at you, sir?' asked the uniformed constable. 'That's what he usually does when he knows he's being watched.'

'No, he didn't smile,' Blackstone said. 'He waved, as if he were a friend and he'd just spotted me in the street.'

'Yes, that's another of his little tricks,' the constable agreed.

'What about the other prisoner? Rilke?'

'Oh, he doesn't wave *or* smile when he knows he's being watched, sir. Well, he wouldn't do, would he? From what I've seen, they're a surly lot on the whole, are your Germans.'

'But does Rilke look worried?'

'I have to say, he doesn't. He seems as at ease about the whole situation as his friend the Yank.'

Why *should* either of them be worried? Blackstone asked himself.

They knew the police would never be able to link them directly to the arson attacks, because there was no such link to find – because, although they were indirectly the *cause* of the crime, they were taking no part in the *commission* of it. And as Mouldoon had been at pains to point out, he was well

170

aware that Blackstone couldn't keep him locked up for much longer.

When Patterson had arrived at the pub, half an hour earlier, the place had been nearly empty, and there had been no trouble securing a table. Since then, however, it had been gradually filling up with costermongers, flower girls and tradesmen – all eager to order a quick shot of something strong to help them get through the rest of the day – and now there wasn't a seat to be had.

Blackstone, when he finally appeared in the doorway, didn't seem to even notice the crush. He spotted Patterson, and made directly for him, cutting a swathe through the sea of other customers.

A bad sign, Patterson thought. A very bad sign.

Blackstone was not usually one of those coppers who used his authority – natural *or* assumed – to get his own way. Unless they were involved in a crime, he was normally the mildest of men with the people he dealt with, because, as he saw it, they were *his* people – and had life hard enough without him making it any worse.

The Inspector jostled a costermonger, causing him to spill his beer. The man swung round, more than ready to slam his fist into the offender's face. Then he recognized Blackstone, and quickly let his arm drop to his side. The policeman, ploughing on, did not even seem to be aware of what had occurred.

Blackstone sank heavily into the chair opposite his faithful Sergeant, and looked at the pint Patterson had ordered him with something closely akin to disappointment.

'Next time you catch the waiter's eye, order me a whisky chaser,' he said despondently. 'In fact, better make it a double.'

'Are you sure about that, sir?' Patterson asked.

'It's the only thing I *am* sure about at this moment, Sergeant,' his boss replied. He sighed heavily. 'What's the point, eh, Patterson? What's the bloody point?'

'Which point are we talking about, sir?'

'What's the point in catching the small fry, when the big fish are simply allowed to swim away?'

171

'Things would be a hell of a lot worse if we didn't catch the small fry either,' Patterson said.

'Would they?' Blackstone said. 'Would they really? I wonder. Why should I lock up a burglar who – if he's left to his own devices – might just decide to rob Lord Lansdowne's house next?'

'And what would that achieve?'

'Some sort of symmetry, I suppose. If I can't catch a robber like His Lordship, I'd at least have the satisfaction of knowing that the robber himself is not immune to being robbed.'

'Strictly speaking, sir, Lord Lansdowne isn't actually a robber,' Patterson pointed out.

'Oh, stop being pedantic,' Blackstone said impatiently. 'You take all the fun out of life.'

'And anyway, as you know yourself, it doesn't work like that, sir,' Patterson said gently. 'The small fry don't go after the big fish. They prey on fry their own size, or maybe slightly bigger.'

'You're right, of course,' Blackstone agreed wearily. 'There are a lot of decent people out there in the city, and they deserve to be protected. But I just wish there was some way we could hit back – some way, however small, that we could make blokes like Lord Lansdowne pay for what they've done.'

'But we can't,' Patterson said.

The waiter had finally noticed them, and came over. 'I'd like a whisky,' Blackstone said. 'A treble.'

'A treble?' the waiter asked.

'A treble,' Blackstone said firmly. He took some coins out of his pocket, and flung them carelessly on to the table. 'Take it out of that.'

The waiter scooped up some of the copper, and walked away.

'Are you sure you want a *treble*, sir?' Patterson asked worriedly.

Blackstone sighed. 'I've had to let them go, you know,' he said, ignoring the question.

'Let who go? Mouldoon and Rilke?'

'Yes.'

'Was that wise?'

172

'They were never going to crack, so it was just a waste of taxpayers' money keeping them banged up. But I've put a team of detectives on both of them. They'll be under observation round the clock.'

'And what do you think we'll gain from that?'

'It might just lead us to McClusky, and through McClusky to Lansdowne,' Blackstone said.

'You don't sound very hopeful that's what's actually going to happen,' Patterson told him.

The waiter returned with the whisky. Blackstone knocked it back in a single gulp, then pointed to the coins on the table and mimed that the waiter should bring him another.

'I said, you don't sound very hopeful,' Patterson repeated.

'And I heard you,' Blackstone said sharply. 'I'm *not* very hopeful. It'll probably be just as much a waste of money as keeping them in gaol would have been. But we have to go through the motions, anyway.'

All the time he had been speaking, his eyes had been fixed on the waiter's progress, as if willing him to return as soon as possible with the second whisky he'd ordered.

'It's only eleven o'clock in the morning, sir,' Patterson said worriedly. 'If I was you, I'd go easy on the spirits.'

'I wish there was some other way I could get at Lansdowne,' Blackstone said, as if he hadn't heard his Sergeant. 'Even if I can't charge him with the crimes he's actually committed, I wish there was some way I could bring him down.'

When Jed Trent entered the morgue laboratory, he found Ellie Carr bent over her desk, examining the photographs of the Honourable Charles Davenport through a powerful magnifying glass.

'Now that it's over, are you finally going to tell me what this experiment of yours was all about?' Trent asked.

Ellie Carr looked up from her work. 'I should have thought that it was obvious what it was all about,' she said. 'It involved firing a piece of metal from a field gun into the chests of dead men. Hadn't you spotted that? I thought you ex-coppers were supposed to be trained observers.'

Trent managed to suppress a grin – but only just. 'You

know what I mean,' he said. 'What is it you're trying to prove?'

'I'm trying to prove that appearances can sometimes be deceptive,' Ellie Carr said. 'I'm trying to prove that the most obvious answer – the one that most people are willing to accept immediately – isn't always the correct one.'

'In other words, however much I badger you, you're not going to tell me,' Trent said.

'Not true,' Ellie Carr said.

'No?'

'Not at all. I'm just not going to tell you *yet*.'

'Why not?'

'Because I don't want you getting any preconceived notions, based solely on my initial findings. I'd much rather wait until I've assembled a completely coherent argument, and then present it to you. *That's* when you'll be really useful, not only because you'll be looking at the results through a fresh pair of eyes, but also because you'll be able to bring into play your considerable expertise.'

'My considerable expertise,' Trent repeated, disdainfully. 'When most people want to flatter a man, they do it with a light touch – so he hardly even notices it's being done at all. But not you, Dr Carr.'

'So what do I do?'

'You use flattery as if it was the traditional blunt instrument.'

'Maybe you're right about that,' the doctor said.

'I *am* right.'

Ellie Carr smiled sweetly. 'But it still works, doesn't it?'

'Yes,' Trent agreed. 'It still works.'

Thirty

The series of crises which had descended on the Prime Minister in the previous few days had meant that he had fallen almost disastrously behind on his paperwork. Now, faced with a veritable mountain of the stuff, he had left strict instructions that he was not to be disturbed for the next three hours. It was not, therefore, unreasonable of him to feel a wave of irritation when he heard the discreet knock on his office door, nor for the irritation to increase when the door opened and his private secretary stepped into the room.

'Yes?' he said curtly.

The secretary looked troubled – and not just by the fact that he was facing the Prime Minister's displeasure.

'I'm sorry to interrupt, My Lord, but I think there's something you really should see,' he said.

'There's *always* something I should see,' the Prime Minister snapped. 'There's a *never-ending stream* of things I should see.'

'This . . . this *is* rather important,' the secretary said.

With a sigh, Lord Salisbury gave in to the inevitable. 'All right, what is it?' he asked.

'It's a letter, Prime Minister. A blind beggar handed it to the constable on duty outside, not five minutes ago.'

'If the man was blind, I presume he is not the letter's author.'

'That is correct, Prime Minister.'

'Then who *is*?'

'The letter is anonymous.'

'For God's sake, Geoffrey, am I now expected – on top of everything else I have to do – to find time to read every anonymous letter that's sent to me?' Salisbury demanded.

'Of course not, Prime Minister. But this one makes some rather serious accusations.'

'Let me see it, then,' Salisbury said, resignedly.

The secretary handed over the letter, and the Prime Minister began to read it. By the time he was half-way through it, the colour was starting to drain from his face, and when he finally reached the end he looked almost ghost-like.

'Good God!' he said.

'Quite!' the secretary agreed dryly.

'I need to speak to Sir Roderick Todd,' the Prime Minister said. 'Get him on the phone at once.'

Before he had left New Scotland Yard to meet Patterson in the pub, Blackstone had ordered the immediate release of Mouldoon and Rilke. But 'immediate' – to those whose lives are based on procedures and red tape – rarely happens very quickly, and it was not until nearly one o'clock that Mouldoon found himself standing in front of the custody sergeant's desk, signing for his property.

'Has Mr Rilke been released?' the American asked, as he slipped his watch into his pocket and scooped up his loose change.

'The German bloke?' the sergeant asked.

'The German bloke,' Mouldoon agreed.

'Yes, we let him out a couple of minutes ago. You should still be able to catch him, if you run.'

'Is that it?' Mouldoon asked.

'Is what it?'

'I've been held without charge for more than a day. Doesn't that merit some kind of official apology?'

'Oh, I see what you mean,' the sergeant said. 'Well, no, I'm afraid you don't get an *official* apology as such – but Inspector Blackstone did leave a verbal message for you.'

'Well, I suppose that's something,' Mouldoon conceded. 'What was it he wanted you to tell me?'

'He wanted you to know that it's only with extreme reluctance that he's letting you go,' the sergeant said. 'He'd like you to understand that, in his opinion, you're still as bent as a corkscrew.'

* * *

176

Rilke had been standing on the Victoria Embankment for some time when Mouldoon finally walked through the gates to join him. For a moment it looked as if the two men were about to embrace each other in a bear hug. On reflection, however, they seemed to decide on a handshake.

The conversation which followed – the watchers recorded – lasted for a little more than two minutes, and seemed to be both earnest and intense. Then the two men separated, and both hailed cabs. Once Rilke had climbed into his hansom, it set off towards the Houses of Parliament. Mouldoon's, in contrast, headed in the opposite direction.

The watchers, having already commandeered two cabs to meet just such an eventuality, set off in pursuit.

Lord Salisbury looked grim, Lansdowne thought as he was ushered into the Prime Minister's office – as grim as he had looked in the earliest, darkest days of the Southern African war.

'I am to take it, Prime Minister, that your summoning me at such short notice means you have changed your mind about paying the ransom?' the Minister of War asked.

The Prime Minister shook his head, almost mournfully.

'No, you are not to make that assumption.'

'Then what . . .?'

'I have recently received a very disturbing report,' the Prime Minister interrupted.

'A disturbing report of what nature?' Lansdowne asked neutrally.

'A report which claims a connection between you and the men who were probably involved in the arson attacks.'

'So that's what this is all about,' Lansdowne said bitterly. 'And did you get this report from the police?'

'No, not from them,' the Prime Minister said. 'Although they have confirmed its contents.'

'The whole thing is just too ridiculous,' Lansdowne said. 'It's true that McClusky works for me, and yes, I once knew Charlie Davenport on a social basis. But the same could be said of any number of people.'

'I have no doubt that any number of people know this

McClusky person, or that any number can claim a previous friendship with Davenport,' the Prime Minister said. 'But, given their vastly different social backgrounds, I doubt that there is anyone other than yourself who is acquainted with both of them. And then there is also the matter of the Austro-Hungary Club.'

'But I've never been to the blasted club in my entire life!' Lansdowne protested.

'Apparently, there are witnesses who are prepared to contradict that statement.'

Lansdowne stiffened. 'Let me get one thing clear, Prime Minister,' he said. 'Are you accusing me of being behind these arson attacks? Are you accusing me of attempting to black-mail my own government?'

'Of course not,' the Prime Minister said hastily. 'The very notion would be absurd.'

'Good. I'm glad that's out of the way.'

'But I *am* saying that there are enough links between you and the arsonists for *others* to draw those conclusions. Mud sticks, Henry, and in politics it sticks more readily than in most occupations.'

'You're asking me to resign,' Lansdowne said bleakly.

'After long and careful consideration, I've reached the conclusion that it would be for the best,' the Prime Minister confirmed.

'The Boer War is the single biggest issue this government is facing at the moment,' Lansdowne said.

'I'm aware of that,' the Prime Minister said gravely.

'And as Secretary of War, I am the man most identified, in the eyes of the public and the press alike, with that conflict.'

'I am aware of that, too.'

'So if I fall, the Government falls, and we let the mealy-mouthed Liberals into power.'

'It isn't that simple,' the Prime Minister said.

'Is it not?'

'No. If you resign, it is perfectly possible, as you say, that the Government will fall . . .'

'Well, then?'

'. . . but if you stay on, and the rumours start to spread, the

Government's fall is inevitable.' The Prime Minister shook his head sadly. 'You have served your Queen and country for most of your adult life, Henry. More than just served it – you have served it well. Your achievements in Canada and India have already earned you your place in history. It would be a pity if those achievements were negated by a scandal now. I am asking you to sacrifice yourself, Henry – sacrifice yourself for the good of your party and for the good of your country. Will you do it?'

For almost half a minute, the Secretary of War stood in complete silence. Then he said, 'When would you like me to deliver this resignation speech of mine, Prime Minister?'

The Prime Minister suppressed a sigh. 'The sooner the better, for all concerned,' he said. 'If you deliver it tomorrow – in front of the House – there is just a chance that we will be able to stop this malicious poison about you spreading any further.'

'And you do believe that, don't you?' Lansdowne asked.

'Believe what?'

'That the poison is nothing but malicious?'

'Of course I believe it,' the Prime Minister said, with not quite as much conviction as the Secretary of War would have liked. 'Even allowing for your gambling debts . . .'

'I have no gambling debts!' Lansdowne said passionately.

'I apologize,' the Prime Minister told him. 'What I should have said was that even if you *did* have gambling debts – and I, of course, accept your word for it that you don't – it would be inconceivable that an honourable man such as yourself would ever contemplate stooping to the depths of which you are being accused.'

'It is encouraging to know that I retain my Prime Minister's confidence,' Lansdowne said. 'And am I to dare to hope that when this scandal eventually blows over, I will be offered another place in the Cabinet?'

But though he spoke the words clearly and forcefully, there was no real conviction behind them.

Nor was there any in the Prime Minister's, 'But of course, Henry,' which inevitably followed them.

Thirty-One

Blackstone returned to Scotland Yard shortly after two o'clock, and had only just entered the main gate when he was informed by the constable on duty that Sir Roderick Todd had been baying for his blood for the previous hour.

The constable had not been exaggerating, Blackstone realized when, a few minutes later, he found himself standing before the Assistant Commissioner's desk. For though he'd seen Todd in some black moods before, he'd never seen anything quite like this.

'You just couldn't keep your nose out of . . .' Sir Roderick began. He stopped for a moment, in order to examine the Inspector more carefully. 'Are you drunk, Blackstone?' he continued, outraged.

Blackstone swayed slightly. 'No, sir.'

Not *quite*, he added, as a mental qualification.

Not *yet*.

But then it was still a long, long time till the pubs closed their doors for the night.

Todd took a deep breath. 'You just couldn't keep your nose out of it, could you, Blackstone?' he said, resuming his planned tirade.

'I'm afraid that I have no idea what you're talking about, sir,' Blackstone said.

And don't really care, either, if truth be told.

'The Prime Minister telephoned me!' Todd said. 'The Prime Minister himself!'

'I always knew you had friends in high places,' Blackstone replied, and only just managed to suppress a giggle.

'He asked me questions. About Lord Lansdowne. *Direct*

questions, you understand! Questions on which it was impossible to be evasive!'

In other words, questions he had to give a straight answer to, Blackstone thought. And that couldn't have been easy for Todd – because it was *never* easy to change the habits of a lifetime.

'Don't you want to know on what he based these questions?' Sir Roderick asked.

'Not particularly,' Blackstone admitted.

'Of course you don't. Because you *already* know! But I'll tell you anyway. They were based on information contained in an anonymous letter – a letter that *you* sent.'

'I didn't send any letter.'

'Yes, you did. You sent it because you were determined to get Lord Lansdowne, whatever it took. Well, you've succeeded. He's going to resign. But you'll pay for it yourself, as well – by God, you'll pay.'

'You can't pin it on me,' Blackstone said defiantly. 'Anyone could have sent the letter.'

'No, they couldn't,' Sir Roderick countered. 'There were only three people who had in their possession the information that the letter contained – me, you and your sergeant. Now I know I didn't send it, so that just leaves the two of you. Do you think your sergeant is responsible?'

'No,' Blackstone said firmly. 'Sergeant Patterson would never even think of doing that.'

'So that leaves just *one* person it could be, doesn't it?'

'I didn't send the letter,' Blackstone repeated.

'I'll break you for this,' Todd promised. 'It may take a few days – it may even take a few weeks – but your days on the Force are numbered. So start getting used to the idea of being a civilian again, Inspector. Start planning for whatever kind of future you hope to have.'

Hope? Blackstone thought, as an image of St Saviour's Workhouse came unbidden to his mind. Hope doesn't come into it!

'Well, what have you got to say for yourself?' Todd demanded.

'Is that all, sir?' Blackstone replied. 'Can I go?'

181

'Yes, you can go,' Todd told him. 'You can go all the way to hell, as far as I'm concerned.'

Patterson was sitting in the office, his feet resting comfortably on the desk, when Blackstone entered.

'What did Todd the Sod want?' he asked.

Blackstone walked over to his own chair, and sank down into it. 'Our esteemed Assistant Commissioner wanted to tell me that my career with the Metropolitan Police is all but over.'

'He's always saying that,' Patterson said cheerfully, 'but he hasn't made it stick yet.'

No, but this time he will, Blackstone thought. This time there's *no doubt* he will.

'Do you have anything to report?' he asked, half-heartedly.

'Do you want to hear about the tails you put on Mouldoon and Rilke?'

'Might as well.'

'Mouldoon went back to his lodgings, Rilke went straight to the Austro-Hungary Club.'

'Did they know they were being followed?'

'Our men don't think so. They say that both suspects seemed so relaxed that they weren't even looking.'

And why was that? Blackstone wondered.

Because they knew they were about to get what they wanted!

Because though nobody had told *him*, the Government was about to give in to McClusky's demands, and hand over the hundred thousand pounds, which he, in turn, would hand straight over to the German!

Yes, that seemed the most likely explanation. Rilke and Mouldoon would get what they wanted. McClusky, no doubt, would be rewarded for his part in the whole thing. And Lord Lansdowne, though he had been forced to resign, would be able to pay off his gambling debts and survive with his reputation intact.

So who had come out of the whole sorry business as the losers? There were only two of them, as far as Blackstone could see.

The first was the Honourable Charles Davenport, who had

182

lost his life as a result of miscalculating the amount of explosives required to set the *Golden Tulip* on fire.

And the second? The second had been an honest – but sometimes foolhardy – police inspector, who had nowhere to go from now on but down.

The American Consul-General was a man who liked to leave no question in his mind unanswered, and ever since the visit by Sergeant Patterson, one particular question had persistently been nagging away at it.

He knew, with something approaching certainty, that the man in the sketch the policeman had shown him was definitely not called Mouldoon. But try as he might he could not put another name to the face, nor say where he had last seen the man.

He walked over to his office window, and looked down on the busy street below.

'Think!' he ordered himself.

The sketched man was not a distant relative of his, nor a friend of a close friend. He was fairly sure of both those things. On the other hand – as he had informed the policeman – when they had met it had been on terms of near-equality, which ruled out at least eighty percent of the people whom he came across in the normal course of events.

Since leaps of imagination had gotten him nowhere, he decided to adopt a more systematic, logical approach. He needed to start his mental search somewhere in the past, he told himself, and perhaps going back five years would not be too much of a stretch.

So what had he been doing on New Year's Eve, five years ago?

He had been at a party in New York, he recalled, and it had been a fairly grand affair. He ran through the people he could remember attending, and searched the corners of his memory in case the man who called himself Mouldoon was lurking there.

No, that was not it. That was not it at all.

By the time the Consul-General had worked forward two years, he was starting to get a headache. Yet, convinced as he was that he had finally developed the right approach, he ploughed on relentlessly.

He began to picture the summer of 1898, and the opening of a new art gallery in Boston. It had been a smart event, he remembered – but not *that* smart. Unlike many similar galas in the city, the committee in charge had not, on that occasion, consulted the Social Register before issuing invitations. In fact, the heavily embossed cards – which were, in fact, also an invitation to take the initial steps towards some kind of social acceptability – had been sent to anyone who had made a considerable contribution to the cost of the project, and as a result there had been more *nouveau riche* gathered together than the Consul-General could ever remember seeing in one place before.

The Consul-General snapped his fingers. That was it! he told himself. That was where he had met the man!

He rapidly crossed his office, and took down a book from the shelf. It was a weighty tome, and bore the ponderous title of *Leading American Industrialists in the Second Half of the Nineteenth Century*.

The Consul-General had never thought of the book by that name. He was, secretly, something of a radical, and to him it had always been *The American Almanac of Robber Barons*.

He laid the book on his desk, and started to flick through the pages. Carnegie, Vanderbilt, Mellon, Rockefeller . . .

There it was – Tyndale! The family had not merited as many pages as some of the other tycoons in the book, but they were still deemed worthy of a sizeable entry, including several group portraits. And it was in one of these portraits that the Consul-General found the face he was searching for.

The laboratory bench was covered with the photographs of the torsos of the corpses which had passed through Ellie Carr's hands in the previous few days.

'Your long – and somewhat impatient – wait is over, my good and faithful servant,' Ellie said to Jed Trent. 'I am now prepared to reveal to you the results of all my labours.'

'And about time,' Trent grumbled. 'What exactly am I supposed to be looking for?'

'The first few photographs are of what's-'is-name – thingamabob – the man the police fished out of the river,' Ellie Carr said.

'Davenport,' Jed Trent said. 'His name's Davenport.'

'Names don't matter to me,' Ellie Carr said airily. 'Now over here, we have the—'

'The photographs of the other cadavers, which I obtained by dubious means – and in all probability at considerable cost to myself – in order that you could carry out your dubious experiments,' Trent interrupted.

'Exactly!' Ellie agreed brightly. 'Now what I tried to do was to replicate the events which led to our first cadaver . . .'

'Thingamabob?' Jed Trent suggested.

'Davenport!' Ellie Carr said. 'And stop distracting me. I've worked very hard at this.'

'Sorry,' Trent said.

'I've tried to replicate the way in which Davenport lost his life. It wasn't easy, because so much of it was guesswork, and if you'd only been able to lay your hands on a few more stiffs—'

'We'd probably both have been behind bars, living on a diet of bread and water, by now.'

'. . . I'd have been able to build in a few more variables,' Ellie said severely. 'Anyway, I think I've done quite well, given the restrictions under which I was working.' She slid another set of photographs over to Trent. 'This is the first corpse we fired at. I told the soldiers not to use too powerful a charge, but you can't expect men who are used to being shouted at to listen to a reasonable, polite request, and they rather overdid it.'

'Poor bloody pauper,' Trent said. 'I'll wager he never dreamed, even during a lifetime of misery he was forced to endure, that after his death he'd be almost blown to pieces.'

'He assisted, albeit involuntarily, in a scientific experiment,' Ellie Carr said crisply. 'He contributed to the advancement of our knowledge, and criminologists in the future will bless him for it, even if not by name. In other words, my dear Jed, he did more that was useful once he was dead than he ever managed to achieve while he was alive.'

185

'You can make anything you do – however horrible – seem reasonable,' Jed Trent said, almost admiringly. 'It's a great talent.'

'Thank you,' Ellie Carr said, ignoring the irony. 'Now the charges we used for the other cadavers were not quite so powerful, and I'm fairly sure that the third of the firings was a fair replication of the accident – if, indeed, any accident did actually occur.'

'What do you mean – if any accident did actually occur?' Jed Trent asked.

'Look closely at the other sets of photographs,' Ellie Carr said. 'Look at the way the piece of iron is embedded in the subjects' chests, and then tell me what you think.'

Trent picked up the magnifying glass, and examined the pictures taken at the second of Ellie Carr's experiments. He spent some time on them, before moving on to the third and last of the cadavers. Finally, he went right back to the other end of the bench, and re-examined the pictures taken of the Honourable Charles Davenport.

'Well?' Ellie Carr asked impatiently.

'The second and third ones aren't exactly the same,' Trent said.

'Well, of course they're not. The amount of charge used was different in each case.'

'But I can certainly see the similarities.'

'And?'

'And they both look quite different to the photographs of the man who was fished out of the river.

Ellie Carr beamed. 'Exactly!' she said.

Thirty-Two

It was a little over two hours after he had entered his lodgings that Mouldoon emerged again. This time he was accompanied by a heavily veiled woman, and since the detectives who were waiting outside in a hansom cab had not seen her enter the apartment, they could only assume that she had been waiting there for him when he arrived.

Mouldoon and the woman were both carrying luggage – he had a heavy portmanteau, she a large carpetbag. Mouldoon hailed a cab, and the two of them climbed in. As it pulled away from the kerb, the detectives instructed their driver to follow it.

They didn't have to follow for long. The cab stopped in front of Victoria Railway Station, and the American and his companion disembarked. They did not go directly into the station, however. Instead they waited outside until they were joined by a third person, whom the detectives instantly identified as Rilke. He, too, was carrying a heavy piece of luggage, which suggested to the watchers that the three of them were intending to take a long journey.

The trio entered the station, and the detectives – now joined by the team which had been following Rilke – followed at a safe distance. Mouldoon, seemingly unaware that he was being watched, bought the tickets, and then he, Rilke and the woman, strode off in the direction of the platforms.

Once they were out of sight, one of the detectives went straight to the ticket office. He showed his warrant card to the railway clerk, then said, 'What did you sell to the man who's just left?'

'Tickets,' the clerk replied. 'Three of them. First class.'

The detective sighed. 'Imagine that!' he said. 'A ticket

office selling tickets! I'd have expected you to sell them a plate of jellied eels.'

'There's no need to be sarcastic, officer,' the clerk said. 'I'm only doing my job, you know.'

The detective suppressed the urge to say that he, too, was only doing his job – and the ticket clerk was making it a lot harder – and contented himself with asking, 'Where were the tickets for?'

'Dover.'

'And were they return tickets? Or just one-way?'

'Just one-way. I told him it would be cheaper if he bought returns, but he didn't seem . . .'

The clerk dried up mid-sentence. There didn't really seem to be much point in saying any more, when the detective was already hurrying away in the direction of the nearest phone box.

'That was Detective Constable Hale,' Patterson said, hanging the phone back on its cradle. 'Mouldoon, Rilke and some woman – as yet unidentified – have just caught the train to Dover. They were all carrying quite a lot of luggage with them. Mouldoon had a portmanteau, and the woman was carrying a big carpetbag.'

'They're leaving the country!' Blackstone groaned.

'That would seem likely,' Patterson agreed. 'I can't see any conceivable reason they would want to go to Dover at all, unless it was to catch a boat to the Continent.'

They wouldn't leave without the money, Blackstone thought angrily. No one would walk away from a hundred thousand pounds. So his worst suspicions were confirmed, and the Government had given way to blackmail after all!

'Have either Mouldoon or Rilke seen anybody who might possibly be McClusky since they were released from custody?' Blackstone asked.

'Not according to our lads with the watching brief. They claim that Mouldoon went straight to his apartment, and Rilke went straight to the club.'

But that proved nothing, Blackstone thought. McClusky could already have been inside the club, waiting for Rilke's arrival. Or possibly it was the woman in the veil who had been the collector. Maybe the money was in the big carpet-bag the watchers had seen her carrying.

Blackstone rose from his seat and strode – only slightly unsteadily – over to the door. He was going to see Sir Roderick Todd again. He knew it was a mistake – that it could only make his already disastrous position even worse – but he was going to do it anyway.

'Bursting in on me like this is making things so much easier for me, Blackstone,' Sir Roderick said. 'This exhibition of insolence alone would be enough reason to get you thrown off the Force.'

'That doesn't matter now,' Blackstone said.

'Doesn't it?'

'No, it bloody doesn't. I've no wish to *belong* to a Force which colludes in giving way to blackmail. Don't you realize what damage you've done? From now on, any serious criminal who wants to raise some cash in a hurry has only to hold the Government to ransom. Because you won't be able to hide from the London underworld what you've done. Trust me, it'll be the talk of the East End pubs by tonight.'

'Then it will be nothing but idle gossip – because no money has been paid,' Todd said.

'If that's the case, why are Mouldoon and Rilke fleeing the country?' Blackstone demanded.

'I have no idea,' Todd said, 'but from what I have heard of them, this country is far better off without them.'

He sounded so sure of himself, Blackstone thought – so convinced of the rightness of what he was saying.

'Perhaps the ransom was paid without your knowledge,' he suggested to the Assistant Commissioner.

'That's impossible,' Todd said flatly. 'I have many friends at the heart of the Government. They would have told me if such a thing had occurred. Besides, the only member of the Cabinet in favour of paying the ransom was Lansdowne himself, and, as you know, he has been completely discredited.'

'Then why . . .?' Blackstone asked, confused.

'You may leave now, Inspector Blackstone,' Sir Roderick said. Then he added, with some relish, 'And if I were you, I'd start packing up whatever personal effects you have in your office, because, after this display, I can almost guarantee that you'll be thrown out of it by nightfall.'

'It doesn't make sense,' Blackstone complained to Patterson. 'None of it makes any sense. The whole operation was about *money*, and yet Mouldoon and Rilke are leaving the country without a penny.'

'Then maybe – just possibly – it wasn't about money at all,' Patterson suggested.

'What else *could* it have been about?'

'I don't know,' the Sergeant admitted. 'But there's been something distinctly odd about this case right from the beginning.'

'Like what?'

'Well, for a start, the arsonists didn't do anything like as much damage as they could have done.'

'We've already explained that,' Blackstone said impatiently. 'Lansdowne wanted to get his hands on the money, but he didn't want to hurt his own country too much – especially when it was at war.'

'Then there's all the clues,' Patterson said.

'What clues are you talking about?'

'The ones that just seemed to fall into our laps. Take the ones that led us to identifying McClusky, for example. He didn't need to *personally* bribe Constable Quail to leave the letter on the fire engine. He could just as easily have used somebody else to do it, but—'

'Maybe he wanted to make absolutely sure that I received the message,' Blackstone interrupted.

'. . . but if he *had* used someone else, Quail would never have smelled the workhouse soap on him. If Quail *hadn't* smelled the soap, you would never have gone to St Saviour's. And if you'd never gone to St Saviour's, you wouldn't have *found* the money and passport wrapped up in the House of Lords notepaper.'

'So McClusky, acting through over-eagerness, made a big mistake,' Blackstone said.

'Then there's the fact that Davenport just happened to have a business card from the Austro-Hungary Club on him when we fished him out of the river. If he *hadn't* had that card, we'd never have gone to the club. And if we hadn't gone to the club, we'd never have met Mouldoon and Rilke, nor got our description of Lord Lansdowne.'

'We always rely on a few lucky breaks in our job,' Blackstone argued. 'You know that yourself. At least half the cases we work on would never be solved without them.'

'You've got a point there,' Patterson conceded. 'But doesn't it strike you – even for a moment – that this case has been just a little *too* easy?'

'It hasn't felt easy at all,' Blackstone countered, his tone an uneasy mixture of irritation and perhaps a little doubt. 'If it had been *easy*, Sergeant, we'd have had all the criminals locked up by now. And what do we have instead? The dead body of one of the arsonists, and the sure and certain knowledge that the rest of them are going to get away with it!'

'But get away with *what*?' Patterson asked. 'If they don't have the money, they haven't actually got away with *anything*.'

It was true, Blackstone thought, suddenly feeling sick. If they hadn't got the money – and he now didn't believe that they had – then they were coming out of the whole business with nothing at all!

The phone rang, and Patterson picked it up.

'Yes, sir,' he said. 'Yes, this is Sergeant Patterson. What can I do for you?' There was a pause, while he listened to what the man on the other end of the line was saying, then he continued, 'I think it might be better, under the circumstances, if you talked to my boss.'

Blackstone shook his head lethargically, but Patterson still held out the phone to him.

'It's the American Consul-General,' the Sergeant mimed.

Lacking the will to fight against Patterson's obvious insistence, Blackstone took the phone. 'How can I help you, sir?' he asked.

'It's more a question of how *I* can help *you*,' the Consul-General replied, chuckling.

191

The man seemed pleased with himself, Blackstone thought. Inordinately pleased.

'I take it you have some information that you wish to impart to us, sir?' he asked wearily.

'Indeed I do. It's about our friend – the one who calls himself Mouldoon,' the Consul-General said, not the least put off by Blackstone's lack of enthusiasm. 'I know who he really is.'

It didn't really matter now whether he was Robert Mouldoon or Billy the Kid, Blackstone thought. Whatever his real name, the man would be on a boat to France within a few hours.

'So who is he, sir?' he asked, doing no more than just going through the motions.

The Consul-General chuckled again. 'He's what I like to call – strictly for my own amusement – a robber baron,' he said.

'A what?'

'A robber baron. Or, to be more accurate, the *son* of a robber baron.'

'I have absolutely no idea what you're talking about, sir,' Blackstone confessed.

'No, I suppose you wouldn't have,' the Consul-General agreed. 'It's kinda complicated. Why don't you and your sergeant come round to the Consulate and I'll tell you all about it.'

The three travellers were sitting in the dining car of the Dover Express. They had done no more than pick at the food they had ordered, but they had already almost drained their third bottle of the best vintage champagne that the railway company could offer.

The train pulled into a small station, and a number of passengers disembarked.

'The Brits have got a real nerve to call this a *main* railroad line,' complained the man who – until now – had been known as Mouldoon, as he looked out of the carriage window. 'Hell, back in the States, our kids have got *model* railroads this size – laid out on the lounge floor.'

192

'*Everything* in America is big,' responded the man who was travelling under the name of Rilke. 'Great Britain, on the other hand, is not "great" at all. It is a mere pocket handkerchief of a country.'

'You got that right,' Mouldoon agreed.

'Yet somehow,' Rilke continued, his voice thick with contempt, 'this pocket handkerchief country has contrived to control the destiny of so many other peoples – including my own.'

'But not for much longer,' Mouldoon said.

'No, not for much longer,' Rilke agreed with a complacent smile. 'And you, my friend, must lay claim to much of the success of our little venture. You have done absolutely splendidly.' He turned towards the third member of the party – the woman – and raised his glass high in the air. 'And you, too, Madam! You also have done splendidly.'

The woman glanced down at the table, with a modesty which was as becoming as it was false.

'It was easy for me,' she said, raising her head again after silently counting three beats. 'I've had the training. But you two have been truly amazing. To take over the leading roles without even having a walk-on part before – that is a dazzling achievement.'

Most men find it hard not to bask in the approval of a beautiful woman, and Rilke and Mouldoon did not even try.

'If you'd played the same roles on Broadway, you'd have had all the critics positively falling over themselves in excitement,' the woman continued. 'The reviews would have been wonderful.'

'Yes, it is kinda sad, in a way, to think that our performances will never get the acclaim they deserve,' Mouldoon said.

Rilke chuckled. 'Come, come, my dear friend, you are not an actor, but a hard-headed businessman,' he said. 'True, you may not get the acclaim which these thespians thirst for, but you certainly get your reward – which is *much more* important to you.'

'Still, a good review would be nice, especially for me,' the woman said wistfully.

'If you ever wish to tread the boards again, that should

present no problem at all,' Rilke assured her. 'My country is truly a land of opportunity, as America once was. Your husband is taking full advantage of that opportunity – so why shouldn't you?'

'That's true enough, honey,' Mouldoon said. 'If you want to appear on the stage, well, hell, I'll just buy you a theatre.'

'Champagne!' Rilke said, signalling to the waiter. 'We need more champagne.'

Thirty-Three

The American Consul-General looked as pleased with himself in the flesh as he had sounded over the telephone.

'Yes, sir, I pride myself on my ability to remember faces,' he said, 'but this has been a real tricky one. See, ever since the scandal broke, people of quality have been giving his family a pretty wide berth.'

'Scandal?' Blackstone said. 'What scandal?'

The Consul-General chuckled. 'I guess that will be obvious to you when I reveal the name of the man in the sketch.' He spread his hands in a flourish. 'The man we're talking about is no other than Lucas Tyndale.'

'Who?' Blackstone asked.

'Lucas Tyndale! The son of Hopgood Tyndale!'

'I'm still not following you,' Blackstone admitted.

The Consul-General looked disappointed. 'Well, I guess our famous families just aren't as well known to you Limeys as we sometimes think they are,' he said regretfully. 'Have *you* heard of him, Sergeant?'

'I'm afraid not?' Patterson confessed.

'This Lucas Tyndale is famous?' Blackstone asked.

'Very,' the Consul-General replied. 'Although some people I know would much prefer the term "infamous".'

For the first time in hours, Blackstone began to feel his interest in the case quickening. 'Tell me about him,' he said.

'A lot of guys made a lot of money out of building the railroads across the States,' the Consul-General said. 'Cornelius Vanderbilt made the most – the last I heard, he was still the richest man in the world – but there was still plenty left over for families like the Tyndales to gather up with their greedy little hands.'

'So these Tyndales own railways?'

'Railroads, we call them.'

'*Railroads*, then.'

'The Tyndales *used to* own railroads, but like I said, that was before the scandal broke.'

'I still don't know which scandal you're talking about,' Blackstone said, hiding his impatience.

'You really don't know much about us, do you?' the Consul-General asked, wonderingly. 'Here we are – the Young Giant, the country set to be the most powerful in the world – and you're as ignorant about us as you are about some tiny country in the Balkans.'

'So educate me,' Blackstone suggested.

'Be glad to,' the Consul-General told him. 'Nearly forty years ago we had a conflict which President Lincoln insisted was no more than a police action, but which most people think of as the Civil War.'

'I've heard of *that*,' Blackstone said.

'Well, that's a start,' the Consul-General said. 'Anyway, after the Civil War was over, the country really started to open up. There were plenty of opportunities for anyone prepared to grab them, and one group of men – I call them the robber barons – were prepared to do just that.'

'Robber barons,' Blackstone repeated.

'Don't quote me on that,' the Consul-General said, suddenly sounding slightly alarmed. 'It's not a very diplomatic thing to say.'

'Your secret's safe with me,' Blackstone promised.

'These robber barons – these *entrepreneurs* – weren't always exactly fastidious in the sort of business methods they used,' the Consul-General continued. 'One of them in particular had a personal motto which ran something along the lines of, "If it's not nailed down, then it's mine. If I can prise it up, then it wasn't nailed down properly." That wasn't the official motto of the Tyndale family – though it might as well have been.'

'Go on,' Blackstone said encouragingly.

'The Tyndales broke so many rules that in the end they couldn't even *bribe* their way out of trouble. So Hopgood

Tyndale found himself faced with two alternatives – give up control of the railroad, or go to jail. Matter of fact, by choosing the first alternative, he managed to come out of the whole mess with most of his personal fortune still intact. But he was still smarting, anyway. The Tyndales don't just want money – they want to build empires. And that path's pretty much closed off to them now.'

'You're sure that this Lucas Tyndale is the man in the sketch?' Blackstone asked.

'I'm convinced of it.'

'You don't happen to know if he's had a falling out with his family – if he might, perhaps, have been disinherited?'

'Far from it. Once I'd worked out who the guy in the sketch was, I rang some people who still know the family, and it seems that Lucas is as much the apple of old man Hopgood's eye as he ever was.'

But that made no sense at all, Blackstone thought. Why should a man who was due to inherit a fortune in America travel to London to become a pimp? Perhaps, despite the Consul-General's assurances, they weren't talking about the same man at all.

'Lucas Tyndale could have changed since the last time you saw him, sir,' the Inspector suggested. 'He might, in fact, look very different to the man in the sketch now.'

The Consul-General chuckled again. 'He'll not have changed,' he said confidently. 'He's like that character in the book by Oscar Wilde.'

'Dorian Gray?'

'That's the guy – Dorian Gray! Sold his soul to the Devil, so he'd never look any older. It wouldn't surprise me to learn that Lucas Tyndale – and his whole family, for that matter – had done just the same thing. They're a good-looking family – angelic on the outside, pure poison from within.'

But a pimp? Blackstone thought. Working as a *pimp*? It just *couldn't* be the same man.

'Besides, it's no more than a couple of years since I last saw the guy myself,' the Consul-General continued. 'It was in Boston. He was with his new wife – a real stunner, I thought. She's probably the reason I remember seeing him there at all

– I couldn't take my eyes off her. Matter of fact, now I think about it, I seem to recall that she was an English girl. I believe she was some kind of actress before she got herself married to Lucas.'

Blackstone felt a shiver run through his body.

It had all been too easy, Patterson had said earlier – and now he was starting to think that perhaps the Sergeant had been right.

'Could you describe the woman to me?' he asked.

'I can do better than that,' the Consul-General told him. 'You really got my curiosity aroused, so while I was waiting for you to get here, I looked through some of the society magazines that my wife likes to read – and I've found an actual photograph of her!'

Blackstone's hands were starting to twitch. 'Can I see it?' he asked.

'Sure. Got it right here on the bookcase.' The Consul-General reached for the magazine, and flicked through it until he came to the right page. 'That's her – Emily Tyndale.'

It was a photograph of a group of women – all wearing large hats and carrying parasols – who were standing in a formal garden. The caption below said that the woman in the middle was Emily Tyndale, but Blackstone needed no such help to recognize her.

'We've met,' he told the Consul-General.

'You have?'

'That's right. But she was using a different name then. Actually, she was using *two* different names.'

'That's incredible,' the Consul-General said.

'But nonetheless true,' Blackstone countered, taking a second look at the photograph of Emily Tyndale – alias Sophia de Vere and Molly Scruggs.

The famous White Cliffs of Dover were no doubt still there, but any visitor wishing to catch a passing glimpse of them would have had that desire frustrated by the sea fog which had rolled in off the Channel.

'We didn't plan for this,' Lucas Tyndale said.

'No one can plan for the weather,' replied the man who

was still travelling under the name of Rilke. 'But there is no cause for concern.'

'If Blackstone finds out—'

'Blackstone will find out *nothing* – or, at least, nothing that we do not wish him to find out. That has always been the beauty of our scheme – it has allowed us to maintain control over every stage of the operation.'

'If he somehow manages to discover who we really are—'

'It will do him no good whatsoever. In this country, for all its other failings, a man may still use whatever name he chooses to. We are perfectly safe.'

'Then why did we leave London?'

'Because that is what *you* wanted to do. For my part, I would have been perfectly happy to stay there, and watch our scheme come to its final fruition.'

'Then you have stronger nerves than I do,' Tyndale said. 'Either that or you have too little imagination to feel what it would be like as the rope tightens around your neck.'

Rilke was about to reply when their female companion appeared out of the fog. 'He's worried, Madam,' Rilke said, in a hearty voice. 'Tell him his fears are groundless.'

'Your fears are groundless,' Emily Tyndale told her husband. 'I've just been talking to the harbour master. The fog's starting to lift, and we should be setting sail within the hour.'

Thirty-Four

The hansom cab pulled up at the main entrance to New Scotland Yard, and the portly Sergeant and his almost gaunt boss climbed out of it.

As Blackstone stepped down, he looked like a man whose mind was elsewhere – and that was not too far from the truth. Ever since the American Consul-General had shown him the photograph, his thoughts – like a desperate eagle which believes itself trapped in a canyon – had been swooping and soaring, soaring and swooping.

He now knew the real names of Robert Mouldoon and Sophia de Vere. More than that – he knew that Mouldoon/Tyndale was heir to a large American fortune, and that Sophia/Emily was his wife. But rather than answering any questions, this merely posed some new – even more perplexing – ones.

Why had Tyndale pretended to be a pimp, and Emily acted as if she were one of his stable of whores?

What could either of them have hoped to gain by becoming involved in Lansdowne's and McClusky's extortion scheme?

Their part in the whole plot – even if only peripheral – seemed meaningless to the point of insanity.

'Excuse me, sir, but there's a woman waiting for you in your office,' the constable on duty at the gate said.

A woman! For a moment, Blackstone had visions of it being Emily, come to unburden herself of her sins by confessing.

But the Emily he had interrogated into the early hours of the morning had too much nerve to break down at this stage of the game. Besides, she'd be in Dover by now.

It was left up to Patterson to ask the obvious question. 'You've left a woman in our *office*?' he demanded. 'Unattended?'

The constable looked down at his boots. 'Yes, Sergeant.'

'But good God, man, she could be anybody. The Fenians have already tried to blow up Scotland Yard once, as I should have no need to remind you. How do you know she isn't working for them?'

'She didn't look to me like she was a mad bomber, Sergeant,' the constable mumbled.

'And how do you *expect* them to look? Do you think they have their intentions painted on their foreheads?

'She said she was a doctor,' the constable protested.

'A doctor!'

'Yes, Sergeant. And she seemed very sure of herself. She insisted she needed to be in your office to prepare what she'd got to show you.'

'And you just took her word for it?' Patterson demanded.

Despite his overall feeling of gloom, Blackstone found that he was laughing. 'The Sergeant here doesn't understand, does he, Constable?' he asked the man on the gate. 'But then, you see – unlike you and me – he's had no opportunity to meet the formidable Dr Carr.'

Blackstone's desk had been its usual cluttered mess when he'd left the office, but now all his papers had been placed on the floor – or possibly *swept* on to the floor – and the desk was laid out with a large number of photographs.

Ellie Carr looked up from her work, and smiled at him. 'Well, this ain't much of a place to look at,' she said in her Cockney voice, 'but I suppose you call it 'ome.'

That was true enough, Blackstone thought – but unless he could pull something out of the fire pretty damn quickly, he wouldn't be able to call it home much longer.

'There was no need for you to come all this way,' he said, knowing that he sounded ungracious and not really caring. 'You could simply have posted me your report.'

'Posted it!' Ellie Carr said. 'And missed the chance of seeing the look on your face when you discover what I've found out?'

Blackstone sighed. 'To be perfectly honest, Dr Carr, I don't really care whether the Honourable Charles Davenport was killed by the projectile or merely drowned.'

'Yes, you do – or, at least, you soon will,' Ellie Carr told him, with a certainty which was slightly unnerving. 'If yer don't believe me, come an' 'ave a butcher's for yourself, Inspector.'

Almost reluctantly, Blackstone walked over to the desk. Patterson, showing no more enthusiasm, followed close behind.

'This is your corpse, the Honourable Charles Thingamabob,' Ellie Carr said, pointing to the first group of photographs. 'Notice how the piece of iron is wedged in his chest.'

'I don't need to look. I've seen it in the flesh,' Blackstone said.

But he did as he'd been instructed anyway.

'Now look at how it's wedged in the chests of the others,' Ellie Carr told him.

Blackstone quickly ran his eyes over the photographs of the other three bodies. 'Who *are* these people?' he asked.

'You're as bad as Jed Trent,' Ellie Carr said. 'It doesn't matter a monkey's who they are – just notice how they *look*.'

Blackstone examined the photographs, first with his naked eye and then with a magnifying glass. 'They look different,' he admitted.

'Which look different to what?' Ellie Carr asked, infuriatingly.

'The last three corpses look different to Davenport's.'

'Excellent. Now could you possibly tell me *how* they look different?'

'The damage seems to have been far more extensive,' Blackstone said. 'There's an edging around the actual wounds – beyond the point of penetration – that isn't evident on Davenport's body.'

'A bit like the crater you find around a meteorite?' Ellie Carr suggested helpfully.

'I've never seen one myself, but yes, I'd assume it's something like that,' Blackstone agreed.

'They all had the projectile fired at them, and they all – more or less – exhibit the same kind of damage,' Ellie Carr said. 'I'd have liked to have done a few more experiments to confirm my finding, but there's no real respect for research scientists in this bloody country and—'

'Get to the point!' Blackstone said impatiently.

'You mean to say that you need more of an explanation?' Ellie Carr asked, incredulously.

'Yes, I need more of an explanation,' Blackstone replied.

'I really would have thought you could have worked it out for yourself,' Ellie Carr said, with just a hint of disappointment in her voice. 'And maybe you still can, if I give you a bit of a nudge in the right direction.' She paused. 'All right?'

'All right,' Blackstone agreed.

'We know for a fact what happened to these three corpses, because I arranged for it to happen. But we only *think* we know what happened to Davenport – we only *assume* that he met the same fate as the others. But if he did, why are his wounds so very different?'

'Because the injuries were not the result of an explosion at all!' Blackstone exclaimed.

Ellie Carr positively beamed with pleasure. 'Go to the top of the class,' she said.

'Then just how did Davenport die?'

'It was the piece of metal itself which first aroused my suspicions,' Ellie Carr told him. 'It didn't look to me like it had been broken off in an explosion. It seemed more as if it had been very carefully *taken* apart. So I took a closer look at it, and what I found was very interesting.' She handed a photograph of the piece of rowlock to Blackstone. 'See what you think.'

Blackstone studied the picture through his magnifying glass. 'There are some curious indentations on the part of the rowlock which was projecting out of Davenport's chest,' he said.

'And?' Ellie Carr asked.

'They seem to be quite regular. Almost as if they were made with some kind of tool.'

'I think perhaps it might have been a ball-hammer,' Ellie Carr speculated. 'But whatever it was, it proves that the piece of metal wasn't *shot* into Davenport's chest – it was *driven* into it by a series of blows. In other words, his death was no accident at all. It was, in fact, cold-blooded murder. What I *can't* tell you, I'm afraid, is just why the killer or killers went to all that trouble.'

'They did it to fool *us*!' Blackstone said.

'You've lost me!' Ellie admitted.

'They wanted to leave us a clue,' Blackstone explained. 'But they didn't want us to know it had been left there deliberately. If we'd thought Davenport had been murdered, we'd have been suspicious about whatever we found in his pocket. But if it had been an accident, we'd just have thought we were lucky – which is exactly what we *did* think!'

'He had something in his pocket that was a clue?' Ellie asked, still trying to make sense of it all.

'Yes. It was the card we found in his pocket that led to the Austro-Hungary Club,' Blackstone said.

'And everything else that happened after that just followed on from there,' Patterson added.

'You were right when you said it had all been too easy,' Blackstone told his Sergeant. 'It was worse than easy – they've been pulling our strings ever since this case started.'

The people standing and waiting on the dock had been able to gauge the speed at which the weather was clearing simply by keeping their eyes fixed on the end of the pier.

At first they could see no more beyond the edge than a black mass which appeared occasionally – and briefly – from within the swirling fog. They believed it to be the cross-Channel ferry, but it could just as easily have been a lighthouse or a rock – or even some part of the fog which, for reasons of its own, had decided to be darker than all the rest.

Then, slowly, a more definite shape began to emerge. It was too soon to say yet that it was definitely a ship, but it was certainly a *something*.

A little more time passed, and the watchers could distinguish the prow, the stern, and even the funnel. Minutes later, they could pick out the railing which ran along the deck, the anchor chain projecting from the water and the gangplank which had just been lowered.

They were not about to spend a night in dank, dark Dover, as they'd feared they might have to. Very soon now they would be on the ship, where there would be food and drink and soft bunks to lie down on. They let out a collective sigh of relief, and none of the sighs were louder than that of the American who was travelling with his wife and their friend with the foreign-sounding name.

'I shall sail from Amsterdam,' Rilke said, as he and his companions approached the gangplank. 'It will be quite a long journey, but I will not mind. I will have the best of everything while I am aboard ship. I have deserved it.'

'We've *all* deserved it,' Emily Tyndale said. 'Isn't that right, my darling Lucas?'

'Talk up the future all you want, but we're not free and clear of the present yet,' Tyndale growled.

'But we soon will be,' Rilke said. 'What a joy it will be to return home – to leave decaying old Europe behind me, and once again breathe the clear sweet air of a young country.'

As they drew level with the gangplank, a customs official stepped forward to block their way.

'If you wouldn't mind, they'd like to have a few words with you in the office,' he said politely.

'Is something wrong?' Lucas Tyndale asked.

'Not really. It's just a minor matter that needs to be cleared up before you sail,' the customs officer said. He smiled. 'Don't worry, we won't let the ferry leave without you.'

They walked back along the pier in procession. It was not until they were well clear of the other passengers that a dozen police constables appeared from out of nowhere.

Rilke dropped his bag, and began to reach into his jacket pocket.

'I really wouldn't go for your gun if I were you, Mr Rilke,' the customs officer said.

He no longer seemed as mild-mannered as he had earlier, and this change of attitude was only underlined by the pistol in his hand.

'I am quite capable of shooting you if I have to,' he continued. 'And even if I were not, we have a number of sharpshooters posted who would be more than willing to do the job.'

Thirty-Five

The square, solid man, who met Blackstone on Dover Railway Station at four o'clock in the morning, introduced himself as Inspector White.

'Arrested them personally,' he told Blackstone as they journeyed in the cab back to Dover Police Central. 'Dressed up as a customs officer for the occasion. The German had a gun in his pocket. He would have used it, too, if I hadn't persuaded him otherwise.'

I'm sure he would, Blackstone thought. But I think you're wrong in assuming that Rilke's a German.

'You've put them in separate cells, have you?' he asked.

'Naturally,' White replied.

'And how are they taking it?'

'Rilke's not said a word since I arrested him. Tyndale was shaken at first, but he seems to have pulled himself together. If I was you, I'd start my interrogations with the woman.'

'That's just what I was thinking,' Blackstone said.

Blackstone was already sitting at the interview table when Emily Tyndale was shown in.

'Sit down, Emily,' he said.

She studied him, then studied the room – almost as if assessing how she should play the part.

'Suppose I don't want to sit down?' she said, after running through her repertoire of responses, and selecting defiance.

'I could force you to sit down, but I don't feel like doing that,' Blackstone told her. 'If you don't want to talk, you can go back to your cell – and I'll have a cosy little chat with your husband, instead.'

206

'He won't tell you anything!' Emily said. 'He's too strong to be broken. Too brave to be cowed by the likes of you.'

She'd cast herself in a melodrama, Blackstone thought – and a badly written one, at that.

'Oh, I wouldn't be sure about him keeping quiet,' he said. 'It's surprising how talkative people can suddenly become when they see the shadow of the rope hanging over them.'

'The rope!' Emily repeated, with a horror which seemed genuine enough for even the most demanding critic.

'Certainly the rope,' Blackstone said. 'Murder's a capital offence. Somebody's got to pay for the killing of the Honourable Charles Davenport, but . . .' He paused.

'But what?' Emily asked.

'But there's no reason why it should be you. Do you still want to go back to your cell, or will you take the seat I've just offered you?'

Emily crossed the room – with a slight stagger to her gait – and sat in the chair.

More dramatics, Blackstone decided. The woman couldn't help acting. It was no wonder she'd been so convincing as a whore.

'You've got it all wrong about Davenport,' Emily said. 'Nobody *killed* him. He was in the skiff when the incendiary bomb blew up and—'

'He might well have been in the skiff, but he was already dead at the time,' Blackstone interrupted her. 'His murder was one of the coldest and most calculated I've ever come across.'

'No, honestly, he was—'

'It won't take the jury more than ten minutes to arrive at their verdict, and the judge will be reaching for his black cap even before they've even come back into the court. But like I said, *you* don't have to be one of those whose neck is stretched – and if you'll just fill in the few details that are still missing, I'll make sure that you're spared.'

'I'll help you,' the woman said. 'It's my duty.'

'Quite right,' Blackstone agreed. 'Where did you meet your husband, Emily?'

'In New York.'

'What were you doing there? Acting?'

207

'Yes. Well, no, actually.'

'Which is it? Yes or no?'

'I was resting. Waiting for the right role to come along. It would have happened, you know. I'd made several appearances on the London stage before I ever went to America.'

'I don't doubt that.'

'I was never given the leading role – but you can't keep real talent down for ever, and if I'd stayed in London a little longer, I'd have been the rage of the West End.' She took a deep breath and puffed out her bosom. 'You may have heard of me, Inspector. My professional name was Emma Moon.'

'That does sound familiar,' Blackstone lied. 'Weren't you in that play . . . oh, what was it called now?'

'*The Sailor's Revenge*,' Emily Tyndale said.

'That's right,' Blackstone agreed. '*The Sailor's Revenge*. I saw that one myself.'

'The critics were very unkind to us. They literally savaged the play, and we closed after a week,' Emily said sulkily.

'But they surely can't have savaged you personally!' Blackstone said, sounding amazed.

'Mine was a relatively minor part,' Emily Tyndale pointed out.

'But, from what I remember, you carried it off magnificently,' Blackstone said.

'Yes, I did, didn't I?' Emily Tyndale agreed.

'And it was after *The Sailor's Revenge* closed down that you went off to America?'

'Yes, it was. I wanted to go somewhere real talent was truly appreciated, you see.'

'And I'm sure you'd have been a big success, given time. But you chose to abandon the bright, dazzling future which lay ahead of you, didn't you? And you did it all for love!'

Emily Tyndale all but simpered. 'You're very understanding for a policeman,' she said.

'Thank you,' Blackstone replied. 'Is Rilke really a German?'

The question threw Emily completely off-balance, just as the Inspector had intended it to.

208

'I . . . I don't really know,' she spluttered.

Blackstone shook his head reproachfully. 'What a pity,' he said. 'What a *great* pity. And just when we were getting on so well. Just when I'd decided that I'd move heaven and earth to stop the hangman putting his rope around that pretty little neck of yours.'

'He's not German at all,' Emily said in a panic. 'He's a Boer. From Southern Africa.'

'A farmer?'

'A lawyer.'

'Where did he meet your husband?'

'In America.'

'And what was he doing there?'

'Trying to raise support – and money – for the Boers' fight against the British Empire.'

'And why did your husband become so interested in him?'

'Because Lucas is a great man! Because Lucas supports the cause of freedom everywhere.'

'The rope, Emily,' Blackstone reminded her, almost gently.

'Southern Africa's very rich,' Emily Tyndale said. 'It's got gold, and it's got diamonds.'

'And if the Boers ever manage to break away from the Empire, they'll need more railways, and they'll be looking for someone – say an American with a great deal of experience in the field – to build and run them.'

'That's right.'

'So someone – perhaps your husband, or perhaps Rilke – came up with a plan which would help the Boers to win.'

'It was all Rilke's idea,' Emily said. She began to cry. 'Lucas and I were sucked into this whole terrible affair against our wills. You've got Rilke now. Can't you let us both go?'

The tears were very convincing, Blackstone thought, but then Emily Tyndale *was* an actress.

'Perhaps I've not made myself clear,' he said. 'Two people will hang. What we're deciding here is *which* two people. Now if your husband and Rilke didn't come up with this plan, then maybe it was Rilke and you.'

Emily's tears stopped flowing. 'Rilke had the original idea, but Lucas helped him to polish it up and refine it,' she said.

'But they can't take all the blame. They had quite a lot of support from some of the leaders of the Boer republics.'

'Unfortunately, they're not here, but your husband and Rilke are,' Blackstone said. 'Would you like to tell me how this man McClusky became involved in the plot?'

'We needed . . .' Emily paused. 'When I said "we" I meant "they". I meant my husband and the evil Mr Rilke.'

'I get the point,' Blackstone said. 'You're personally as pure as the driven snow. But I still need to know the mechanics of the plot.'

'They needed to recruit somebody who had a close connection with Lord Lansdowne,' Emily said. 'We – they – drew up a shortlist of possible candidates. McClusky was chosen because of his military connections – and because it soon became obvious that he's a very greedy man.'

'Who was working with him?'

'Working with him?'

'On the arson attacks. We know now that it wasn't Davenport, but McClusky couldn't have done it alone. So what's his partner's name?'

'I don't know,' Emily said. 'I swear I *don't* know. He said he'd be happier putting his own team together. I think he probably used people he'd served in the Army with.'

'But the Honourable Charles Davenport was definitely not part of that team, was he?'

'No, he wasn't.'

'So tell me how he fitted in.'

'It happened almost by accident,' Emily said. 'Rilke had already bought the Austro-Hungary Club. We needed it because—'

'I know why you needed it,' Blackstone said.

'They knew that once they'd lured you there, you'd have easily spotted if it had been nothing but a fake. So it had to be a real gambling club, which was why Rilke began to run it as if it actually *was* his business.'

'Why me?' Blackstone asked.

'Why you?' Emily repeated. 'What do you mean?'

'The blackmail notes were addressed to me personally. Was there a reason for that?'

'Of course. Rilke said it was the best way to be as certain as we could be that you were in charge of the investigation.'

'And he *wanted* me in charge?'

'Yes. Because Rilke was afraid that, once they saw the way the investigation was heading, most inspectors would try to fudge it. But he'd heard that you wouldn't do that. He'd heard that once you got your teeth into a case, you'd stick with it to the bitter end, whoever was involved.'

'I'm flattered,' Blackstone said.

'Lucas didn't like the idea,' Emily continued. 'He said you might be smart enough to see through whole thing. But Rilke told him not to worry. He said that dogged determination shouldn't be confused with brains, and you were probably just as stupid as all the other officers in Scotland Yard.'

'It's always a mistake to underestimate the enemy – and it's one I've made a few times myself,' Blackstone said. 'Let's get back to Charles Davenport. A few days before the operation was due to begin, he came into the Austro-Hungary Club, didn't he?'

'Yes, that's right.'

'Why?'

'To gamble, of course.'

'Was that the only reason he was there?'

'Yes. His family paid him an allowance, on condition that he lived in Italy. But he just couldn't keep away from the London clubs, so he secretly returned to Britain.'

'And what happened next?'

'He ran out of money, and asked for credit. When Rilke refused it, he threw an absolute fit. He said he had powerful friends, and threatened to use their influence to have the club closed down.'

'He mentioned Lord Lansdowne as one of these powerful friends of his, did he?'

'Yes.'

And that, Blackstone thought, had pretty much sealed his fate.

'What did Rilke do?' he asked. 'Drug him?'

'Yes. At least, for most of the time.'

'And then you kept him locked away until you needed him?'

211

'*Rilke* kept him locked away. In the cellar of the club. Maybe Lucas had something to do with it, too – I can't say for certain – but *I* didn't know anything about it.'

Ah, how little spousal loyalty meant when the threat of the rope fell across it, Blackstone thought.

'The night the *Golden Tulip* was set on fire, Rilke killed Davenport,' the Inspector said. 'He did it by hammering a specially prepared piece of metal into his chest. Then Davenport was left in the water for us to find. He was the perfect clue for you to leave, because he served not one, but two, functions – to both lead me to the door of the Austro-Hungary Club, and to establish a link between the arson attacks and Lord Lansdowne.'

Blackstone thought back to his own visit to the club. At the time, he had congratulated himself on pulling off his impersonation of a rich, rough millionaire. But Rilke hadn't been fooled at all. The Boer had been expecting him, and however bad his impersonation had been, Rilke would have let him in – because, for the plan to work, it was necessary for him to be introduced to Emily.

'Your only job – your only part in the whole thing – was to describe Lord Lansdowne to me,' Blackstone said.

'And to say that I'd seen him in the company of Davenport and McClusky,' Emily replied.

'Of course,' Blackstone agreed. 'Had you ever actually met Lord Lansdowne?'

'No, but I'd studied several photographs of him, and watched him enter and leave the House of Lords.'

I'm about to save Lansdowne's career, Blackstone thought – the career of one of the Privileged Few, of an Empire builder. If my mother was still alive, she'd be ashamed of me.

Under other circumstances, he'd probably have been quite content to step aside and let Lansdowne look after himself, he reflected.

And why not?

He had no brief for the British Empire, and some sympathy for the Boers' desire for independence. But Rilke and Tyndale had killed a man as part of their plot – and that couldn't go unpunished, even if, in the process, it meant getting the Minister of War off the hook.

'So let's be perfectly clear about this,' he said. 'Lord Lansdowne has never set foot inside the Austro-Hungary Club.'

'He hasn't.'

'You didn't try to lure him in?'

'No.'

Of course not. Why run the risk, when they didn't need to? It mattered not a jot whether he had, or hadn't, been in the club. All that was necessary was that enough people – enough of the *right* people – *believed* that he had.

'Was it Rilke or Lucas who sent the anonymous letter about Lansdowne to the Prime Minister?' Blackstone asked

'What anonymous letter?' Emily asked.

She wasn't going to admit to any more than she had to, Blackstone thought. And it didn't really matter, in terms of putting his case together, which of the two men had sent it. But it had to be *one* of them, because – aside from Sir Roderick Todd, Sergeant Patterson and himself – they were the only ones who knew enough about the whole affair *to* have penned it.

'The first fire burnt down a single warehouse, when it could have gutted a whole street,' Blackstone said. 'The second destroyed a single ship when it could have spread through the entire eel fleet. The explosion on Tower Bridge never happened at all. Why were they all such failures?'

Despite herself, Emily smiled. 'Is that what you think they were, Inspector? Failures?'

'No,' Blackstone agreed. 'They weren't failures at all, were they? They achieved exactly what they set out to achieve. You didn't want to do *too much* damage – because you were afraid that if you did, the Government might panic and pay the ransom. And you weren't interested in money. What you wanted was the investigation into Lord Lansdowne to continue until we'd collected enough of the fake evidence you'd planted to make our case against him.'

Emily nodded.

'Tell me what was supposed to have happened?' Blackstone continued.

'Lansdowne was meant to resign,' Emily said.

And he'd come damn close to doing so, Blackstone reflected – another twelve hours and he'd have been gone.

'And since, with the war going on, he's just about the most important person in government at the moment, the rest of the Government would probably have fallen with him,' the Inspector said.

'Yes, that's what was supposed to have happened.'

'With the Government's fall, the Liberals would have taken power. And as they've been against the war right from the start, they wouldn't have carried on pursuing it as this government has been doing – they'd have sued for peace with the Boers.'

'That's what we hoped for.'

'So the Boers would have gained virtual independence – and your husband would have been rewarded for the part he played in it all by being given control over the railways.'

'You make it sound as if he were doing it all for purely selfish reasons,' Emily said.

'And wasn't he?'

'No, he was not.' Emily's voice rose to a dramatic trill, as if she were delivering the final speech in the play. 'Lucas was driven by the instinct of a true pioneer – the spirit of free-dom. Southern Africa lay at his feet. The whole of Africa was just on his doorstep. He would have been a power to be reck-oned with!'

She fell silent. She did not actually bow, but she was clearly waiting for applause.

'And now, instead of being a power to be reckoned with, he's just another jailbird,' Blackstone pointed out.

'A great tragedy!' Emily said. 'A great waste of talent.' She shrugged her shoulders. 'Still, I've done all I could for him – all any wife could be *expected* to do. May I ask you one question?'

'Why not?'

'How long do you think I'll go to prison for?'

'That depends on how well you play it,' Blackstone said. 'You need to convince the jury that you had only a minor role in the affair. And you need to charm the judge. If you can do all that, you might get away with four or five years.'

'Four or five years,' Emily repeated thoughtfully. 'Then it won't be too late.'

'Too late for what?'

'For my comeback, of course! I won't even have to audition for roles. Theatre companies will be falling over themselves to take me on – because they'll know that they'll be hiring someone famous, someone who can pull in the crowds.' She paused. 'Lucas was holding me back, you know. He was denying me my destiny. But all that's over now.'

'True,' Blackstone agreed. 'And I suppose you could say that crime's loss is the theatre's gain.'

'Beautifully put,' Emily agreed.

Thirty-Six

'Just look at yourself, Inspector,' Sir Roderick Todd said. 'You're unshaven. Your suit's crumpled. You're a positive disgrace.'

'I haven't had much sleep in the last thirty-six hours,' Blackstone replied. 'And I didn't go home to change, because your message said that you wanted to see me the moment I got back to London.'

'Even allowing for all that, I still think you could have made more of an effort,' Sir Roderick said peevishly.

'I'll try to do better next time,' Blackstone said. 'That is, if there's to *be* a next time.'

'You almost cost Lord Lansdowne his career,' Todd said. 'You almost brought the Government down.'

'It was Rilke and Tyndale who did that,' Blackstone pointed out. 'All the clues they left clearly pointed to Lansdowne being involved.'

And Lansdowne himself hadn't actually helped his case, the Inspector thought. Of course, it may have been because he was feeling under the weather that he didn't recognize the sketch of McClusky immediately – but it had still looked suspicious.

'Granted, Rilke and Tyndale did their best to implicate His Lordship,' Sir Roderick conceded. 'But a good detective – even a merely competent one – would have seen through it all from the start. That's my considered view of the matter, at any rate.'

'But it isn't everybody's view?' Blackstone guessed.

'Lord Lansdowne has interceded on your behalf,' Todd admitted. 'I can only put it down to his very generous nature and his complete ignorance of how a police force is supposed

216

to work. Of course,' he added hastily, 'we can't really condemn His Lordship for his lack of knowledge on that particular front.'

'Of course not,' Blackstone agreed.

'Nevertheless, the upshot of Lord Lansdowne's no doubt well-meaning intervention is that you are to be given another chance,' the Assistant Commissioner continued. 'Another chance, Blackstone! Mark those words well. That is not the same as saying that the slate is wiped clean of all that has gone before.'

'I'm sure it isn't,' Blackstone said.

Patterson and Dr Carr were waiting for him in the pub.

'How did it go?' the Sergeant asked.

Blackstone shrugged, then reached for his pint. 'As well as could be expected,' he said.

'Archibald here's been explaining the whole thing to me,' Ellie Carr said. 'You're really not as dense as you look, are you? In fact, I'd say you've got quite a good brain – for a flatfoot.'

'Compliment noted and accepted,' Blackstone told her.

'Well, I 'ave to be nice to yer, don't I?' Ellie Carr said, slipping back into her Cockney. 'I mean ter say, I was rather 'oping that yer'd throw more of yer cases my way.'

'Considering you saved my bacon on this one, I don't see how I could refuse,' Blackstone said.

'Good, I'm glad that's settled,' Ellie Carr said. She turned her attention back to Patterson. 'Archibald?'

'Yes, Ellie?'

'Would you be an absolute sweetheart and go and buy us another round of drinks?'

'I'd be glad to.'

Ellie Carr reached across the table, and ruffled Patterson's hair. 'Good lad!' she said.

'My Sergeant's engaged to be married,' Blackstone said, when Patterson had gone to the bar, and was thus out of earshot.

'So he was saying before you arrived.'

'She's a nice girl, his Rose. No match for you, admittedly, but still a *very* nice girl.'

217

'You're making some kind of point, aren't you?'

'Yes, I am.'

'Would you care to spell it out?'

'I don't think I need to. I think you've got it already.'

'You're saying that I should leave young Archibald alone, are you?'

'Exactly.'

Ellie Carr laughed. 'You need have no worries on that account, Inspector,' she said. 'When it comes to my meat, I like it young and fatty. But if we're talking about my men, I prefer them older – and much stringier.'